WORTHY
of
DEATH

A MAGNIFICENT EPIC OF
SEVEN TRAGICALLY ENTANGLED LIVES

NOR THINGS TO COME:
A TRILOGY OF THE AMERICAN WEST: BOOK 3

BY

RICH RITTER
THE NEW VOICE OF THE AMERICAN WEST

PUBLICATION
CONSULTANTS
We Believe In The Power Of Authors

ISBN 978-1-59433-934-9
eBook ISBN 978-1-59433-935-6

Manufactured in the United States of America.

For I am persuaded, that neither death, nor life, nor angels, nor principalities, nor powers, nor things present,

NOR THINGS TO COME

…shall be able to separate us from the love of God…
Romans 8: 38-39

TABLE OF CONTENTS

LIST OF EXCERPTS FROM
MUIREALL ANNE RAVENSCROFT'S
ONE-VOLUME HISTORY OF THE AMERICAN WEST

A Synopsis of Book 2:
Gathering of the Clans

by Muireall Anne Ravenscroft,
award-winning author of *A Concise History of the West*
and other acclaimed works of nonfiction.

W hen Rich Ritter asked me to write a synopsis of the first book of *Nor Things to Come: A Trilogy of the American West*, I initially thought the task unnecessary. After all, I reasoned, why would any serious reader commence the second book of a trilogy without having read the first? But as I considered what I should write to briefly outline the magnificent story presented in *The Perilous Journey Begins*, it came to me one evening during a pleasant autumn thunderstorm that readers of the first book would almost certainly appreciate a "refreshing of the memory" before diving into the second. Now that Mr. Ritter has asked me to write a synopsis of *Book 2: Gathering of the Clans*, my opinion on this matter has not changed. However, if you are indeed reading this final book of the trilogy without any knowledge of the first or second, then I advise you to go no further. I believe with all my heart and mind that you have an intellectual obligation to find *The Perilous Journey Begins* and *Gathering of the Clans* and read them before commencing this conclusion of the story. But it is not my right to tell you what to do. If you insist on proceeding, then the following synopsis—which only covers the second book—will offer only incomplete and superficial preparation.

Silver City, Idaho Territory, September 1871. Priscilla Kimball skips to the centerline juncture of Washington Street and Avalanche Avenue. A freight wagon rumbles up behind her. One of the local "Cousin Jennies" (the wife of a Cornish miner named Tressa) admonishes Priscilla to get out of the road before another wagon runs her over. Priscilla strolls over to the woman and tells her that she is looking for a job because the wagon family she is living with can no longer afford to keep her. Tressa tells Priscilla that she can stay with her family, but Priscilla declines. Later in the day, Priscilla finds a sign on the wall of the two-story saloon on the corner of Washington and Avalanche advertising work for one (or maybe two) women. Priscilla enters the saloon and meets Nadia—a slender woman wearing a colorful dress—standing at the bar. Nadia tells Priscilla that she is not the type of woman the saloon is looking for, but Priscilla explains that she is desperate to find a job. The owner of the saloon, a stocky woman dressed in black named Margaret, overhears the conversation and walks up to the bar. She tells Priscilla, "There'd be some in this town who'd pay good money for a young one like you, but there's others who'd try to run me out of Silver City for offering the opportunity." Nadia intervenes and asks Margaret to give Priscilla a cleaning job because no one else wants to do it. Margaret finally agrees, but says if Priscilla breaks anything it will come out of Nadia's wages.

Silver City, Idaho Territory, September 1871. Manfred Herrmann meets Father Nero Aguilar at the War Eagle Hotel for breakfast. As they walk into the lobby, Father Nero suggests they might find a way to work together, because: "There is more than enough sin to go around. Another man of the cloth, even one who is not a Catholic, may be a useful addition to this town." The two are seated at a table by a window with views to Jordan Avenue, and are served hot coffee, scrambled eggs, and bacon by a Chinese waiter dressed in a white apron splattered with tomato soup. They discuss Martin Luther's Ninety-Five Theses, the Spanish Inquisition, the Thirty-Years War, and Martin Luther's marriage to a nun. Father Nero asks Manfred if he has any plans to take advantage of this " ... trivial distinction between Catholic and Lutheran clergy." The recollection of Alexandra Smythe running along the train platform in Chicago flashes into his mind. Manfred says he has thought of marriage, but has no one in mind. Father Nero segues to the point of the meeting, and reports that the Bishop has denied the use of *Our Lady of Tears* Catholic Church to hold Lutheran services. He suggests the idea of holding services in the back room at the saloon on the corner of Washington and Avalanche. After finishing breakfast, Manfred meets with the owner of the saloon, an incorrigibly surly woman named Margaret. She reluctantly agrees to allow use of the backroom for church services, but only if there are no sermons about the sins of swearing or gambling or drinking or whoring. Manfred agrees, and shakes Margaret's hand to seal the contract.

Silver City, Idaho Territory, October 1871. Conrad Airingsail—wide-brimmed hat scrunched down on top of ears and spectacles to block the afternoon sun…unraveled hem of a gray bandana stretched beneath a small dirt-smudged nose…cowboy spurs with the rowels filed down strapped to boots splattered with dried mud—stops his buckboard in front of *The Sommercamp Emporium & General Store*. When he hops to the ground, the spurs jingle and the 12-gauge-sawed-off-pistol-grip-double-barreled shotgun secured to his back in a quick-release harness he had fabricated himself swings into view. Another weapon, a small-caliber five-cylinder revolver carried in a shoulder holster, is concealed beneath his sweat-stained vest. He finds Mr. William F. Sommercamp at the back of the store and hands him a note with a list of items including flour, bacon, coffee, and other needs. Conrad then hands a sack of fresh vegetables to Mr. Sommercamp for his children. In a small cabin south of town, Manfred Herrmann is busy writing notices advertising his new church. When he leaves the cabin to hand out the notices, a cat rubs his leg. Manfred tells the cat to never come back and tromps into town. He approaches over 100 residents, but not a single person takes one of his hand-written notices. Dejected, he runs into William Sommercamp and an odd cowboy in front of the general store. Without speaking, the cowboy grabs one of the notices and quickly rides away in the buckboard. When Manfred asks why the man didn't say anything, William Sommercamp explains that Conrad Airingsail is a mute who keeps to himself, never drinks or plays cards, and always smells like he's slept in a pile of fresh manure. When Manfred returns to his cabin, the cat is waiting for him—with a dead shrew.

Silver City, Idaho Territory, October 1871. Roshan Kuznetsov loads another heavy scoop of dirt into a gold rocker near the gravelly banks of Jordan Creek. He complains to his business partner, Tseng Longwei, that they have not found a speck of gold with the gold rocker and they should, "...use this piece of shit to build of the fire tonight, if you agree with my think, and you should say to it." Longwei replies, "I say we should work for three more days with the gold pan and the gold rocker. If we still do not find any gold, we should track down this man who sold the gold rocker and ask him to tell the instructions of its use to both of us at the same time." After a spirited discussion of the man's appearance and how to find him, they agree to wait three days. Three days later, Roshan Kuznetsov warms his blistered hands near the flaming relic of the piece-of-shit gold rocker and nudges a cast iron pot of simmering beans into the hot coals now glowing below the collapsing mining implement. As they continue to argue about whether or not they were using the gold rocker correctly, a grizzled old man rides up on a burro and asks if he can join them for dinner. Roshan says they have many beans and he is welcome. The old man also asks if they have any whisky. Longwei says they have no whisky but plentiful water from Jordan Creek. The man introduces himself as Gustus De Angeles, and asks Roshan and Longwei if they'd be interested in helping him work his claim on War Eagle Mountain, near Mahogany Gulch. When they hesitate, Gustus offers to pay them each five dollars a day.

Silver City, Idaho Territory, October 1871. Csongor Toth admires the sign that will announce his new business with understated grandeur. He asks the young man holding the heavy sign to lift it higher so he can properly examine it.

CSONGOR TOTH, ESQUIRE
MINING CLAIMS LAW
(PAYMENT IN GOLD PREFERRED)

Csongor tells the boy to have the sign installed by the end of the day. But as the boy leaves, Csongor demands to examine the other side.

Csongor Toth, Esquire
Mining Claims Law
(payment in gold preffered)

Upon reading the text, Csongor slumps into his chair. The boy asks if he likes the sign. Csongor replies, "Tell your master I am overjoyed with the quality of the sign. Not only will it announce my new law firm with appropriate verve, but it will also allow me to judge the literacy and powers of observation of potential clients without having to ask directly." Later in the day, Csongor meets with three of the more celebrated miscreants of Silver City: Seth, who claims no surname; Bill Jackson, who goes by Jackson; and Miguel Cervantes, who does not know how to read or write. Csongor asks each man if he has ever killed. After affirming they have, Seth demands that Csongor reveal how many people he has killed. Csongor answers, "I suppose I could offer an exact count if I cared to think about it, but unfortunately the delicious exhilaration of killing has blended the individual deaths into a composite rapture that has blurred specific details." Csongor presents a business proposition involving blackmail, larceny, extortion, bribery, and similar endeavors. He offers each man ten dollars a day, a bottle of Old Pulteney whisky, and a fifty-dollar advance to buy clothes, shave, and take a bath. The three men accept and agree to report back Friday morning to commence the first endeavor of this fledgling business enterprise.

Silver City, Idaho Territory, November 1, 1871. Tseng Longwei considers four options ranging from staying in the wagon and enduring the rump-thumping, teeth-cracking, back-slamming abuse of this so-called "road" to Silver City to getting off the wagon, sitting on a comfortable rock or stump, and waiting for Roshan to drive the wagon to town and return with supplies. He decides instead on a fifth option: stay in the wagon and appreciate the mystical gift of life and the serenity of a land not torn asunder by the ravages of the brutal civil war in China. When the wagon begins the final steep grade toward Jordan Creek, Roshan snaps the reins and startles the mules into a wild descent. A large boulder shatters the wagon tongue, separating the mules and throwing Roshan and Longwei into the back of the wagon. The mules drift behind the wagon before it plunges chaotically into a shallow ravine. The next day, after paying the blacksmith a week's wages for repairs, they drive to a general store to buy supplies. Roshan enters the store, but Longwei goes for a walk because the store does not allow Indians or Chinamen. He meets a man dressed in a black suit who is handing out ragged shreds of paper advertising church services in the back room of a saloon. Longwei accepts one of the notices, returns to the general store, and finds that Roshan has loaded the wagon with the supplies. As they head back to Mahogany Gulch, Longwei suggests that Roshan allow the mules to select the speed and route because, "...this is the only way to allow the possibility of arriving at Mahogany Gulch alive."

A few miles north of Silver City, November 6, 1871. Joshua Hotah and his beloved appaloosa both sniff the crispness of an autumn breeze and squint into the hazy rim of sun drifting low along the mountainous horizon to the southwest. A stagecoach rumbles by; Joshua tells the appaloosa, "You are lucky to not have to pull a stagecoach for a job." Joshua glimpses a slender column of bluish smoke to the west and rides towards it. They find a Nez Perce woman tending a fire next to a teepee. Because Joshua only speaks enough Nez Perce to buy a horse, the woman initially brandishes a large knife. Joshua calms the woman, and she allows him to examine her son, who has a swollen belly and is very sick. After Joshua uses sign language for "white man, chief, and medicine," (which together means "doctor") and "die and sleep" (which together means "dead"), the woman allows him to take the boy to Silver City. Joshua finds Doctor Guinevere Dupree in the same building as the undertaker. Joshua is suspicious because he thought all doctors were men, but Guinevere explains that she graduated from New York Women's Medical College in 1868. After examining the boy, she determines that he has appendicitis and requires an immediate operation. Joshua asks if she has done this before, and she says, "...I had the good fortune to observe Dr. William Parker of New York perform an appendectomy on three different occasions." Joshua replies, "I have watched men skin and gut a buffalo many times more than three, but this does not mean I know how to do the same." Joshua agrees to assist, and as Guinevere begins the procedure, she asks, "Is it really true you do not know how to skin and gut a buffalo?"

Saloon on the corner of Washington and Avalanche, November 6, 1871. Priscilla Kimball suppresses the urge to retch when she involuntarily gulps a big whiff of stale vomit. She fishes around in a bucket of soapy water, snags the torn rag sticking to the bottom, wrings it out, and falls to her hands and knees to clean up the mess left by one of the establishment's more important clients. A strapping miner named Jacque—sufficiently drunk to blur his vision—shuffles quietly into the dim room. He blinks twice before locating Priscilla's enticingly-naked legs and youthful derrière. He drops to his knees and yanks her skirt up. After twisting her arm behind her back, he speaks to her in slurred tones: "No need to get upset, little missy. This'll only take a minute…or maybe two." Wearing the exotic lingerie of her trade, Nadia bursts into the room and slaps the side of Jacque's head with a hickory axe handle. When Jacque releases Priscilla, Nadia tells him he's in the wrong room again and Priscilla is not a whore. Priscilla retires to Nadia's pleasant little room where she washes her face and rests. Nadia tells Priscilla, "I was supposed to be a school teacher, but something terrible happened before I started." She also says, "…my dream is to make enough money to move to California and buy a nice home with a view of the ocean. I'd like to have my own garden too. It's either that or marry a fine gentleman of means, which I don't really believe is likely given my current occupation. I hope to raise a family someday too." Priscilla asks if she thinks this will happen anytime soon. Nadia says that she hopes so, because she's not sure how much longer she will last.

A masked ball before winter, November 7, 1871. Sitting in a bentwood rocking chair next to a barrel of pickles in The Sommercamp Emporium & General Store, Manfred Herrmann pulls an enormous pickle out of the barrel and gnaws off a big chunk. William Sommercamp approaches and says, "I thought you hated pickles." Manfred replies, "I can hardly stand to even look at one. I'm just punishing myself for sulking." William Sommercamp suggests that Manfred attend the masked ball at the Masonic Hall to cheer himself up. After arguing about the logic of this idea, William Sommercamp gives Manfred a plain black mask—perfect for a preacher—and sends him on his way. Manfred sticks a second pickle in his jacket pocket (just in case). After arriving at the ball, Manfred slouches on a three-legged stool and sulks. Two men begin pushing each other at the main entry. Before it escalates into a brawl, a young woman wearing a dress the color of a clear morning sky and a mask the color of fresh clouds steps through the doorway, touches each man on the shoulder, says a few words (which Manfred cannot hear), and the men immediately separate and remove their hats. Csongor Toth later introduces the young woman to Manfred and asks him to dance with her. To his astonishment, she is Alexandra Smythe, who he met on the train from Chicago. After the first dance, Alexandra asks, "What is it you have in your coat pocket?" Manfred explains that it is a pickle. Alexandra suggests he remove it before the next dance. Manfred says, "Yes, Miss Smythe. I'll get rid of it. Right away." Alexandra replies, "Please call me Alex." Manfred fingers the pickle as he searches the room for an appropriate place to discard it before answering, "Yes, Miss Smythe."

Commotion at the masked ball, November 7, 1871. Waiting patiently on the second floor of the Masonic Hall, Tseng Longwei listens to Roshan "negotiate" with the burly doorkeeper who has informed them that Chinamen are not allowed. After an angry exchange, Roshan shoves the doorkeeper; the doorkeeper pushes back. As Roshan prepares to push even harder, a young woman wearing a dress the color of a clear morning sky and a mask the color of fresh clouds steps briskly through the doorway and asks if she has arrived safely at the masked ball. The two men separate and remove their hats. Tseng Longwei bows to the doorkeeper and thanks Roshan for his effort, then goes for a walk. He discovers a bonfire on the banks of Jordan Creek with three old men, two old women, four young men, six young women, and nine children of various ages and genders—all Chinese—gathered around the flames. The old man informs Longwei that he must tell a story if he wishes to stay. After studying the constellations, Longwei tells of a mythical land where a blue dragon rules the eastern kingdom, a black tortoise rules the wintry northern kingdom, a white tiger rules the autumn lands of the western kingdom, a fiery red phoenix rules the southern kingdom, and a powerful emperor rules the lands of the middle kingdom and watches over all the lands. A dispute arises between the blue dragon and the emperor and war breaks out. The blue dragon asks his most trusted colonel to guard his most valued possession: a young princess of the most astonishing beauty. The emperor's armies defeat the blue dragon and the colonel is overcome by fear and flees. As he leaves the castle, he discovers the blue dragon in chains and the princess stripped naked and bound in heavy wood stocks. The princess implores the colonel to save her, but he turns away in shame. The old man says, "Not exactly a story for young children, but very good nonetheless. You may stay, Tseng Longwei."

A bath at the War Eagle Hotel, November 7, 1871. Gordania Sinclair plunges to the bottom of the copper bathtub when heavy footsteps tromp beyond the locked door separating the second-floor bathing room from the hallway. She gradually emerges and arranges the floating mounds of soap foam to conceal her torso. When the water has cooled and no longer provides adequate pleasure, she steps out of the tub and dries herself with a white cotton towel. She shifts her gaze to a full-length mirror and gently runs an index finger along the hideous scar from her neck down to its jagged termination a few inches below the right clavicle, then begins to dress. After sliding a derringer (the one Csongor gave her in Chicago) into a cotton holster she had sewn into her bloomers just above the right knee, she reaches for her dress. She asks the hotel clerk for directions to the masked ball. When she arrives at the Masonic Hall, a commotion between two large bearded men prompts her to touch each one on the shoulder and ask if she has arrived safely at the masked ball. To her surprise, the men instantly separate and remove their hats. She finds Csongor Toth and asks him if he was successful in luring Mr. Herrmann to the masked ball. Manfred unexpectedly approaches, and Csongor introduces him to Miss Alexandra Smythe of Liverpool, England, and asks him to dance with her. After dancing until after midnight, Manfred and Alexandra relax and drink glasses of sour lemonade. Manfred pulls his chair around and sits directly in front of Alexandra, his knees separated from hers by an electrified gap of only two inches. In an apparent display of modesty, Alexandra slides her hand over her right knee and rests it on top of the derringer.

An English lesson … of sorts, November 8, 1871. Two hours after the grandfather clock chimes twelve, Roshan gives the burly doorkeeper a final stern look before tripping and bouncing down the stairs in a rhythmic series of comical "harrumphs." Finding Roshan's hat at the top, the doorkeeper wads it into a little ball and throws it with every ounce of strength he can muster, hitting the back of Roshan's head. The burly doorkeeper yells, "You forgot your hat." Roshan stumbles through the front door of the

Masonic Hall and begins looking for the wagon and Tseng Longwei. After wandering around and failing to find the wagon, he ends up at the saloon on the corner of Washington and Avalanche. Roshan meets Margaret, and asks if she can tell him "... of the owner to see my question of the look for the something of the strangest you can't believe it when your lips hear of it." She answers, "You're looking at the owner. Now what is this strange request? I can hardly wait to hear all about it." Roshan says he is looking for a whore who can speak both English and Russian. Margaret sends for Nadia, who is less than pleased and chastises Roshan in fluent Russian. Upon hearing the beauty of his mother tongue, Roshan's heart swells with affection for Nadia. They retire to the bar. Roshan drinks hot coffee and Nadia explains that she was once a teacher. Upon hearing this, Roshan asks if she will give him English lessons. Margaret arrives and tells Nadia it is time to get upstairs. Nadia informs her that she plans to give Roshan English lessons. Margaret sneers, "Go ahead, Nadia. You show him how to stick his subject into your predicate. The rate's still the same and my cut's still the same."

A business meeting after the masked ball, November 8, 1871. The hour of two in the morning has arrived, and Csongor Toth waits with Seth, Jackson, and Miguel. At exactly 2:02, the door opens and Elijah Brown enters the room. Csongor says he is two minutes late. Elijah rests a hand on his Smith & Wesson revolver and explains dryly, "I had a little business to clean up in Dodge City, otherwise I would have arrived on time." Csongor says he was not expecting an African shootist. Elijah offers to leave, but Csongor tells him to stay because his credentials are impeccable. Csongor offers whisky and a cigar, but Elijah declines. Csongor lights a cigar for himself and presents the reason he has sent for Elijah. Because of a truly gruesome affair in 1864, a deep-seated fear of Indians still persists to this day. His plan is simple: he will offer protection from the Indians to the locals, particularly those with outlying mining claims. But to guarantee financial success, he must first create a new incident to adequately intensify fear in every heart. He then asks Elijah Brown to dispatch an innocent family, burn their wagon to the ground, and mutilate the bodies using Indian weapons and techniques. He adds casually, "There must be scalps." Surprised, Elijah exclaims that he will not kill women and children and declines the offer. Disappointed, Csongor pays

Elijah for his time and askes Seth, Jackson, and Miguel to escort him from the office. Later in the morning, while followed by a mongrel of a dog, Tseng Longwei approaches his wagon after leaving the bonfire on Jordan Creek. To his surprise, he finds a black man covered in blood in the wagon. Longwei lifts the man onto his shoulders and heads to the new doctor—with the mongrel of a dog still trotting by his side.

The Strange Dream of Joshua Hotah, November 8, 1871. Smudgy penumbras flitted beyond the diaphanous veil of mist but Joshua Hotah could not make them out even though the shadows appeared at times to drift closer when he glimpsed them from the corner of his eye but they also appeared to move away at the same time when he saw them from the corner of his other eye.... So begins the strange dream of Joshua Hotah in which a white raven guides him to vacuous apparitions of his parents. His mother tells him, "Do not trust the white raven my son or you will surely die." But when his father—who stands in a vast opening in the mist littered with many dead carcasses of buffalo covered with countless white ravens—attempts to give him the same warning, Joshua is awakened by agitated pounding on the door across the hallway. He checks the Nez Perce boy, opens the door, and discovers a very small man carrying a very large man on his shoulders speaking to Guinevere Dupree. After the very small man walks out of the clinic, he apologizes to Joshua for waking him. Joshua replies, "You do not need to apologize to me. I was having a very unpleasant dream. I am happy it is over, even if I did not hear the final words of my father." Longwei says that when he lived in China, he often told people the meaning of their dreams. The two men reconvene outside and sit on the covered boardwalk. They each tell stories of their past before Joshua describes his dream. Longwei asks if Joshua has seen this white raven before. Joshua says, "What does it matter if I have seen the white raven or not?"

Saloon on the corner of Washington and Avalanche, November 10, 1871. Reeking of stale sweat, Andrew asks, "What don't seem right about it? It's my idea in the first place, not yours, and I promise you're gonna make a lot of money 'cause me and some other fellows I knows about would be willing to pay top dollar for the privilege." Sitting across the table, Margaret explains that plenty of people might not take kindly to it, especially Father Nero and the new preacher, Manfred Herrmann. Andrew pressures Margaret to reconsider and asks why she has a problem with the idea. Margaret responds, " ... because she's only fourteen. If she was a little older it wouldn't bother me at all." Andrew exclaims that his friends might be disappointed because he told them she was thirteen. Margaret spots Priscilla Kimball by the piano, calls her over, and explains that she is thinking of giving her a promotion. When Priscilla asks what she has to do for the promotion, Margaret says only entertain a few special customers from time to time. A testy negotiation ensues. When they are about to agree to a dollar-fifty for each satisfied customer and every other Sunday morning off, Nadia steps in and prevents them from shaking hands. Her voice trembling, she tells Margaret, "There's no way I'm letting you turn Priscilla into a whore." Enraged, Margaret tells Nadia that she has cost her a lot of money, and to make up the difference she will take three dollars out of her salary every day. Nadia calls Margaret a witch, but then understands implicitly that her beautiful dream to move to California and live in a cozy home with a view of the ocean has vanished. Forever.

He that is without sin among you, November 28, 1871. An agitated mob gathers in front of the Idaho Hotel to listen to Samuel B. Peters, an upstanding deacon of a congregation in Boise City. With theatric aplomb, he exclaims, "Why, the very idea of offering up a thirteen-year-old girl as a prostitute ... to be abused by older men in the most unspeakable ways ... sends shivers up my spine and fills me with deep shame for my fellow man." The mob is joined by Jackson, Seth, and Miguel before marching to the saloon on the corner of Washington and Avalanche. Priscilla sees the mob gathering in front of the saloon and calls for Nadia because Margaret is out on an errand. Nadia steps out to the boardwalk, and someone in the crowd asks to see the thirteen-year-old whore. Nadia says she's never heard of such a thing. After finishing a cup of coffee with Father Nero at the War Eagle Hotel, Manfred walks outside and notices an unusual commotion near Avalanche Avenue. He heads down the street and stands by Nadia's side. Encouraged by Jackson, Seth yells, "Strip her! Teach the whore a lesson she will never forget. Burn the saloon. Burn it!" Manfred steps in front of Nadia and says, "He that is without sin among you, let him first cast a stone at her." Jackson picks up a stone and throws it, hitting Nadia above the left eye. But when he picks up a second stone, Conrad Airingsail appears behind him and fires his shotgun in the air. Manfred steps between the two to avoid an escalation of violence, but is forced to punch Jackson in the face when he tries to pull his gun. Startled (and impressed) by what they have just witnessed, the unruly mob slowly disperses.

War Eagle Mountain near Mahogany Gulch, December 1, 1871. The first bona fide snowstorm of winter has rendered the mountain road between town and Mahogany Gulch impassable. Carrying a load of hand-split firewood on his back, Tseng Longwei trudges back to the cabin in knee-deep snow. After Gustus De Angeles opens the door, Longwei stumbles into the cabin and finds Roshan and the black man—the one he carried to the doctor—sitting on rough-hewn chairs at a rough-hewn table playing cards. The black man arranges his cards with great skill, even though he cannot recollect where he learned to play the game. "I can't explain it, but I just don't remember a dang thing. Can't remember my name or where I came from or even why I ended up here." As Gustus begins frying up some potatoes and bacon for breakfast, Longwei commences a long soliloquy about his journey from China to Mahogany Gulch. He concludes by stating, "…the glorious poverty and splendid deprivation I have finally achieved in this small cabin with the three of you has finally crushed my pride into worthless dust and convinced me to appreciate the life I have been given." Before the men eat, Longwei suggests the name "John Smith." The black man agrees, but asks if he can change back to his real name—when he remembers what it is. Roshan replies, "Roshan will not stop in your way when you remember of the real name." Gustus smacks a slab of bacon on a metal plate and says, "Call him whatever you want, but I don't give a shit because I'm getting hungrier by the minute. Who wants bacon?" The mongrel of a dog tilts his head and thumps the floor with his tail.

Sunday morning at the back room of the saloon, December 3, 1871. In Nadia's skilled hands the concertina wheezes out a reedy but convincing accompaniment to *A Mighty Fortress is Our God,* as Manfred Herrmann waves his arms in a useless attempt to teach his "congregation" the words. Half-way through the third verse, the upright piano in the next room bursts into a rousing performance of *Camptown Races* and the entire musical extravaganza disintegrates. Manfred surveys the room and finds a Chinaman with long black hair, a muscular black man with an impressive shiner and a cauliflower ear, a grizzled old geezer who swears a lot, a fellow who speaks a nearly indecipherable version of the English language, the enigmatic Conrad Airingsail, and a young lady named Priscilla. He yearns to see Alexandra again, who he had invited at the masked ball. He reads the 23rd Psalm: "The Lord is my shepherd...." A lively discussion ensues about the difference between a psalm and a salami. After the service, Manfred cleans the room then sits in a chair. Alexandra Smythe unexpectedly enters the room and says, "Oh dear. Have I arrived too late for the church service?" They retire to the dining room of the Idaho Hotel. In a moment of introspection, Manfred tells her that he still has nightmares about the hundreds of men he killed during the war, particularly a young boy. Alexandra replies that he had to kill to survive, and asks why this is so important. Manfred stutters, "Because...you see...the problem is...the problem is this...I enjoyed it." He then tells her about the mob in front of the saloon and the man he punched and that he really wanted to kill him. Alexandra says she admires him even more for sharing his story, then adds, "But you are not alone. I can assure you that we all have secrets." After she says this, she does not speak more of herself.

A visit to the doctor, December 4, 1871. A subterranean blast rumbles in one of the deep shafts of War Eagle Mountain. Roshan Kuznetsov asks Nadia, "Did you hear of the noise which is of the now?" Before Nadia can suggest a more graceful sentence, Dr. Guinevere Dupree opens the door to the back room of her two-room clinic and explains that it will take at least half an hour to treat a man who shot off his toe demonstrating his quick-draw technique. Roshan asks Nadia about her plans for the future so that he can practice his English while they wait. She tells her story, and finishes with, "A wealthy gentleman will someday arrive in Silver City and ask me to marry him. This gentleman will provide the financial means to fulfill my dreams, and we shall move to California and buy a beautiful home with a view of the ocean and sit in rocking chairs outside on warm summer evenings next to the garden and watch the sunsets and crashing waves and raise a family of at least two boys and two girls and go for long walks on the beach and live happily ever after, just like in a fairy tale." Disappointed, Roshan asks if love is not enough if the man has no wealth. Nadia says she is confident she will love the children, whether or not she loves the father. Dr. Guinevere Dupree removes Nadia's stitches.

As they depart the clinic, Roshan insists on escorting Nadia safely back to the saloon, and she insists on giving him a free English lesson in return. Roshan declines, but is tricked into a free lesson during the walk. At this moment, when he thinks of Nadia's dream to buy a home in California with a view of the ocean and have a family with four children and go for walks on the beach with the crashing waves and sunsets, he decides to pay her double for the next lesson.

The time for action has arrived, May 5, 1872. With the promise of favorable weather now fully upon the cusp of a luminous spring morning, Ferd Tucker struggles to adjust the leather harnesses of the four oxen lollygagging in front of the prairie schooner while Joniah rearranges the family's meager possessions in the back. About sixty feet away, Seth and Clarinda play a spontaneous game of slap tag in a narrow alley. Miguel appears and asks the children about the wagon in front of the livery. Clarinda exclaims, "Father and mother are getting ready to head out today. They said we'll be in Boise City before we knows it." Miguel tells them to have a safe trip and hustles away. Ferd, Joniah, Seth, and Clarinda depart Silver City in the wagon a short while later. Back at the law office, Miguel finishes his report to Csongor, Seth, and Jackson about the wagon family. Csongor declares, "Gentlemen, at long last...the time for action has arrived." He orders Jackson to round up the horses; Seth to collect the Indian clothing, bows and arrows, and related accouterments; and Miguel to follow the wagon. Later, Ferd and Joniah watch four horsemen—and one heavily-laden mule—gallop by the prairie schooner and vanish around a switchback about a half-mile down the road. The four men dress in Indian clothing and wait. After the wagon rolls over the top of a hill and begins a steep descent toward a tree-lined bend in a narrow creek, the sharp crack of a rifle shot resounds off the mountains. Ferd slumps to his left without releasing the reins, a stream of blood drooling from a ragged hole in his back. Csongor chastises Jackson for using a rifle instead of arrows or knives. Joniah screams at the children, "Run back to town and get help. Run now! Run! Run!" She grabs an axe, jumps off the wagon, and marches toward the four men. Csongor tells Jackson to take the axe away from the approaching woman and tie her to the wagon—exactly as he has instructed. He orders Seth and Miguel to apprehend the children and bring back their scalps. After Jackson ties Joniah to a wagon wheel and cuts off her dress, she tells Csongor of her hope that he will burn in hell. Csongor thanks her for the charming sentiment, then says, "Now, my unfortunate darling, it is time to begin." Csongor pulls the bowstring back and takes aim.

An unexpected act of kindness, May 5, 1872. The Nez Perce woman impales four thick cuts of fresh elk backstrap on a sharpened juniper stick and cooks them over a fire. Joshua Hotah and the Nez Perce boy return from a hunting trip, and the boy explains in English, "We no shoot elk today. We see elk, but we no shoot elk. Elk far away." Joshua tells the Nez Perce woman that she should try to say more English words like her son, but she can only manage, "Thank you, Joshua Hotah. Good morning." The sharp crack of a rifle shot rings out in the distance; Joshua rides away to investigate. The appaloosa stops fifty feet downhill from a wagon. Joshua pulls his Henry repeating rifle from its sheath, dismounts smoothly, and approaches the wagon. He sees a dead man awkwardly bent over. He walks around the wagon and finds a dead woman tied to the wheel and pierced with arrows. When the dead woman's eyes open, he swears in Sioux and jerks back. He asks her who has done this terrible thing. She says it was white men dressed like Indians, then begs, "Please help my children. I don't know what happened to them." Joshua jogs up the road to find the children. When he returns, he tells the dead woman he has asked her children to wait by a big tree because he does not think it is right for them to see their mother in this way. The dead woman asks his name, then thanks Joshua for saving her children. She then asks him to kill her, because Seth and Clarinda are safe and she does not want to suffer any more. When Joshua raises his rifle and aims at her heart, she says, "My name … is Joniah Tucker, and I want you to know … I already … forgive you for this … unexpected act of kindness." He pulls the trigger; her eyes flutter briefly before she dies. Joshua rides up the road and fetches Joniah's dead children. He finds a rusty shovel and a dull pick in the back of the wagon, hikes down the road to a pleasant stretch of ground overlooking the tree-lined bend in the narrow creek, and begins digging. The appaloosa follows Joshua down to the creek and keeps him company, but does not say anything.

CHAPTER ONE

A fortuitous stroke of luck
May 5, 1872

B efore an inexplicable chill of nostalgia erupted from beneath his skull and shuddered down the core of his spine to his sweaty lumbar, Csongor Toth reminisced of his childhood as an impoverished peasant frolicking in the pastoral lands of eastern Hungary—although he did not appreciate the vigor of his peasantry nor the depth of his poverty until the eventful years of adolescence. He recalled his father sitting on a shabby chair with three wobbly legs and telling colorful stories of the great Hungarian Revolution. The event had played out in 1848, three years after Csongor's birth, and consequently meant little to him. He remembered a dreary vision of his mother stumbling across a plowed stretch of dark ground on a bright spring morning with a large bag strapped over her shoulder, but he could not recollect the cheerless expression on her face or the pointless contents of the bag. He remembered his infatuation, at the age of 14, with a flirtatious peasant girl, his elder by three years, and he recalled with delicious clarity the savagely-prurient dreams that began emerging from the murky subliminal folds of his pubescent mind following the night she spurned him. He remembered the days after his sixteenth birthday when the startling epiphany erupted into his thoughts that his unfortunate birth into an impoverished peasant family was an absurd cosmic error demanding immediate rectification. He recalled his promise to take whatever actions were necessary to remedy the error. He subsequently made plans to procure the wealth necessary to finance both travel to a larger city and a suitable female tutor who could provide for his education and play a central role in his increasingly ravenous dreams. He remembered the night he entered the home of the wealthy family, only a few miles away from the disgusting little hovel his own family had lived in from the time before his birth. He did not originally intend to take anyone's life, but after emptying a box of jewelry and precious coins rather noisily, his discovery by the father had left him no other choice. After using his fists to beat the poor gentleman nearly unconscious, he had employed a length of curtain cord as a garrote to finish the job. It was regrettable that he had wandered into the man's bedroom across the hallway, because he was thereby obligated to asphyxiate the man's deliciously-plump wife with her own nightgown—an act that had required equal measures of dexterity and strength. But in both instances, he had experienced a curious surge of euphoria, which he later discovered could not be replicated in any other way—although the euphoria soon faded and usually vanished altogether within a day. He discovered the children, a boy and a girl, in separate rooms at the end of the hallway. He decided to let them sleep after suffering a fleeting twinge of conscience. This surprised and amused him at the time. He remembered the primal urge to look up the peasant girl who had rejected him a few years earlier. After several inquiries he learned of her unfortunate demise from cholera. He recalled weeks of depression following the discovery of this wasted opportunity. He eventually recovered from his emotional muddle and began his journey to Budapest. He soon found living quarters appropriate to his recently improved financial status. He placed an advertisement in the newspaper for a female tutor with expertise in philosophy, languages, and mathematics. After interviewing six highly-qualified (but rather unattractive) applicants, a woman in her late twenties who possessed the requisite intellect and physical presentation arrived on his doorstep in desperate need of a job. It turned out that she was also on the run from an avaricious suitor and needed a place to hide, but this petite nicety was not revealed during the interview. Csongor had hired the young lady on the spot with the understanding that she would tutor only him and that she would teach him something new every day—unless some dramatic calamity allowed the possibility of a day off. He remembered his sacred pledge to control the full expression of his salacious appetites until he had achieved mastery of advanced mathematics, English, German, and philosophy. Regrettably, he fell somewhat short of this promise on a rainy Friday afternoon during a contentious debate on Immanuel Kant's[1] notions of ethics. Although the exquisite rapture temporarily assuaged the tiresome consequences of this untidy business—another newspaper advertisement, more interviews with disagreeable women, arduous negotiations over petty details, and, of course, the inconvenience of—

A distant gunshot crackled from the site of the Indian massacre. Csongor glanced in the direction of the gunshot and stiffened. He could not immediately deduce the meaning of the shot and experienced an uncharacteristic stab of doubt when he imagined a few unfavorable possibilities. After staring silently into the cloudless sky above the distant carnage, he spoke to his men in soothing tones belying his anxiety. "It would be sensible for one of you gentlemen to ride back to the Indian massacre and sort out the meaning of the gunshot. I am quite fatigued from the rigors of today's ordeal and really don't care who makes the trip. But whoever goes should change into his traditional attire and ride with utmost haste."

Jackson, a grimace twisting his heavy brows, barked angrily at Seth and Miguel, "You heard the man. One of you get finished changing your clothes and get on your horse and ride back to the wagon and find out what's going on."

Seth lifted his hands in protest. "I ain't riding back there. It's probably already haunted with the ghosts of that family. And those ghosts are probably going to want revenge on the men who killed them in the first place."

Miguel initially appeared rather blasé, but after hearing Seth suggest the possibility of vengeful ghosts also rejected the idea. "If there's a bunch of ghosts looking for revenge, then I'm not riding down there either. You should just go check it out yourself if you think it's important."

Jackson's shoulders contracted and he clenched his fists into quivering balls. "What a couple of babies. There ain't no such a thing as ghosts. Now one of you get your ass on your darn horse and ride back to the wagon and figure out why someone's shooting down there when they got no business doing anything of the sort."

---

[1] Immanuel Kant (1724-1804) was a German philosopher who is considered the central figure in modern ideas of metaphysics, epistemology, ethics, political philosophy, and aesthetics.

Seth folded his arms belligerently and stomped his foot. "I ain't going back there. You're full of bullshit if you don't believe in ghosts. I heard stories the miners tell of running into evil spirits down deep in them hard rock mines. One fellow said the ghost nearly caught him when he got all tangled up in a coil of rope and tripped over a shovel." He stomped his other foot to add an exclamation point to the end of his sentence.

Miguel scraped the toe of his Indian moccasin along the ground. "Like I said, if you're so cocksure there ain't no ghosts, then you go down there. I'm staying here with Seth."

The scowl on Jackson's brow erupted across his forehead and cheeks. "Well if you're so scared of ghosts, then why don't the both of you get on your horses and ride down there?"

Seth began drumming on his right elbow with his fingers. "Nope. Not gonna do it no matter what you have to say about it."

Miguel tapped his moccasin. "Nope neither."

Jackson rested his hand on the gun wedged behind the rope he had used to hold up his Indian pantaloons and struck a relaxed pose, but then exploded. "That there's enough. There ain't no such a thing as ghosts. Now the two of you change your clothes and get your asses on your darn horses and ride down there afore I get angry and do something I might regret." Jackson's hand squeezed the wood and metal grip of the gun and his index finger slid inside the trigger guard.

Csongor Toth spoke when Jackson began pulling the gun out of his pants. "Oh, for goodness sakes. I've never heard anything like this, and during my limited time with you gentlemen I thought I had heard everything." Csongor stifled a small yawn with the fingertips of his left hand. "I must say...I find myself inexplicably refreshed after listening to the three of you bicker about the possible existence of vengeful spirits. Might I therefore suggest that we all change our clothing and ride down to the massacre together to determine the meaning of the gunshot? Now, is this acceptable to everyone? If not, Jackson may end up shooting someone, which I believe might discourage further discussion."

Seth glanced bitterly at Jackson's gun hand. "I ain't staying here all by myself when there might be ghosts about. They can fly, you know. They can fly right through you." He shivered. "And they can see in the dark, better than a cat."

Miguel kicked at a rock sticking out of the dry ground. "If Seth's going, I'm going too, 'cause I'm not staying here by myself neither. I didn't know they could fly."

Csongor pressed the fingers of his hands together. "Excellent. Then we're all agreed. Finish removing your Indian clothing, gather up the weapons and other artifacts, and hide everything in yonder bushes. We must depart as quickly as possible, for we have already wasted too much time discussing the epistemology of the otherworld. Make haste gentlemen, make haste, for time is precious and there is precious little time to spare!"

Jackson reluctantly pulled his hand away from the gun. The scowl continued to furrow deep lines into the weathered skin of his forehead, and he spit his words angrily at Seth and Miguel. "You heard the man. Time to stop talking about piss geology. Ghosts or no ghosts, we're all heading down there together."

Joshua Hotah examined the broken shaft of the shovel he now gripped in his right hand and then the other half of the shovel lying splintered near his feet. He pointed with the broken shaft and spoke to the appaloosa. "I think we are not digging more graves today. And this is not good news because I still have more work to do on the first grave." Joshua tossed the splintered shaft toward the creek; it spun smoothly until the first skip imparted a lazy wobble then splashed into the water near the far bank.

The appaloosa's nose followed the arc of the shaft down then up a little then down again. After it dove into the creek she snorted and wiggled her head.

Joshua visually measured the shallow grave he had excavated into the rocky soil. "No my friend, there is not enough room in this grave for all of the bodies. There is not even enough room for two bodies, and I do not want to separate the mother from her children because I made a promise. I think it is possible to fit the father into it…if I bend him a little. Lucky for us he was not a large man because the grave is not a large grave either." Joshua kicked a rock into the hole, then immediately regretted it because he had made the grave smaller. "I do not think he will care if he is straight or not." Joshua dropped to his knees, reached down, and pulled the rock out. He stood and rolled the rock around in his hand.

The appaloosa stomped a hoof lightly on the ground and whinnied a soft whinny.

Joshua thought of an idea for the mother and children. "I could build a travois and take them to the town. I could ask someone to bury them in the white man's graveyard. I remember seeing an ax along the road. I do not know who dropped it there. I saw some rope in the wagon." Joshua listened but the appaloosa said nothing. "This is what we will do. I will get the ax and the rope, bury the father who is not a large man in this grave which is not a large grave so he can rest by the creek, and carry the mother and her children back to town on the travois, which I will build after I bury the father." He tossed the rock into the creek. "I think it is a good plan."

The appaloosa nodded vigorously and let out a small snort at the same time.

Csongor Toth, his elbows resting near the top of a craggy ridge, squinted though the twin-telescope binoculars he had ordered from Munich last December—and which had finally arrived at the Sommercamp Emporium & General Store only a week ago. After thoughtfully inspecting the wagon—and observing the strange proceedings of a lone man and his horse on the road below his position—he nudged the center focusing knob until the peculiar image of the man conversing with the horse settled into focus. After watching a little more, Csongor realized that the horse appeared to understand the man's words and gestures.

Jackson squirmed his knees against the hard earth and grunted, "What are you seeing though them expensive telescopes? I'm getting pretty tired of sitting here up on this ridge and doing nothing but watching you fiddle with that thing when I can't see much of what's going on anyway."

Csongor spoke without lowering the binoculars. "Patience, my surly companion. I regret to inform you that the man has destroyed my glorious work of art and relocated the bodies down by the creek. He has just finished digging one grave and he threw something into the creek. But more interesting than any of this, he appears to be talking to his horse. And even more interesting, the horse appears to be talking back."

Jackson sniffed back a drool of dirt-streaked snot. "Talking to his horse and the horse talking back? How can you tell by looking through them metal tubes? If you ask me, it don't much matter who he's talking to or what he's doing to them bodies. If there's just one man and his horse, we ought'a ride down there right now and shoot them both before they spill the beans and we all get hanged for killing the family."

Seth cleared his throat. "Maybe he's not talking to his horse. Maybe he's talking to the ghosts of the family. They wouldn't be angry at him, 'cause he's not the one who did it. They might be asking him where they can find us, and he might be telling them right now."

Csongor lowered the twin-telescope binoculars and rested them on top of his forearm to protect them from the ground. "Your obsession with ghosts is becoming quite annoying. Nonetheless, I must disagree that this man might 'spill the beans' as you so eloquently put it. This man's arrival is, in fact, a fortuitous stroke of luck."

Jackson snorted, "A stroke of luck? How do you figure?"

Csongor lectured: "Simple, my well-intentioned but dimwitted compadre. First, judging from the man's attire and hair, he is almost certainly a real Indian. Second, the man is digging graves to bury the family, which gives us time to ride back to Silver City and fetch the sheriff and lead him directly to one of the perpetrators of this heinous act of violence against humanity." Csongor rolled to his side and began storing the twin-telescope binoculars in a leather case. "Let me explain more precisely. Miguel, you stay here and keep an eye on this man…and his horse. Jackson and Seth, you ride back to Silver City and find the sheriff. Volunteer to help. And make sure he deputizes both of you. I will ride to Silver City after you have departed to attend a meeting with an upstanding citizen of Silver City, a meeting I arranged previously to provide myself with an alibi— although it seems I no longer need one because this Indian has arrived to save the day."

Miguel stood and began vigorously slapping the road dust from the front of his pants. "What's an…alley bye?"

Csongor stood and did the same, but with a more effeminate brushing motion. "It is a sophisticated legal word of which you do not need to concern yourself at this time."

Miguel pouted, "Just asking."

Now that Csongor had resolved the problem of the man and the horse, he swung his arm in a dramatic flourish as he strode towards the horses with renewed confidence. "Onward men. We each have our assignments. Onward! Onward to take full advantage of this fortuitous stroke of luck, which, I might add, has presented itself so gloriously on this finest of days."

Miguel asked Seth after they had mounted the horses, "Do *you* know what an alley bye is?"

Seth sneered, "Go to hell, Miguel."

Joshua picked up the ax about a hundred feet back up the road. He trudged to the wagon and, after rummaging through the family's meager possessions, found a sufficient coil of worn rope. He walked down to the spot where he had broken the shovel and spoke to the appaloosa. "I have everything I need to make the travois. You stay here and guard the family while I find some good trees to cut down."

The appaloosa nodded her agreement—or at least Joshua thought she had before he disappeared into the trees beyond the curved edge of the road. After a while the appaloosa heard chopping sounds and the crackling noise of trees falling to the ground and then more chopping sounds. Joshua returned dragging two slender trees, completely bare of any branches, under his sweaty arms. Joshua dropped the trees next to the grave. "Since it is you who must pull the travois, I have found trees slender and strong. If you will watch the family a little longer, I will make the travois and load the mother and her children. When I am finished, I will bury the father in the one grave I dug before the shovel broke and we will ride into town to find the white man's graveyard. Do you have any questions to ask?"

The appaloosa stomped her hoof, and Joshua began the task of building the travois so he could transport the mother and her children to Silver

City. The afternoon grew hotter and he had to drink from the creek many times before he had finished his work.

After a hard ride, Jackson and Seth staggered breathlessly into the jail of Sheriff Wendell Boyle and immediately began stomping their feet on the wood floor and slapping off dust with their hats. Sitting on a creaky swivel chair behind a small desk, Sheriff Boyle crumpled a sheet of paper and threw it into a waste basket. "What's wrong with you boys? Can't you see I just swept the place clean? Now you've gone and brought in a bunch of dirt and I'll have to sweep the place up again. A man my age shouldn't have to sweep the floor more than once a day."

Jackson stopped slapping at his vest and bowed his head to feign the appearance of regret, even though he didn't really care about the cleanliness of the Sheriff's office. "We're really sorry we messed up your nice office Sheriff, but we got news and you need to ride out of town and check on it right away. As a matter of fact, me and Seth are willing to ride along with you as deputies so you don't have as much work on your hands."

Sheriff Boyle stood and set his hands on the desk. "What kind of news would make me want to deputize the likes of you and ride out of town on what sounds to me like a wild goose chase?"

Seth could not conceal his excitement and broke in before Jackson could answer. "There's been a massacre. Indians did it. We saw the whole thing. And now the Indian who did it is digging graves to hide the bodies so nobody will ever find out about it. You gotta deputize us quick so we can ride back and arrest him before he gets away."

Although not particularly fond of Seth's characterization of the news of the day, Jackson had no choice but to work with the story as presented. "That's right, Sheriff. Indians massacred this family when they was leaving town in a wagon, and there's still one of them trying to bury the bodies … because he doesn't want anyone to find out about it." He offered a solemn oath to strengthen his story. "I swear it's the truth. We seen the whole thing, just like Seth says."

Sheriff Boyle barked, "Why didn't you try to do something about it, if you was standing there watching the whole thing?"

Confused, Seth twisted his toe against the floor. Jackson fabricated a hasty clarification. "What we meant to say, Sheriff, is we saw the whole thing of this one Indian trying to bury the bodies so no one would find out about it, and he's still there...as far as we know. The other Indians was gone by the time we got there, but we were afraid they might be hiding nearby and come right back and we rode into town to tell you as quick as we could."

Sheriff Boyle stroked his moustache. "I see. I guess it makes some sort of sense, if I think about it the right way." He pulled open a drawer and retrieved two tarnished badges and tossed them on the top of the desk. "Alright then, I'm deputizing the both of you." He slammed the drawer closed. "But I think we'll need a few more men just in case the other Indians return. You two run across the street to the saloon and ask if anyone wants to ride out of town to apprehend the Indian responsible for this massacre. I'll walk over to the saloon down the street and do the same. If we work fast, we can raise a good-sized posse within the hour."

Jackson cleared his throat. "I think we might want to leave a little sooner. When we left, the Indian was just starting on the second grave. He might be nearly finished by now and who knows when he might get away."

Sheriff Boyle pounded the desk. "Alright then. We leave in thirty minutes. Meet me back here with whatever men you can scare up and we ride. Thanks to the both of you, I'll have to sweep the office again after we get back."

Miguel Cervantes rode in a furious gallop back to Silver City. He had watched the strange man who talked to his horse for quite awhile before dozing off. When he snorted himself awake and lifted his chin off his tingling arms the sight of the man riding up the hill in his direction shocked him completely awake. When the man had approached within a hundred yards, Miguel observed that he had not buried the entire family as everyone originally thought, and for some inexplicable reason was now pulling some of the bodies behind his horse on some sort of Indian contraption he must have built while Miguel napped. Csongor had given him specific instructions to keep an eye on the man and his horse, but didn't tell him what to do if the man changed his mind and decided to ride away with the bodies. Miguel had no idea what to say when he got back to Silver City, but this problem resolved itself with the arrival of Sheriff Boyle and his new deputies and the makeshift posse rounded up from several of the local saloons.

The posse and Miguel both slowed as they approached each other. The posse halted completely when Sheriff Boyle held up his hand. Miguel and the sheriff briefly stared at each other before the sheriff finally spoke. "And who might you be, standing out here by yourself in the middle of nowhere?"

Miguel removed a glove halfway then pulled it back on. Csongor had not told him how to make up a good story to tell the sheriff if the Indian and his horse changed their minds. He made a valiant attempt nonetheless. "My name is Miguel Cervantes. I have been watching the Indian who massacred the family. He's riding this way with some of the bodies … which surprised me because I thought he was going to bury the bodies to hide them … but then he changed his mind when I did not see it and now he's riding this way with some of the bodies instead of burying them … like we thought in the first place."

Sheriff Boyle coughed up some phlegmy dust then spat it to the side. "That don't make a darn bit of sense. You say he was going to bury the bodies but now he's bringing the bodies this way? Why would anyone in their right mind do that after a massacre?"

Jackson coaxed his horse forward until he was next to Sheriff Boyle. "Miguel works for me. I told him to watch this Indian fellow while we rode into town to fetch you. He's probably decided to take them bodies somewhere for one of them strange Indian rituals I've heard about. Probably why he decided not to bury all the bodies. If you ask me, it don't make any difference one way or the other. We still need to catch him before he gets away."

Sheriff Boyle complained, "This whole thing is getting more peculiar by the minute, but I guess I can see your point. We'd better ride fast and catch this fellow before something else happens that don't make any sense." He twisted in his saddle and yelled at the men of his makeshift posse, "Let's ride, men, before this fellow gets away with the bodies and does something else we don't care to know about." Sheriff Boyle kicked his horse into a gallop and propelled the posse forward with a gallant wave of his arm. Miguel Cervantes mounted his horse and joined in after the last man had passed by.

Without a working shovel, Joshua Hotah wedged the father's body into the grave and covered the blood-stained corpse with smooth rocks gathered from the creek. When he had finished, he observed the western skies and judged the time of day a little after three o'clock. He walked to the creek and knelt down for one last drink before heading to Silver City. He checked the ropes securing the mother and her children to the travois before mounting the appaloosa.

The appaloosa whined when she felt the travois rub against her haunches.

Unsympathetic, Joshua Hotah said, "There is no reason for you to complain. This is only the second, or maybe the third time I have asked you to pull a travois, and this is not much of a load so there is no reason for you to complain." Joshua touched his heels against the sides of the appaloosa and the animal began pulling the travois up the road toward Silver City. When they reached the top of the hill and began descending, Joshua noticed a distant cloud of dust moving along the road. At first he could not discern the direction of the cloud, but after studying it a little more he realized that the cloud moved steadily in his direction. Joshua and the appaloosa continued riding on, and the cloud disappeared behind a bend. When the cloud reappeared, Joshua observed the first of many riders. He patted the appaloosa on the neck. "Good news, my friend. Men are riding from Silver City to help us. We can give them the mother and her children. It will save us the trouble of finding the white man's graveyard. We can return to camp sooner than I thought."

When the men arrived, twenty-three in all, Jackson and Seth rode at the front with Sheriff Boyle. Jackson waved the rifle Sheriff Boyle had given him in the air. "There's the bloodthirsty savage who massacred the family. He's trying to hide the evidence right in front of us. We saw the whole thing. Drag the murdering varmint down off his horse before he gets away."

Sheriff Boyle raised his hand. "I don't want any shooting before this man gets a fair trial. Then we can hang him proper. Just get him down off his horse and tie him up. I want to ask him a few questions. I want to take a look at what he's pulling too."

To Joshua's surprise, Jackson and Seth rode forward and dragged him sidewise off the appaloosas before he could say anything. Three other men quickly jumped on top of him and beat him around the face and shoulders and kicked him in the side. They tied his arms behind his back and looped the rope three times around his chest and pulled it painfully tight, and then Jackson slammed a rifle butt into Joshua's stomach. Jackson and Seth lifted Joshua up and dragged him in front of the posse.

Sheriff Boyle eyed Joshua suspiciously. The other members of the makeshift posse closed in behind to hear the conversation. The sheriff spoke loudly and distinctly so the Indian could understand. "I hear from my deputies you just murdered a family on the way out of Silver City this morning. I'm told you are trying to hide the bodies so we won't find out about it. What do you have to say for yourself?"

Joshua tried to straighten up, but the ropes binding his arms behind his back prevented it. "It was not me who killed the family. I spoke to the mother. She told me white men dressed like Indians killed her family. She said the same men who did this tied her to the wagon wheel and shot her with arrows."

Sheriff Boyle scoffed, "Well then, that makes everything a lot easier to understand. Why don't you just take us to see this woman right now and we can hear what she has to say for ourselves?"

Joshua tried to look back, but the ropes cut into his arms. "I can't take you to see her. She is dead, like the rest of her family. She is tied to the travois behind my appaloosa."

Sheriff Boyle grinned. "Well, ain't that mighty convenient. And I don't suppose you know who killed the woman, since you claim to know who killed the family?"

Joshua answered, "I killed her because she was in much pain and asked me to do it."

Sheriff Boyle pounded one hand into the other and exclaimed, "That's the most peculiar story I ever heard. First you tell me white men dressed up like Indians did it, then you confess to killing the woman yourself because you say she asked you to. Son, you're going to need a really good lawyer to get out of this one." He spoke directly to Jackson. "Get him back up on his horse. I got a nice warm jail cell waiting for him in town." Jackson grinned and muttered something profane no one could hear.

Manfred Herrmann had just walked out of the saloon on the corner of Washington and Avalanche when Sheriff Boyle and his new deputies (Jackson and Seth) and the makeshift posse of men rounded up from the saloons and Joshua Hotah and the appaloosa dragging the travois paraded down the middle of the street. Manfred saw the bloodied face of Joshua Hotah before he beheld the travois and the lifeless bodies of a woman and two children tied to it. When he focused more closely on the boy and girl, he realized that someone had scalped them. He prayed that the scalping had not occurred before death. Farther down the street, some of the citizens of Silver City began gathering to observe the grim procession for themselves.

Excerpt from

A Concise History of the West

by Muireall Anne Ravenscroft

Lawmen, Judges, and Vigilantes

The various systems of jurisprudence existing in the American West during the latter half of the nineteenth century were spotty affairs at best, particularly given the inconsistency of — or in most cases the complete absence of — codified laws to guide the professional conduct of the lawmen, judges, and other judicial officials of the times. Lawmen were typically underpaid, often inexperienced, and in general poorly trained to face the myriad dangers and rigors confronting them. Judges were often self-proclaimed as such, even though they frequently brought little or no genuine legal training or background to judicial proceedings. This lack of experience could quickly result in a death sentence for the accused without any opportunity for appeal. Vigilante groups flourished throughout the American West, particularly in the mining towns and areas where lawlessness and retribution reached levels difficult to comprehend in the twentieth century. But perhaps a few pithy examples will illustrate these points better than a dry narrative, for the story of the American West is replete with an endless cast of colorful characters to choose from, as the following will surely reveal.

David C. Updyke (1830-1866), also known as "Big Dave Updyke," narrowly won election as Sheriff of Ada County, Idaho in March 1864, likely due to his political connections. Prior to this auspicious event, the highpoints of his resume included two years of experience as a stagecoach driver in California, prospecting and working a claim on Ophir Mountain in Boise County, purchase and operation of a livery stable in the middle of Boise City, and travels to British Columbia; Yuba County, California; and Virginia City, Nevada. There was never any hard evidence that David Updyke had committed a crime prior to his purchase of the livery stable, but many suspected him of participation in a stagecoach robbery near Boise City in 1864, and also of aiding in the illegal circulation of stolen gold dust. The livery stable soon became a common meeting place for many of the more despicable characters of Boise City, prompting the locals to call the ad hoc gathering of men "Updyke's Gang." Nonetheless, no actual proof of illegal activity by the gang was ever found. On July 26, 1865 David Updyke and three other men robbed a stagecoach in Portneuf Canyon, killing four passengers in the process before absconding with $86,000 in gold — a massive sum at the time. A local vigilante group from a settlement near the Payette

River — a group Sheriff Updyke had tried to break up and arrest soon after his election — immediately pursued the three men who had accompanied Updyke, but decided to approach the punishment of the elected Sheriff of Ada County with more caution and therefore waited for a better opportunity. The opportunity presented itself on September 28, 1865 when the Payette River Vigilante Committee detained Sheriff Updyke for failing to arrest an outlaw named West Jenkins, among other charges. However, Updyke quickly made bail and fled to Boise City where his political connections and influence provided protection from further arrest. Accompanied by an outlaw named John Dixon, Updyke left Boise City April 12, 1866 to avoid another confrontation with the vigilantes. Unfortunately, the vigilantes captured both men during the night in an abandoned cabin thirty miles out of town. The hanged bodies of Big Dave Updyke and John Dixon were found two days later. One of the vigilantes had pinned the following note to Sheriff Updyke's chest: "an aider of murderers and thieves." The $86,000 in gold from the stagecoach robbery was never recovered.

Judge Roy Bean (c. 1825-1903) dispensed his own peculiar brand of justice during court sessions held in his saloon near the banks of the Rio Grande River in the desolate Chihuahuan Desert of West Texas. Born in Kentucky around 1825, Roy Bean walked away from his family home at the age of fifteen and headed west in search of adventure. After travelling to New Mexico on a wagon train, he crossed into Mexico and established a trading post in Chihuahua. He killed a man and fled to San Diego to live with his brother, Josh. After becoming the first mayor of San Diego, Josh Bean appointed Roy a lieutenant in the state militia and hired him as the bartender of his saloon. Roy was arrested for wounding a man in a duel. He escaped back to New Mexico and joined his brother Sam who had found work as a sheriff.

For the next several years Roy tended bar at his brother's saloon and smuggled guns from Mexico through the Union blockade. After the Civil War he married a Mexican teenager and moved to San Antonio, Texas. He supported his wife and five children during the 1870s by selling stolen firewood and watered-down milk to the locals. Roy Bean abandoned his family around 1882 and travelled to Vinegaroon in the desolate Chihuahuan Desert, where he operated his own saloon from a tent to service workers building a new railroad line from San Antonia to El Paso. Eager to establish some sort of law enforcement in the area, the County Commissioners appointed Roy Bean "Justice of the Peace" for Precinct Number 6 in Pecos County, Texas. Likely under the influence of alcohol at the time, Roy accepted the appointment and transferred to Langtry, a tent city overlooking the Rio Grande River. Roy built a saloon, named it the "Jersey Lillie" after an attractive British actress, and posted several signs on the front announcing "Ice Cold Beer" and "Law West of the Pecos." Judge Roy Bean's judicial rulings where characterized by avarice, preconceived bias, and only a modicum of common sense, all delivered in excessively dramatic language. An example of one of his colorful rulings is as follows: "It is the judgment of this court that you are hereby tried and convicted of illegally and unlawfully committing certain grave offenses against the peace and dignity of the State of Texas, particularly in my bailiwick. I fine you two dollars; then get the hell out of here and never show yourself in this court again. That's my rulin'." Legend holds that Judge Roy Bean sent dozens of men to the gallows, but in fact there is no historical evidence proving he hanged even one man. Despite his oddly personal manner of jurisprudence, he was officially elected as a judge in 1884, and then reelected several times thereafter. He conducted judicial proceedings and served customers whiskey in his saloon until 1902. He died a year later in 1903.

The Missouri Bald Knobbers, a remarkably brutal organization which rendered its own version of justice during the years 1883 through 1899, in many ways typified the conduct of many of the vigilante groups that flourished in the American West. Formed under the leadership of one Nathaniel N. Kinney in direct response to the profound lawlessness and rampant legal corruption that had spread across Missouri in the chaotic years following the Civil War, the first meeting, held in secret, involved twelve prominent leaders of Taney County, Missouri. Membership in the organization had expanded to over 200 when the group met on April 5, 1885. During the week following this meeting, over 100 Bald Knobbers marched to the Taney County Jail in the town of Forsyth, battered down the doors, and carried away two brothers, Frank and Tubal Taylor. Although generally known as outlaws and law breakers, the sheriff had arrested the brothers on this particular occasion for wounding a local storekeeper during a dispute about credit and a pair of boots, a storekeeper who was also a member of the Bald Knobbers. The vigilantes hauled Frank and Tubal south of town and hanged them. This shocking act of violence prompted several of the original members to resign. Participation in the group continued to grow nonetheless and ultimately reached well over 500 men. In the years following the hanging, the Bald Knobbers expanded into other law enforcement activities including night rides to discourage the illegal behavior of drunks, gamblers, and prostitutes; flogging or branding men suspected of thievery; and belligerent threats to men accused of beating their wives or failing to support their families. There is also historical evidence that the Bald Knobbers hanged men — or simply beat them to death — for the less serious crimes of assault, disturbing the peace, or destruction of property. The expanding activities and violence of the Bald Knobbers divided the citizens of Taney County into either supporters or detractors and prompted the formation of an opposition group calling itself the "Anti-Bald Knobbers." Unfortunately, the Bald Knobbers often reserved the harshest punishments to those who publicly spoke out against the vigilante group. Stories about the Missouri Bald Knobbers ultimately reached the national press, and in 1887 one journalist called the group the nation's largest and fiercest vigilante movement. A member of the Anti-Bald Knobbers named Billy Miles assassinated Nathaniel Kinney on August 20, 1888, but was later judged not guilty because the court declared that he had killed Kinney in self-defense. The Missouri Bald Knobbers disbanded in 1899.

Judge Isaac C. Parker (1838-1896), also remembered as the "hanging judge" in popular western novels and similar contexts, held the bench of the U. S. Court for the Western District of Arkansas for twenty-one years. During this long tenure Judge Parker heard thousands of criminal cases regarding disputes between Indians and non-Indians. He sentenced 160 people to death, many of these during a fourteen-year span when defendants had no right of appeal. Although he promoted reform of the criminal justice system and became a strong advocate for the rights of the Indian nations, a number of sensationalized cases and mass executions ultimately tarnished his legacy and....

John Ravenscroft pressed down hard on the pedals of his bicycle, accelerating until he pulled even with Muireall. He spoke to her in an artificially-loud voice to overcome the sound of the cool afternoon breeze whooshing in his ears. "I finished the section on lawmen, judges, and vigilantes before breakfast this morning."

Fearful of losing her balance, Muireall squeezed the handlebar grips tightly and spoke without turning her head. "Did you? I didn't see you reading this morning. What did you think of it?"

John steered around a divot in the road before answering, "I liked it. But I found it difficult to fathom such rampant violence and lawlessness when I consider our world in the year 1907. I'm not expressing myself very clearly, but you know what I mean."

"Yes, I know what you mean. The vigilante groups are particularly disturbing when viewed from a twentieth century perspective. Such brutality is beyond comprehension."

John maneuvered a little closer to Muireall. "Yes, the vigilantes. I never even knew they existed until I read your manuscript."

Flashes of sunlight sparkled though the trees flourishing along the road. "Neither did I until I began the research. Where would you like to eat dinner tonight?"

A bug glanced off John's cheek and buzzed past his ear. "Nearly swallowed a bug. How about that cute little restaurant we visited a few months ago, the one with the tiny round tables outside by the street? If I remember correctly, they had an excellent wine list, and I don't think there's any danger of running into any vigilantes there."

"Nor do I. Maybe a judge or lawman, but surely no vigilantes." A gust lifted Muireall's bonnet, but she adroitly tugged it down without losing speed.

CHAPTER TWO

An unusual friendship
May 6, 1872

Priscilla Kimball held a dainty hand against her dainty lips and coughed a dainty cough after sniffing in a healthy whiff of the bluish haze floating across the saloon from the ceiling down to her dainty arm-pits. When she approached within three steps of the table where Margaret impatiently drummed her stubby fingertips, a wizened man sitting at the same table and wearing a filthy derby and pants tucked into his boots and a shaggy vest with a tarnished metal star pinned on it expanded the bluish haze by exhaling a vast plume of smoke from a thick cigar. When Priscilla arrived at the beer-and-tobacco-stained table, she folded her hands in front of her apron and waited for Margaret to finish her conversation with the cigar-smoking man.

Margaret appeared quite relaxed in the hard chair and waved her hand around dispassionately as she spoke. "Like I was saying, Sheriff, I don't really care what color he is or what he's done. Red, white, yellow, or green with too much whisky, they're all scoundrels as far as I can tell. If the price is right, we can feed him for you. Of course, we don't have a big fancy kitchen like some of the larger establishments in town, but we shouldn't have any trouble getting the job done to everyone's satisfaction."

Sheriff Boyle puffed the thick cigar, then started chewing on it. "That's good news Margaret, since I can't convince anyone to feed this fellow because after they found out he killed the whole family and scalped the children nobody will have a thing to do with him. I'm as upset about it as the next fellow, but I don't want him to starve to death before he gets a fair trial and hanged proper."

Margaret rested her fingers after tapping out a lively five-stroke roll. "I see your point, Sheriff. It *would* be a downright shame if he starved to death before you get to hang him. Well, I've got just the gal to take care of this job, and she's standing right here in front of us. Priscilla, introduce yourself to Sheriff Boyle."

Priscilla curtsied without moving her feet. "Nice to meet you Mr. Boyle. My name's Priscilla Kimball." She curtsied again.

Sheriff Boyle shoved the cigar in his mouth before asking, "Ain't you the young gal I heard rumors about, the one who was working as a whore?"

Margaret quickly interceded. "Course not Sheriff. I run a respectable business here. We even have church services in the back room … every Sunday. I wouldn't ever let someone young as Priscilla do any whoring. Just wouldn't be right." She punctuated her declaration with a presumptuous grin.

Sheriff Boyle chewed on the cigar as he said, "Church services in the back room? Never heard of church services in a saloon before."

Margaret smirked. "They call themselves *Lutherans*. They meet every Sunday morning and make quite a racket. Come see for yourself sometime if you don't believe me."

"No need to see such a thing for myself, Margaret. When can you get started? This fellow hasn't eaten since yesterday, and I don't know when he ate before then." Sheriff Boyle gnawed off a small chunk of the cigar and spat it under the table.

Margaret pressed the tips of her stubby fingertips together. "We can start by serving him dinner tonight. I'll have Priscilla make all the arrangements and deliver the meal by seven. That way she can be doing something useful around here and actually make me a little money." Margaret grunted to Priscilla, "Maybe start paying back a little of the debt you accumulated since you started working here."

Priscilla curtsied a third time. "Yes, ma'am."

Margaret pulled her hands apart and spoke to Priscilla in a kinder voice. "You understand what to do? I suppose you were listening to the whole conversation."

"No, ma'am. I only clean up in the kitchen from time to time when there's a special mess. No one ever asked me to cook anything before."

"It's not hard to figure out. It's half-past-five and you have to deliver the meal by seven. Go talk to the cook and tell him to have some food ready for you to deliver to the jail by half-past-six. When he hands it to you, deliver it to the jail. When this Indian fellow finishes his meal, bring the plate back here. Do the same thing at breakfast tomorrow, say around eight after you finish your morning chores. Deliver breakfast and dinner to the Indian until I tell you not to do it anymore. He's on his own for lunch." Margaret moved her stubby fingers to the table and resumed drumming. "You got any questions?"

"Yes, ma'am. What should I ask the cook to make for the Indian?"

Margaret sputtered, "How should I know?" Then she remembered Sheriff Boyle was still sitting next to her and her voice softened. "Tell him to make bacon and eggs, dear. Cook knows how to do it."

Confused, Priscilla blurted, "For dinner? Then what should I ask the cook to make for breakfast tomorrow morning?"

"Have him make bacon and eggs for every meal. We're not running a fancy restaurant with menus. Now go back to the kitchen and talk to the cook before he disappears or gets too drunk to fry an egg."

Priscilla curtsied a fourth time. "Yes, ma'am," and before leaving to find the cook said, "Nice to meet you, Sheriff Boyle."

Before the sheriff could say anything, she skipped away to the kitchen and found the cook—a scruffy man of 34 named Edward who supplemented his spotty prospecting income by cooking—frying up three eggs and a slab of bacon for one of the customers. Priscilla recited Margaret's instructions to the man. Then she asked if he had a tray or basket she could use to carry the meal over to the jail.

Edward wiped a greasy hand across his greasy forehead. "I can fry up some eggs and bacon and slap 'em on a plate for you, but if you want to carry the plate over to the jail on a special tray or in a pretty picnic basket, you'll have to figure that out for yourself. Come back a few minutes before seven and I'll have it ready for you."

But when Priscilla returned to the small kitchen ten minutes shy of seven, she had failed to locate a tray or picnic basket because people had mostly laughed at her when she asked them where she could find one or the other. After she told Edward of her dilemma, and explained why she didn't have a good way to carry the meal over to the jail, he scooped the eggs and bacon from the frying pan with a greasy spatula and slapped them on a plate like he had promised and handed the plate to her and said, "Looks like you'll have to carry the plate over to the jail all by its lonesome. Don't let the dogs get it. They'll probably come running after you when they smells the bacon."

Priscilla balanced the steaming plate of eggs and bacon in her little hands and heat from the bacon started to tingle her fingertips a little. When Edward told her to get out of his kitchen because he had other customers to feed, she carried the plate into the saloon and hurried past the potbelly stove and through the front doors. She scampered off the boardwalk into Washington Street and stopped because she didn't know where to find the jail because during all the commotion looking for a tray or picnic basket she had forgotten to ask anyone for directions. She crossed Washington and walked south past an imposing two-story building with big stone arches. She asked four different people where to find the jail. The fourth person finally told her the jail was located in the county courthouse on Washington Street: the two-story building with the big stone arches just down from Avalanche. She eventually arrived at the jail with a cold plate of bacon and eggs around ten minutes after seven.

Sheriff Boyle scattered some paperwork across his desk when Priscilla Kimball slammed the door open and stumbled into the jail. He growled, "You're late."

Priscilla explained the events of the last fifteen minutes between panting breaths. "I'm truly sorry...Sheriff Boyle but...I didn't know the way... and I had to ask and finally...after walking a really long...way this nice man wearing a...black suit told me where to go...and...and he said...I was going in the wrong direction...way down the street and...when I was coming back two...big dogs ran out of an alley...and tried to get the bacon from me...and I had to run and...I almost spilled the eggs... and the bacon too but then I caught them...just in time...by holding the plate against...my chest and the dogs were still chasing...after me when I finally—"

Sheriff Boyle stood and rattled a big ring of keys. "I think I've heard just about enough for tonight. Make sure you're on time for breakfast in the morning. Maybe you should think of carrying the food in a picnic basket so you can run easier when the dogs come after you. Now follow me and you can deliver them eggs and bacon to the accused murderer waiting for it in his cell. He's likely pretty hungry. Don't think he's eaten anything for two days." Sheriff Boyle used one of the keys to unlock a heavy wood door at the back of the office. He led Priscilla into a narrow hallway with three jail cells with iron bars and heavy iron doors along one side. A glowing kerosene lantern hanging on an iron hook provided a wavering light. The accused murderer waited silently inside the last cell on a rough-sawn wood bed with his knees drawn up and a frayed wool blanket pulled around his shoulders.

When Priscilla walked to the front of the cell the wood floor creaked and the Indian raised his chin and looked directly at her. Frightened, Priscilla's voice trembled when she asked Sheriff Boyle, "How do I give him the plate? There's bars in the way."

Sheriff Boyle huffed impatiently, "I'm not opening the door with no deputies around. Just set it on the floor and he can eat them bacon and eggs through the bars."

Priscilla slid her hands beneath the plate. "I forgot to bring a knife and fork. Do you have some you can spare?"

Sheriff Boyle sneered, "You must think I'm crazy if you think I'm giving that murdering redskin a knife or a fork. You just set the plate down on the floor by the bars like I told you. If he's hungry enough he can eat with his fingers."

Priscilla glanced at the Indian—he was still looking at her—then snapped her eyes to Sheriff Boyle. "I have to bring the plate back after he finishes. Can I wait out front with you?"

Sheriff Boyle rattled the big ring of keys. "I don't need a pretty young gal sitting in my office distracting me while I'm trying to read my paperwork. You'll just have to wait in here for him to finish." He walked back to the heavy wood door. "Knock when you're ready and I'll unlock the door for you. That is ... if I'm not busy doing something else."

Priscilla shivered when the hinges squealed and the door swung closed. Her index fingers tapped the sides of the plate. The Indian was still looking at her. She cautiously lowered the plate to the floor by the bars and shuffled back until she bumped against the wall. She found the courage to speak to the Indian when a splinter pricked her shoulder. "I have to wait for you to finish so I can take the plate back to the cook.

If you wouldn't mind getting started, I'd appreciate it." The Indian said nothing. She offered an apology. "Sorry it's kind of cold. I went the wrong way and on the way back some dogs chased me and I had to run."

Without saying a word, the Indian jumped off the bed, kneeled on the floor next to the bars, and quickly devoured the eggs and bacon with his fingers. When he had finished, he returned to the bed and resumed the same posture as before.

Priscilla waited until the Indian had finished wrapping the frayed wool blanket around his shoulders. She lunged forward and dropped to her knees and reached for the plate then stood and quickly backed up until she bumped the wall and the same splinter pricked her again. She ran to the heavy wood door and knocked. When the door did not immediately open, she knocked again. When the door still did not open, she knocked a third time. She raised her fist to knock a fourth time—

Sheriff Boyle unlocked the door and pulled it open. "Hold your horses, little miss. I heard you the first time."

Priscilla rushed out of the narrow room, ran across the office, and skittered though the front door without closing it. The next day, a Tuesday, she arrived at eight in the morning, but this time she carried a plate of steaming eggs and bacon in a picnic basket Nadia had found for her. After she set the plate on the floor and pushed it against the iron bars, she said, "I didn't get lost today and I didn't get chased by those big dogs either so this time your bacon and eggs are nice and hot." But the Indian ate the meal in silence and Priscilla did not say anything more. Neither of them spoke at dinner that night, nor during breakfast or dinner on Wednesday. Priscilla offered a few words on Thursday morning, but the Indian did not acknowledge her.

On Thursday night, Priscilla lifted the plate of hot eggs and bacon from the picnic basket and slid it across the floor. After rising up from her knees she said, "I found two carrots for you because I thought you might be getting kind of tired of eggs and bacon every meal. I didn't have time to cook them, but they are washed."

After munching down the carrots, but before starting on the eggs and bacon, the Indian said his first words to Priscilla. "My name is Joshua Hotah. I am not the one who killed the family in the wagon. I spoke to the mother before she died."

Stunned by hearing the Indian's voice, Priscilla could not think of anything to do except introduce herself. "My name is Priscilla…Priscilla Kimball." Impulsively, without thinking of the potential risk, she offered her hand. "Pleased to meet you, Mr. Joshua Hotah." When Joshua reached through the iron bars to grasp her hand, she thought of pulling it back.

Joshua squeezed Priscilla's little fingers with a surprisingly gentle touch. "Pleased to meet you, Priscilla Kimball." Joshua released her hand, dropped down to the floor, and did not speak again until he had finished the bacon and eggs. "Thank you for the carrots. I have only eaten bacon and eggs a few times before my arrival in this jail. I usually eat other things."

Priscilla stepped closer to the iron bars and rested her hands on a horizontal bar after Joshua settled down on the wood bed. "You spoke to the mother? How'd you do that? I heard everyone in the family was dead."

Joshua wrapped the frayed wool blanket around his shoulders. "When I arrived, she was not dead yet. I found her tied to a wagon wheel shot with many arrows and one through the belly. She was suffering from much pain when she spoke to me. She had lost much blood."

"She was still alive?" Priscilla pushed her face between the bars.

"Yes. She told me white men wearing Indian clothes killed her husband and children. She asked me to help the children. I went up the road to look for them. When I found the boy and girl, they were dead. Someone had scalped them."

"That's awful. Why would someone do such a horrible thing?"

"I do not know why. When I saw the woman again, I said her children were safe. She was happy to hear it."

"You lied to her?"

"Yes. I could see from her many wounds…she was going to die very soon. She did not need to know her children were scalped. I said her little girl was pretty."

"Then she died?"

"Yes. She asked me to kill her because she did not want to suffer more and she was happy her children were safe. I shot her in the heart with my Henry rifle. She died quickly."

Priscilla gasped, "*You* killed the mother?"

Joshua pulled the blanket a little tighter. "Yes, but she asked me to do it because she was in too much pain. She was going to die very soon anyway." He recalled an important detail. "She thanked me, and called it an 'unexpected act of kindness' before I shot her. I thought the words were strange when she said them. I understand now."

Priscilla remembered something she had heard in the saloon. "Why were you trying to hide the bodies, if someone else killed them and the mother asked you to do it?"

This claim surprised Joshua, because he had not heard it before. "Hide the bodies? Why would I do this?"

"I don't know, but I heard men talking about it in the saloon. They said it was a good thing the posse caught up with you when they did because you were trying to hide the bodies."

"I was not hiding any bodies. I buried the man in a grave too small for him because the shovel broke and I could not dig more graves for the mother and her children. I had to bend him a little, but he did not mind because he was dead. I was bringing the mother and children to town for someone to bury them in the white man's graveyard."

"That makes sense … I suppose. But why were you all covered in blood? I heard the men say this too."

Sheriff Boyle unlocked the heavy wood door and flung it open. "What's going on back here?" When he saw Joshua sitting on the bed and Priscilla hanging onto the bars, he relaxed. "I just realized you've been in here nearly half-an-hour. I thought maybe he'd dragged you through the bars and strangled you or something."

Priscilla faced the sheriff and crossed her arms. "I'm just fine. No need for you to worry about such things."

Sheriff Boyle noted the empty plate. "I see he's finished eating, so there's no need for you to hang around my jail neither. I got better things to do than keeping track of a young gal who shouldn't be here in the first place."

Priscilla picked up the plate, dropped it into the picnic basket, and marched out of the jail. The next day, a Friday, she arrived in the morning with bacon and eggs and an apple. She continued the previous night's conversation with Joshua Hotah, but within five minutes the heavy wood door opened and Sheriff Boyle entered the narrow hallway accompanied by a man wearing a black suit. When the light of a lantern splashed across the man's face, she recognized him as the one who had given her directions to the jail the first night.

Sheriff Boyle spoke derisively to Joshua Hotah. "You got a visitor today, and I don't think he wants to hang you like most everyone else in town."

The man in the black suit moved to the front of the cell and addressed Priscilla first. "I see you found your way to the jail."

"Yes sir. Thank you for the directions."

"You're welcome." He turned to the man sitting on a wood bed inside the jail cell. "My name's Manfred Herrmann. I heard a judge is arriving from Boise next week for the trial. I thought I might come down here and offer you some comfort."

When the man in the cell did not answer, Priscilla explained, "He doesn't like to talk when Sheriff Boyle's around."

Sheriff Boyle rubbed his chin and sneered, "Well then, I'll just lock the two of you in here with the murdering savage and you can talk all night long, if it suits you." He stomped through the door and slammed it closed and locked it. After a fair bit of coaxing, Priscilla convinced Joshua Hotah to tell his side of the story to the man in the black suit.

CHAPTER THREE

Billiards at the Idaho Hotel
May 14, 1872

Waves of gray-streaked clouds rolled over the Jordan Creek valley a few hours before daybreak. While most people slept—some drank whiskey or played poker or whored through the night (only a few of the possibilities)—the clouds drizzled pleasantly across the roofs and streets and alleyways of Silver City. When the first freight wagons rumbled through town after sunrise, the iron-rimmed wheels churned up muddy ruts and splattered the boardwalks and the sides of buildings and anyone who got too close with ragged flecks of mud. Soot-blackened chimneys puffed grayish swirls above the variegated rooftops; within a few hours of daybreak the pungent smells of acrid smoke and rain-moistened air settled into the valley. By mid-morning the gloomy clouds and showers had vanished to the west and the rising sun emerged above the southeastern mountain peaks to bathe the town with an agreeable warmth and sparkle off myriad panes of window glass. During the noon hour the sun ascended to its greatest altitude of the day, and the few buildings still veiled in mountain shadows crept into the light and the last of the dampness steamed off the roofs. By mid-afternoon the overlapping tracks engraved into the muddy streets by the freight wagons dried into hardened ruts. By dinnertime only the rim of the descending sun remained visible above the irregular horizon of the western mountains, and the comforting radiance of fading sunlight filled the valley and glowed pleasantly on the bony slopes of the eastern mountains.

Her hair still moist from bathing, Alexandra Smythe pushed through the front door of the War Eagle Hotel and strolled into the cool evening air. After tugging on the sleeves of her gray dress and adjusting the high collar to a comfortable fit, she pivoted right and walked along the boardwalk beneath the canopy fronting the hotel. At the northern end of the hotel she stepped off the boardwalk, crossed a narrow alley, stepped up to the continuation of the boardwalk at the next building, and turned right again into a slightly wider alley. She walked past a one-story-shingle-roofed general store and a one-story-tin-roofed stage and harness supply business. When she reached the eastern end of the alley, she angled northerly across Jordan Avenue and turned left at a Chinese shop offering an eclectic assortment of hand-painted merchandise. She continued north down Jordan and glided along the front of a livery, a storage building, a women's boarding house, a vacant building with boarded-up windows, another women's boarding house, a hardware store, and a business specializing in candies and fine cigars. When she arrived at the boardwalk fronting the Idaho Hotel, she reduced her pace and pulled on the sleeves again. Alexandra stomped the dirt off her black leather shoes and patted the front of her gray dress before entering the hotel lobby. She walked to the center of the lobby and stood just outside a loose circle of six Victorian parlor chairs and two small round tables (each with a smoldering kerosene lamp).

An elderly man wearing black lace-up shoes, dark wool pants, a striped vest, and a white shirt with a wrinkled collar and long sleeves lounged in one of the parlor chairs and read yesterday's newspaper. When he heard the delicate footsteps of a woman, he lowered the newspaper and stroked his thinning gray hair. "Can I help you, ma'am? You look to be a little lost."

Alexandra gazed above the man's head at a round clock hanging on the back wall of the lobby: because the bath had required more time than she had anticipated, she had arrived twenty minutes late. She spoke to the man without lowering her eyes from the clock. "I was supposed to meet a friend here for dinner, but I fear I may have arrived too late. He probably grew tired of waiting for me and has already gone home."

The man folded the newspaper lengthwise on his lap and rested his hands on the chair arms. "What's his name? Maybe I know him and can say whether he's in the hotel or not."

Alexandra stared at the man's wrinkled shirt collar. "Are you staying here at the hotel?"

The man fidgeted with the corners of the newspaper. "Course not. I work here. I'm the hotel clerk. I'm the one who checks people in and takes their money and tells them what room to go to."

"Then you very well might have seen him come in."

"I might of, but there's no way of knowing for sure if I did or not unless you tell me the man's name."

"Of course. How silly of me. His name is Csongor Toth, but I can't imagine you've ever heard of him."

"I've heard of him alright. He did some legal work on a mining claim for my brother-in-law; although at the time I told my brother-in-law that he was a fool to waste any more money on that worthless piece of ground. Only problem is, I don't know what he looks like because I never met him, so I can't tell you if he's in the hotel or not. But if you tell me what he looks like, I might be able to tell you if I saw him or not."

Alexandra tapped her chin with an index finger. "He's quite distinctive, actually. Hard to miss when you consider the other residents of Silver City. Quite slender. Always well dressed. Clean shaven except for a meticulously-thin moustache." And then she added without thinking, "And he always smells very nice."

The man folded the newspaper into a square and set it on the table next to the brass base of the kerosene lamp. "There's a man and a woman in the parlor. I know they're still in there because I hear them laugh every now and again. About a dozen folks showed up and headed for the dining room in the last half-hour. A couple of men, and a few women too, came and went from upstairs. But if I had to guess, I'm thinking the man you just described is in the billiards room. Saw him hanging around the front doors for a while before he went in there. Never said a word to me about anything, so I don't know what he smelled like."

Alexandra raised her freshly-washed chin and scanned the room. Within seconds she heard the distinctive sound of clacking billiard balls emanating from the doorway at the back of the lobby (to the right of a narrow stairway). "Thank you for your assistance. I know exactly where to look for him." Alexandra walked briskly to the back of the lobby and through the doorway into the billiards room. Two glowing kerosene lamps, both hung with chain from hooks screwed into the dark wood ceiling, illuminated the green felt surface of a large billiards table with ornately-carved legs. A solitary man reclined over the table to line up his next shot.

Csongor Toth continued to line up his shot while he spoke. "It pains me to observe that you are late, my dear Alexandra. But fear not, I have found a way to entertain myself while waiting for your arrival." He stroked the cue ball smoothly, drove a red ball into one of the corner pockets, watched the cue ball carom off another red ball, and straightened up. "I am still learning the rules of this American version of the game. However, it is very similar to English Billiards and should not take much longer to master." [2]

Alexandra apologized for her tardiness. "I'm sorry to arrive this late. I should have finished my chores earlier in the day."

Csongor slid to the other side of the table and began calculating his next shot. "Not to worry, my darling. I doubt that I could ever be angry with you. Would you like me to teach you to play billiards before we dine? I've heard the game is very popular with the women of Boston."

Alexandra moved closer to the table. "I wouldn't mind, but we have several important things to discuss, and I thought we could talk over dinner. Do you think we have time?"

Csongor waved his hand over the table. "All the time in the world. As the name might suggest, American Four-Pocket Billiards is played with four balls, two white and two red. The white balls are called cue balls, and one strikes them with a cue stick." Csongor held up his cue stick and gestured down its length with his free hand. "It would please me to dine with you anytime you wish. What, specifically, did you want to discuss?"

Alexandra squeezed her hands together. "It's Manfred. I'm quite worried about his safety after the dreadful events of last week."

Csongor resumed his discussion of the game of billiards. "One scores points by simply pocketing balls, scratching the white cue ball, or by making carom shots off two or three balls. It's really quite uncomplicated." Csongor gripped the rail cushion, bent his knees, and targeted one of the cue balls. "What events are you speaking of? Certainly not the unfortunate massacre of that innocent pioneer family."

---

[2]   The game of American Four-Pocket Billiards was very popular until the 1870s. The rules were similar to English Billiards, the leading game in Great Britain from around 1770 through the 1920s.

Alexandra frowned. "Csongor, it's exactly what I'm speaking about."

Csongor stood and retrieved the red ball he had just pocketed and rolled it slowly across the table with a flick of his fingers. The ball kissed the cushion in front of Alexandra. "As I explained, the rules are very similar to English Billiards, a game I learned to play during my college days in Budapest, days which I now remember with surprising fondness. Why should you be concerned about Manfred's safety? I have not heard that he had anything to do with the massacre. Certainly you are not suggesting—"

Alexandra picked up the red ball and pressed it against her breast. "Of course he didn't have anything to do with it. How silly of you to suggest it. I'm worried about his safety for other reasons." She squeezed the ball until her fingers turned white.

Csongor placed the cue stick on the table and rolled it back and forth with the palm of his hand. "It is of the utmost importance to select a straight cue if one wishes to ensure an accurate stroke. You can test the straightness of the cue by rolling it on the table like this. Those who merely sight along the cue to determine this quality are fools. Other reasons? Whatever do you mean?"

Alexandra relaxed her hand and pointed the red ball at Csongor and spoke more quickly. "What I mean is…he's been walking all over town this week asking people to donate money for the Indian's legal defense, the one they say killed the family. I'm very concerned for his safety. First there was the incident with the stone throwing in front of the saloon, and now this. I fear he is not making any friends in this town, and may very well be making some dangerous enemies."

Csongor raised his chin slightly and sniffed. "After finding a cue that is both straight and true, the next step is to properly chalk the tip to increase friction against the ball." Csongor picked up a small piece of chalk from the rail near the corner pocket and applied a thin coating on the leather tip of the cue. "This step is necessary if one wishes to impart spin on the ball, which is often required by some of the more sophisticated shots. Manfred is a grown man who, I assure you, can take care of himself. I shouldn't think you need worry about him."

Alexandra pressed the red ball down on the table and rolled it back to Csongor with an aggressive push. He caught the speeding ball before it hit the cushion. "Csongor, you should know how perilous this town can be. We haven't seen too many killings or beatings in recent months, but it is clear to me the town has turned against this Indian. And now Manfred is trying to help him. If he doesn't stop, I'm afraid the town will turn against Manfred too."

Csongor set the red ball on the table and spun it like a children's top. "I have heard that a two-piece cue is all the rage because one can carry it anywhere in a small leather case. I should look into the possibility of ordering one from England, although it would likely arrive sooner if ordered from New York or Boston. I do see your point, but what is it you expect me to do? I am but a simple lawyer who desires nothing more than to eke out a decent living in this unforgiving land without drawing attention to myself. And, I should point out, my friendship with Manfred is in its infancy. I therefore doubt he will listen to anything I might say to dissuade him from this unfortunate defense of an individual who is clearly guilty of murder."

Alexandra tilted her head slightly and blinked. "How is it you are certain of this man's guilt? I heard a judge would be coming to town this week to start a trial." She pressed both hands down on the table and squinted. "Do you know something you have not told me?"

Csongor pressed two fingers against his lips. "The stroke is the next important issue. The forward hand must embrace the cue in a relaxed manner that promotes an unfettered natural stroke. At the same time, the gripping hand must advance the cue without hesitation or wavering. One must also keep the back straight and the knees slightly bent." Csongor demonstrated his technique on the red ball Alexandra had rolled at him. "Quite so, my dear Alexandra. It was inappropriate to announce the Indian's guilt before his trial has even commenced. I can't imagine what I was thinking. I do hope you will forgive me, and that this unfortunate remark will not taint the rest of our evening together. I do detest the indigestion that often results from a mealtime argument."

Alexandra flicked her hand. "It's not me who needs to do the forgiving. But I will accept your apology anyway. Now…what are we going to do about Manfred? I agree he's a grown man who can take care of himself, but I still believe he is in great danger and in need of our help." An ominous darkness flowed across her face. "What are your thoughts on the matter?"

Csongor placed the cue on the table and set his hands on the rail and mocked Alexandra's gloomy expression. "Regrettably, it appears the billiards lesson is over. Perhaps we should continue at some other time when we are both in a more jovial mood. Shall we retire to the dining room and resume our discussion over dinner and wine?"

Alexandra sighed, "Yes, we should play billiards some other time." Her tongue slid across her upper lip. "Strange. I was not at all hungry when I arrived, but now I'm absolutely famished."

Csongor walked to the opposite side of the billiards table and offered his arm to Alexandra. "Then let us proceed to our repast. We have much to talk about." He proffered a fleeting smile to encourage her. "And I shall definitely take you up on your offer to play billiards another time. I shall look forward to our first game together with deep longing."

Alexandra rested her palm on Csongor's arm and inhaled deeply. "Then I shall look forward to it too." As they stepped away from the billiards table, she noticed that he smelled very nice.

CHAPTER FOUR

A message delivered
May 15, 1872

T seng Longwei propped the grimy hickory handle of the sledge-hammer against the battered wheelbarrow, spit on each of his calloused palms, and rubbed his hands together to spread the slimy mess as evenly as possible. When he had finished drying his hands on his pants, he raised his sweat-glistened face upward until his nose reached a point six inches shy of the jagged ceiling. He breathed deeply of the dank tunnel air. The flames of two pale candles secured in wrought iron holders spiked into narrow cracks—one to each side of the work area—cast a wavering light that did not assuage his growing claustrophobia. He had never complained about working alone in a tunnel when he could still see the pleasant glow of daylight shining into the mine entrance. But this particular tunnel had slanted downward after only 20 feet and then broke sharply to the left after another 30 feet, and now the tenuous flames of the candles offered the only alternative to an otherwise stygian gloom. Tseng Longwei retrieved the sledgehammer with both hands, swung the heavy tool upward until it rested momentarily above his right shoulder, and skillfully guided the blackened steel head in a smooth arc until it plummeted downward and fractured a modest boulder into three chunks. He balanced the sledgehammer on the tunnel floor before bending down and lifting one of the chunks into the wheelbarrow. When he reached out to retrieve the second chunk, he heard the distant sound of another wheelbarrow rattling down the tunnel. And he heard singing.

Roshan Kuznetsov, his attitude uplifted by the improving weather, maneuvered an empty wheelbarrow through the wood-framed mine entrance and began singing—the new song Gustus De Angeles had taught him—in his deep, gravelly voice:

> Down by the river, there lived a maiden,[3]
> In a cottage built just seven by nine,
> And all around this lubly bower,
> The beauteous sunflower blossoms twine.

As he approached the sharp turn to the left, he squeezed the handles of the wheelbarrow and sang the refrain with even more gusto:

> Oh! my Clema, Oh! my Clema,
> Oh! my darling Clementine.
> Now you are gone and lost forever,
> I'm dreadful sorry Clementine.

Roshan yanked the handles hard to the right, steered the wheelbarrow smoothly around the sharp turn to the left, and burst lustily into the second verse. He finished the last line after arriving in front of Longwei.

> Her lips were like two luscious beefsteaks
> Dipp'd in tomato sauce and brine,
> And like the cashmere goatess covering
> Was the fine wool of Clementine.

Longwei rolled the third and final chunk of the fractured boulder over the side of his wheelbarrow. He slapped his hands together and wiped them on his shirt. "You speak English much better when you sing. Maybe you should sing all the time."

Roshan released the handles and the wheelbarrow clanked against the tunnel floor. "It is of the much Roshan speaks good in the song, but I do not to think it is of the truth when singing all the time, if you know of what I speak to you in the now."

---

[3] Roshan is singing *Down by the River Liv'd a Maiden*, published by H. S. Thompson in 1863. This song provided the basis for the familiar *Clementine* written by Percy Montrose in 1884.

Longwei rested his hand against the tunnel wall. "Yes, I know of what you speak to me. I was attempting to make a small joke to lighten the work, but I see how my joke was not funny."

Roshan laughed, but not at the joke. "You must tell Roshan in front of the time for a joke, and I will greet you with the laugh you wish most to hear when a joke is over the end. This is the must to you do it."

Longwei pulled his hand from the wall and stroked the rolled edge of his wheelbarrow. "I did not expect you to arrive this soon with another wheelbarrow. I believe the tunnel is not wide enough for the two wheelbarrows to pass. You will have to move your empty wheelbarrow to the entrance to allow me to push my wheelbarrow filled with stones out of the tunnel."

Roshan massaged his chin and studied the two wheelbarrows in the flickering light of the candles. "I see what is meaning of your words." He pointed an index finger in the air, nearly jamming it against the tunnel ceiling. "But it is not of the problem for you because now as we speak of the two wheelbarrows who do not fit in the tunnel I must tell of you not to worry of this because a man of black is arrived with his buggy horse and must ask to speak of you and now you must leave the anyway to be the sure."

"A man of black? Are you speaking of John Smith?"

"No, of course it is not of the who I speak. I am talking of the man from Silver City of the black coat and of the black shoes who speaks in the church of the saloon on the corner of Avalanche and Washington. You know of it, I think."

Longwei breathed in a deep whiff of dank air. "Yes, I know of it. And I know of this man too. I have seen him several times walking the streets of Silver City inviting people to attend his church. But why would he ask to speak with me? There is no logic in it."

"Do not ask of this for Roshan to think of the logic or not think of the logic. I only do the messenger to deliver the message of the man of black. But I can tell you this for much is sure: I will take much care of the two wheelbarrows who do not pass and you do not worry about it if you care to speak to the man of black because he waits of you this very now and you should hurry when I say to do of it."

Longwei briefly pondered what Roshan had said. "Then I will leave you to solve the riddle of the wheelbarrows which will refuse to fit in the tunnel." Longwei patted Roshan on the shoulder when he walked by and an extraordinary plume of dust erupted from his business partner's vest and nearly extinguished the candles. "Thank you, my friend, for your thoughtfulness. I will return as soon as possible to continue my work. There are still many stones to remove from the tunnel before we set another charge."

Roshan nodded, and, while Longwei trudged out of the tunnel, he began singing the third verse of his new song. But without any awareness of it, because the number of syllables worked out perfectly (not that he would have known the difference), he unconsciously modified the lyrics of the second line of the refrain:

> *Her foot, Oh! Golly! Twas a beauty,*
> *Her shoes were made of Dig-by pine,*
> *Two herring boxes without the tops on*
> *Just made the sandals of Clementine.*

> *Oh! my Clema, Oh! my Clema,*
> *Oh! my darling Nadia.*
> *Now you are gone....*

Longwei surfaced through the heavy-timbered mine entrance into the midday light. The bright skies temporarily blinded him. He slowed his pace and shaded his face with a dirty hand. When the clarity of his vision had sufficiently improved, he spotted two men standing in front of a horse and buggy near the large pile of rocks he and Roshan had excavated from the new tunnel. When he walked closer, he recognized Gustus De Angeles and the man in the black jacket and black shoes Roshan had mentioned. Longwei stopped in front of the two men and lowered his hand.

Gustus De Angeles turned away from the man wearing the black jacket and spoke directly to Longwei. "Longwei, this here's Mr. Manfred Herrmann. Seems that Indian fellow the town's getting ready to hang sent him to speak with you. Strangest thing I ever heard of, but I told him he could talk to you all he wants...as long as you get your work done for the day."

Manfred Herrmann bowed respectfully. "Pleased to meet you, Mr. Sing Longway."

Longwei bowed with matching respect. "My name is Tseng Longwei. I am also pleased to meet you, even though I do not know the reason you wish to speak with me."

Gustus snapped one of his suspenders. "Well then, I'll leave the two of you to go about your business. I've got to check on how John and Roshan are getting along before the whole day is all used up." He backed away without shaking Manfred's hand.

Longwei slid his hands into opposite sleeves. "How do you know of Joshua Hotah? I did not know the town had plans to hang him. What has he done to deserve such a thing?"

Manfred thrust his hands into his trouser pockets. "Your English is very good, Mr. Longwei. Where did you learn to speak so well?"

Longwei nodded his appreciation of the compliment. "I learned to speak English from missionaries when I was a young boy in China. My English improved during the long passage across the ocean and my time building the great railroad across the mountains, although I have learned many new words which I have not found much use for."

Manfred yanked his right hand from the pocket and used it to gesture. "I met Joshua Hotah at the county jail, just last week. Since then we have talked on several occasions. After hearing his version of the story, I do not believe he is guilty of this horrible crime."

Quite uncharacteristically, Longwei asked excitedly, "Guilty? Guilty of what crime?"

Manfred yanked his other hand from the pocket and crossed his arms. "He's been accused of murdering an entire family on the road out of town. The sheriff and his deputies claim to have caught him trying to hide the bodies of the mother and her two children. The mother was shot full of arrows and the children were scalped."

"This is truly hard to believe."

"Unfortunately, I witnessed the entire spectacle when the sheriff and his men rode back to town with Joshua Hotah beaten and bound and a horse dragging the mutilated bodies of the mother and children behind. It was the most horrible sight you can imagine." Manfred shifted his feet.

"I think over half the town must have lined the street to see the same thing. Frankly, it did not bode well for Joshua Hotah."

"Then why have you come to Mahogany Gulch to speak with me? I talked to Joshua Hotah once many months ago. He told me of his strange dream and I told him of the dream's meaning. I have not seen him since then."

"He mentioned that you had interpreted his dream. But he also mentioned the Indian woman who lives with her son a few miles out of town. He said you would know where to find her."

Longwei slouched. "Yes, he told me of the Indian woman and her child. He also told me when he first met this woman she tried to stab him with a large knife. I think it might be very dangerous to find her when she has a large knife and does not speak English."

"Joshua mentioned the knife. He did say it was very large…and very sharp. But he also told me he has taught her a little English, and that her son has learned much English. He does not believe there will be any problem."

Longwei blinked, even though his eyes had fully adjusted to the light. "Problem? What kind of problem do you speak of?"

"He doesn't think there should be any problem when you tell the Indian woman he's in the county jail waiting for the trial to start."

Longwei's shoulders squirmed beneath his clothing. "Why should I be the one to tell her about Joshua Hotah's unfortunate news? Why don't you tell her? You are the one who spoke to him. And it appears you know more about the danger of the large knife than I do."

Manfred acknowledged the argument with a nod but refused to yield. "Therein lies the problem. Joshua Hotah thinks the Indian woman will likely come after a white man with that knife before he gets a chance to explain himself. He thinks you will have a better chance of not getting stabbed because you are not a white man."

Longwei fabricated a handy excuse. "This may be true, but I have much work to do here at Mahogany Gulch. I am certain Gustus De Angeles will not allow me to leave on such a foolish errand, especially when I may never come back."

"I wouldn't worry about it. I don't think I'll have any problem talking Mr. De Angeles into giving you the afternoon off. And if everything goes well, you'll be back at work in the mine before you know it."

"Even if you do talk him into giving me the afternoon off, I do not believe he will let me take the wagon when it is much needed here."

"He doesn't need to lend you the wagon. I will take you to the Indian woman's camp in my buggy. When you are finished talking to her about Joshua Hotah, I will bring you back."

Longwei gulped. "But what about the large knife, the one you say is also very sharp?"

"Joshua Hotah said you were a great warrior in China before you came to America. He didn't think you would have any problem dealing with a small woman who has only a knife to defend herself." Manfred grinned widely.

Longwei slumped into a pose of defeat. "I see. It appears I have run out of arguments to avoid this small woman and her large knife, which is also very sharp."

"Good. Then let's go talk to Mr. De Angeles. We should leave as soon as possible so I can bring you back here and return myself to Silver City before sunset. I wouldn't want to be traveling on that road after dark."

Tseng Longwei bowed graciously. "Yes, the road can be quite dangerous, even more so when it is not dark and one is filled with too much confidence."

CHAPTER FIVE

Manfred retains an attorney
May 16, 1872

M anfred Herrmann rocked in his favorite bentwood rocking chair
next to his favorite pickle barrel near the front door of The
Sommercamp Emporium & General Store, and, proving he was predes-
tined to be a Lutheran from the day of his birth, indulged in a rather ugly
episode of cerebral self-flagellation. At the same time, he engaged in a
more public exhibition of self-flagellation by gnawing big chunks off an
enormously sour pickle and chewing each chunk to a vile pulp before
gagging it down.

William Sommercamp detected Manfred out of the corner of his eye
while he restocked a rack of wall-mounted shelves with canned oysters,
canned meats, canned fruits, canned vegetables, and a box of newfangled
can openers just shipped in from San Francisco. After he slid the last
can of vegetables into place and aligned the cans by running his fingers
across the front of each row, he walked to the front of the store and leaned
against the pickle barrel. William Sommercamp allowed Manfred to rock
back and forth a few times before speaking to him. "I see you've decided
to come into my store again and eat a pickle." William Sommercamp
crossed his ankles and chewed a hangnail off his thumb. "Must mean I
should assume something's gone awry, because I know you hate pickles
and the only time you eat one is when something's gone awry."

A tear rolled off the tip of Manfred's nose when a small chunk had
trouble squirming down his throat. "Of course something's gone awry.

Why wouldn't there be something awry?" He bit off another chunk and rocked with increased enthusiasm. "As far as I'm concerned, I should come in here and eat more pickles because so many things have gone awry I can hardly keep track of them."

William Sommercamp opened the lid on the barrel, reached in, and pulled out a juicy pickle for himself. "I'll join you then. Unlike you, I actually like pickles. Nothing better on a hot day to quench the thirst than a nice dilled pickle."

Manfred rocked a little more aggressively. "Nothing better? I'd rather die of thirst than eat one of these abominations on a hot day." He shoved the last of the pickle into his mouth and scowled as the sour morsel flopped against the side of his tongue. He crushed the chunk between his wisdom teeth before swallowing it whole, then reached into the barrel and grabbed a second pickle.

William Sommercamp sucked some juice off his pickle before biting into the tasty gherkin. "Are you going to tell me what's bothering you, or are you going to just sit there rocking in that chair feeling sorry for yourself and diminishing the sales potential of my pickles?"

Manfred stopped rocking. "Do you want me to tell you what's bothering me?" He glared straight ahead and continued rocking.

"I certainly do. I wouldn't have come over here if I didn't want to know what's bothering you. I have plenty of work to keep myself busy without spending time talking to you about what's bothering you."

A young woman wearing a yellow bonnet entered the store. She observed Manfred's sour visage before asking, "Something wrong with the pickles?"

William Sommercamp nibbled the end of his pickle. "Nothing wrong at all, ma'am. As a matter of fact, I think this is my finest batch of pickles ever. It's just that Manfred really hates pickles, so he frowns when he's eating one."

The woman shook her head and walked away toward the back of the store to find fabric for a new dress for one of her five daughters.

William Sommercamp feigned displeasure because he thought this might improve Manfred's gloomy disposition. "Now see what you've gone and done. Mrs. Simpson will probably never buy another pickle from my store. And if you've ever seen the size of her family, you'd know we're talking a lot of pickles I could've sold. Oh well, I guess I'll just have to survive by selling other things, like newfangled can openers from San Francisco."

Manfred did not care a whit about lost profits on pickles or the sale of can openers. "Do you want to hear what's bothering me, or do you want to complain about lost pickle profits?"

William Sommercamp smirked, "You know how much I like to talk about pickles, but I guess we can change the subject to something else, if it makes you happy."

Manfred stopped rocking. "Makes me happier than you can imagine. What's bothering me is that I've been trying to raise money for the legal defense of Joshua Hotah all week, and I haven't had much success."

"Who's this Joshua Hotah fellow? Never heard of him."

A wiry miner named Samuel, who frequented the general store about once a month, burst through the front door and began stomping his boots on the wood floor. A small slab of dried mud broke off the bottom of his right boot before he pulverized it into a plume of dust.

William Sommercamp shook a finger at Samuel. "Samuel. How many times have I told you to clean your boots before you come into the store? Now I've got to sweep again."

Samuel removed his dusty black hat with a wrinkled brim and clutched it with both hands in front of his tarnished belt buckle. "Sorry Mr. Sommercamp. I only comes in once a month, and I keeps forgetting." Samuel noticed Manfred's expression and the half-eaten pickle in Manfred's hand. "Something wrong with them pickles?"

William Sommercamp protested, "No, Samuel. Nothing's wrong with the pickles. The problem is Manfred doesn't like pickles in the first place. Why don't you buy one and find out for yourself?"

Samuel squashed the dusty black hat onto his head and shoved his thumbs behind his belt. "No thanks. Mr. Sommercamp. Not sure I likes pickles either."

Annoyed, William Sommercamp sucked in a deep breath. "Then why don't you buy something so I can make a living, especially since it's obvious to me I'm not going to make a living by selling any pickles." Samuel nodded respectfully. He stomped his boots a few more times as he walked by the pickle barrel.

Manfred waited until Samuel had finished his boot stomping before explaining, "He's the Indian fellow Sheriff Boyle's holding in the county jail, the one they say massacred the wagon family last week."

William Sommercamp uncrossed his ankles and stomped his foot on the floor. "The Indian in the jail? I heard he was guilty and the whole town wants to lynch him. You sure it's wise to be going around town asking folks for money to defend him? They might decide to lynch you too."

Manfred resumed rocking. "Doesn't matter if it's wise or not. I've talked to Joshua Hotah on several occasions. I have come to believe he's been falsely accused. I therefore feel compelled to do something about it."

William Sommercamp brushed some lint off his sleeve. "You think he's innocent?"

"I have no doubt in my mind at all. He *is* innocent."

"Any luck raising the money?"

"Not much. That's what's bothering me."

"How come you haven't asked me for a donation?"

"After being turned down so many times I guess I just forgot."

William Sommercamp fished around in his pocket and pulled out a five-dollar bill. "Here, take this. How much do you have now?"

Manfred accepted the donation. "Let me think. I got ten from Conrad Airingsail, five from you, two from a Chinaman named Tseng Longwei, and…" He pulled a small wad of folded bills and two quarters from his coat pocket and began counting. "…adding it altogether it comes to… exactly… exactly… twenty-one dollars and fifty cents." He squeezed the money in his hand. "Not bad for a week's work and making a lot of enemies."

William Sommercamp reached into his pocket a second time. "Not bad, I'd say, but there's no way I'm letting Conrad Airingsail give more than me. Here, take another five. At least we're even now."

Manfred stood and the rocking chair bumped against the back of his legs. "Thank you. Thank you very much. I don't know if I have enough, but I think it's time to hire a lawyer. The trial starts tomorrow. I'm afraid I've run out of time."

"Who'd you have in mind?"

Manfred shoved the money into the inside pocket of his black coat. "The only man I would trust for such an important job: my good friend Csongor Toth."

William Sommercamp asked skeptically, "You think he'll agree to do such a thankless job for twenty-six dollars and fifty cents?"

Manfred sighed. "I pray to God he does, because this is all the money I've got."

"Well then, you'd better track him down right away and find out if he'll even consider defending that Indian fellow."

"I intend to. And I'm taking the rest of this pickle with me just in case."

"Fine with me, but only if you don't come back here to eat it."

Csongor Toth scrutinized Manfred's agitated demeanor with keen interest as his friend described his various meetings with the Indian named Joshua Hotah, his week-long effort to raise money for the man's defense, and his absolute confidence of the man's innocence.

Csongor pushed away from his desk when Manfred had completed his presentation. "Without a doubt, a story of personal conviction and perseverance in the face of great adversity. Nonetheless, how can you really be sure of the man's innocence? I have had the opportunity to speak with Sheriff Boyle directly, and he has informed me that the evidence is overwhelming in every regard."

Manfred pulled the money from his coat pocket and dumped it on Csongor's polished desk. "I cannot explain to you why I believe so deeply in Joshua Hotah's innocence. It is enough to say that I believe it with my entire heart and my entire mind. But why I believe it is not the question. The question is whether or not you are willing to represent him in court. I've raised twenty-six dollars and fifty cents. It's all I have: no more, no less. Will you take the job?"

Csongor examined the little pile of money, touched the tip of his index finger to the tip of his nose, and sniffed. "The amount of money you have offered to defend a man who is most likely guilty of the crime falls substantially short of my usual retainer, let alone the full cost of mounting a vigorous defense in front of a hostile jury."

Manfred pushed the money closer to Csongor. "I know it's not enough. I was hoping you'd take the case anyway."

"And why, pray tell, would I do such a thing?"

"Because, my friend, it's the right thing to do."

Csongor lowered his hand and sniffed a second time. "Yes, I imagine it is when one considers the issue from a certain narrow perspective. But you are asking much from someone who has very little experience in criminal law."

"Criminal law?"

"Yes. If you had come to me with a case involving a dispute over a mining claim, or perhaps a disagreement about some financial matter, then I would not have hesitated to take it, but in this instance—"

Manfred interrupted, "Whether or not you have the experience doesn't matter. I want you to take the case anyway."

Csongor tapped his fingers next to the little pile of money and breathed. "For twenty-six dollars and fifty cents?"

Manfred grinned. "Yes, that's exactly what I want you to do."

Csongor pulled his hand back. "The problem is, I charge a minimum of fifty dollars to draw up the paperwork for a simple mining claim. And I prefer to receive payment in gold dust as well. It's far more reliable than paper money."

"I don't have any gold dust. You'll just have to settle for this less-than-reliable paper money. Oh, and don't forget the fifty cents."

"I did not forget the fifty cents."

"It's the right thing to do."

"Yes, you said that before."

"I wasn't sure you heard it the first time. I thought I'd better say it again."

Slowly—very slowly—Csongor opened the topmost drawer, reached across the polished surface of his desk, rested his hand on top of the money, then swept the twenty-six dollars and fifty cents into the drawer. He closed the drawer soundlessly. "I will likely regret this decision before the week is over." He tapped the desk with his knuckles. "No, *likely* is not the right word. I will almost certainly regret this decision, probably within minutes after you walk out of my office."

Manfred Herrmann quickly stood and thrust out his right hand. "And I know in my heart you will not. You are doing the right thing. God will bless you for it."

Csongor stood too and grasped Manfred's hand lightly with his fingertips. "My fondest hope is that God does not find out about our meeting today."

Manfred seized Csongor's hand and shook it vigorously. "Thankfully, you have not lost your sense of humor. I'll be on my way then. Thank you, and see you in court tomorrow. I heard the trial starts at noon, but you should check with Sheriff Boyle."

Csongor released his hand from Manfred's strong grip. "I'll be sure to check with him, first thing in the morning."

Manfred began to leave but then pivoted back. "And you may want to drop by the jail tonight and have a talk with your new client. I'm pretty sure he's still in there." He waited for approval of his suggestion.

Csongor finally answered, dispassionately, "Without a doubt."

CHAPTER SIX

The night before the trial of Joshua Hotah
May 16, 1872

C songor Toth poured a dark swirl of Old Pulteney whisky into a spotless glass then pushed the cork into the mouth of the bottle. After reading a few words from the elegant label, he displayed the bottle near the front of his polished desk—next to the room's only light: a well-maintained and flawlessly-clean kerosene lamp. He tilted the rim of the glass to his lips and sipped. After savoring the whisky's peaty aroma and pleasant burn, he cradled the glass in both hands and supported his elbows on the padded leather armrests of the chair. The potbelly stove squatting near the back of the office crackled pleasantly. The Seth Thomas[4] clock mounted on the wall directly behind his chair chimed eleven times. Csongor held the glass in one hand and retrieved a gold watch from a vest pocket with the other. His thumb clicked open the spring-loaded cover of the watch. He noted the time: ten fifty-nine. As Csongor restored the watch to the vest pocket and adjusted the chain, a mysterious gentleman emerged from the shadows into the atmospheric illumination of the kerosene lamp. The gentleman stroked his moustache, nodded precisely, and touched the brim of his shiny top hat with the eagle-headed grip of his walking cane.

---

[4] The Seth Thomas Clock Company was incorporated in 1853 at Plymouth Hollow, Connecticut. However, Seth Thomas (1785-1859) had manufactured clocks at that location beginning in 1814. Plymouth Hollow was renamed "Thomaston" in 1865.

Csongor did not appear surprised by the unexpected appearance of the mysterious gentleman and began speaking to him directly. "Monsieur Hector Faure. How kind of you to visit, because I must tell you something quite upsetting. One of my expensive time pieces is not telling the correct time, and I have no way of knowing which one is to blame. When the clock chimed eleven, the watch indicated one minute before the hour." Csongor raised the glass and poured a delicate splash of whisky across his tongue. He slowly squeezed the whisky to the back of his mouth before swallowing. "Yes, yes, I know perfectly well that the clock may be fast or the watch may be slow, which could mean both are to blame, but your observation does nothing to help me solve the problem. In fact, you have only added to my confusion."

Monsieur Hector Faure shrugged indifferently before suggesting another possibility.

Csongor set the glass on the desk and scoffed, "Of course I've considered the possibility that both the clock and pocket watch may be wrong. Do you think so little of my intelligence? Do you really imagine I'm incapable of simple calculation?"

In an ersatz display of contrition, Hector Faure lowered his eyes and apologized, but his tone lacked conviction.

Csongor braced his forearms on the polished desk. "It is good you did not intend to imply that I was a fool, but the presumptuous tone of your voice did suggest otherwise."

Hector Faure inquired if Csongor had met the Indian face-to-face.

Csongor listened to each word, then meditated briefly before answering. "Yes, I did visit the Indian. In fact, I just returned from the county jail…less than an hour ago. Did you not see me when I came in? I know you've been hiding in your favorite corner the entire time. You *must* have assumed I was returning from the jail when I arrived." Csongor stood and hooked his thumbs into his coat pockets.

Hector Faure tapped his lips repeatedly with an index finger and asked if Csongor was aware of the man's name.

"Of course I know his name. It's Joshua Hotah, if you must know. And another interesting discovery, which I believe will surprise even you. The man is not a full Indian: he is a half-breed. His mother was Sioux, but his father was born in England. He evidently travelled to America to hunt the wild buffalo. I have no idea how they found each other out on the prairie. Who would have imagined such a combination was even possible?"

Hector Faure asked if Csongor had completed preparations for the trial.

"You should know better. I have not prepared for the trial because I only just met with the man." Csongor took a small key from a desk drawer and strolled over to the Seth Thomas wall clock. He calculated the time down to the second from his pocket watch and adjusted the wall clock to match.

Hector Faure asked if Csongor was certain of the pocket watch's accuracy, and then reminded him of their earlier conversation.

"No, I can't be sure the pocket watch is the correct time, but sometimes one must make decisions in life without adequate information. This is one of those times."

Monsieur Faure tapped the tip of his cane on the floor with a brisk downward motion, and asked why Csongor had agreed to defend the half-breed named Joshua Hotah in the first place. After all, the man is innocent.

"Yes, I would agree. Because of an unfortunate moment of indecision, I have allowed my friend Manfred to lead me into a potential trap, a trap from which I do not yet know how to escape. But you must admit: I still have the advantage."

Hector Faure asked why, because he saw no advantage at all.

"Why? It is simple. I still have the advantage because there is no proof of Joshua Hotah's innocence. There is, of course, only circumstantial evidence that he had anything to do with the murders. However, the sheriff and most of the town believes he is guilty, and this will be enough to win the day. Now, if only I could—"

Hector Faure quickly interrupted, and suggested the possibility of other evidence.

"I can assure you there is absolutely no evidence, circumstantial or otherwise, linking me or my men to this shocking crime. And if you must know, I am rather pleased of the way I conducted the entire affair, particularly the manner in which I supervised those three unpredictable malcontents who work for me. I must also point out the obvious: it is not my fault the half-breed blundered along at the wrong time. I cannot take responsibility for the bad luck of others. To do so could drive one mad."

Monsieur Faure smirked and offered the possibility that Csongor had already gone mad.

"What a silly thing to say. There is no evidence to suggest anything of the sort. Do you really believe a person overcome by insanity could have planned and executed such an exquisitely devious plan? I think you have underestimated me again." Csongor lifted the glass and sipped at the whisky.

Hector Faure twirled his moustache and snorted that the difference between sanity and madness was often a fine line easily traversed by vanity.

Csongor took exception to this suggestion and retorted, "If this is what you believe, then you are a bigger fool than I ever imagined. Although it is clear my opinions have failed to win the argument, is there nothing more I can say to convince you otherwise?"

Hector Faure answered that nothing would change his opinion.

"Then I am afraid we must simply move to another topic."

Hector Faure calmed himself and nodded at the bottle of Old Pulteney.

Csongor noticed the change in posture and offered an olive branch. "Would you care for a glass of whisky? Although I don't think I've ever mentioned it to you, I have grown quite fond of this Old Pulteney, particularly the exquisite aroma."

Hector Faure nodded and set his top hat on the desk.

Csongor filled a second glass with approximately two ounces of whisky and pushed it across the polished surface of the desk. "Excellent. Then we shall have no hard feelings over our disagreement?"

Hector Faure's tone softened as he confirmed their friendship.

"This confirmation pleases me too. Then we shall drink to our eternal friendship."

After picking up the glass, observing the light of the kerosene lamp through the amber liquid, and throwing back a significant swallow of whisky, Monsieur Faure decided to explore a different subject. He spoke at great length before his conclusion.

Csongor listened to the new proposal with keen interest, but did not betray any particular reaction. "I do suppose you are right. It serves no purpose to argue. The limited time remaining before my mind and body are overcome with exhaustion is better spent planning the defense of Joshua Hotah." Csongor finished the last of his whiskey and slammed the glass down on the desk. "But therein lies the rub! How do I plan the man's defense when the most auspicious result would be his conviction?"

Hector Faure wagged a finger and chided Csongor.

"Yes, yes…and his subsequent death by hanging. I assumed this intended outcome was clear, but if I must state the obvious, I must. Nonetheless, my point remains intact. Let me ask the question in a different way. How do I *appear* to defend him with determination and passion when my real purpose is to do everything possible to ensure his conviction? And, before you say a word, his subsequent execution."

Hector Faure threw back the last of the whisky and clinked the empty glass down on the desk next to the bottle of Old Pulteney. After a moment of thought, he proffered a strategy.

Csongor jumped at the sharp sound of the glass, but then relaxed when he listened to his friend's ideas. "I see. What you say does make sense. Simply put him on the stand and, with the proper questioning, let him incriminate himself. Joshua Hotah is so deeply honest that no one could possibly believe his wild story. I commend you for your legal insight. Bloody brilliant."

Monsieur Faure offered a sincere word of caution.

Csongor stroked his neck just below the chin. "I understand how much preparatory work will be required before I put Joshua Hotah on the stand." Csongor lowered his hand and tapped the desk. "What do you think of this approach? First, I pretend to attack the accounts of Sheriff Boyle—and his so-called 'deputies'—but I do it in a manner that only amplifies the believability of their stories." Csongor grasped his hands behind his back and paced behind the desk. "This will require subtle transition from one argument to the next. I must not give the jury, or anyone in the courtroom, the impression of deliberate incompetence. I must question the witnesses aggressively, while at the same time undermining the credibility of the story Joshua Hotah will present when I call him as a witness to testify on his own behalf. A tricky business, to be sure, but I do not see a better choice."

Hector Faure peeled a white glove from his left hand, tapped his bare knuckles on the desk, and declared that Csongor did have another choice.

Csongor peered into his empty glass. "Do you really think so?" Csongor sniffed. "Do you really believe I should turn myself in and confess to this heinous crime? What purpose could this possibly serve?"

Monsieur Faure set the eagle-headed cane on the desk, pulled up a chair and sat, then clapped his hands together and laughed.

Csongor was not amused by this abusive display of mockery. "You are making fun of me? I should have known you would have offered such a ridiculous suggestion only in jest. I should have known."

Hector Faure leaned back in the chair and crossed one leg over the other. Then he straightened up again, raised his hand with the index finger extended, and offered a more serious thought.

"No, I do not think it is risky to question my own men on the stand. I believe this will be necessary to seal the fate of Joshua Hotah."

Hector Faure questioned the reliability of Csongor's men.

"What if one of them says something stupid? Like what?"

Hector Faure offered several examples, each more chilling than the previous one.

"I agree. Incredibly stupid. Do you really think they are so thoroughly dimwitted?"

Hector Faure chortled and exclaimed that he did.

"You do? Then I will have to speak to each man before the trial, to be sure they know what I will ask and how they are to respond. But there is so little time...."

Monsieur Faure rose up from the chair, slowly pulled on the glove, placed the top hat gently on his neatly-groomed head, retrieved the eagle-headed cane from the desk, and offered his free hand to prove that the meeting had ended.

Csongor stood and grasped Hector Faure's hand and shook it vigorously. "Must you go now? I had hoped you would stay a while longer and help me prepare some questions for the sheriff."

Hector Faure explained that he had two more appointments before dawn and had already stayed too long.

"I know you have other business to attend to, but nonetheless, I was hoping you would—"

Hector Faure held up a hand and tilted his head.

Csongor fell back into his chair. "I understand, but your departure saddens me. I have always enjoyed your company, even if we do argue from time to time. But I do understand. Adieu my dearest of friends. Adieu."

Without offering a spoken farewell, Monsieur Faure nodded once before vanishing through the front door into the eerie darkness of the empty street.

Csongor slid his coat off and draped it over the back of the chair. He strolled to the potbelly stove, opened the iron door, stirred the glowing coals with an iron poker, and tossed in three pieces of neatly-split wood. He pushed the iron door shut and rubbed his hands together. He walked back to his desk and sat in the chair. He removed several sheets of paper and a fountain pen[5] from a side drawer and positioned them neatly on the desk. He folded his hands together and brooded until the Seth Thomas clock chimed twelve times. And then he seized the pen and began to write. He worked unceasingly until the Seth Thomas clock chimed four times and the potbelly stove no longer adequately warmed the room. When he had finished his work, he donned his coat, blew out the flame of the kerosene lamp, and withdrew from the gloomy office. When he bent down to extinguish the lamp, he did not notice the curious sight of one empty glass and one full glass next to the bottle of Old Pulteney.

---

[5] Although the first practical fountain pen was patented by New York insurance broker Lewis Waterman in 1884, a fellow named John Jacob Parker patented the first self-filling fountain pen in 1832.

CHAPTER SEVEN

Mahogany Gulch, the day of the trial of Joshua Hotah
May 17, 1872

Roshan Kuznetsov pressed a smudgy finger against the side of his nose and blew a gob of snot from deep inside the left nostril. The snot stretched into a wavering string over Longwei's knees and the end of the wagon seat before arcing to the ground a few feet in front of Gustus De Angeles. Roshan sniffed and wiped his nose on his sleeve. "We are on the way of the trial to see as I told of you. We could think of the night if the trial takes too much of clock. Thank you for the wagon to take us on our way on this morning of weather of the good more than you can see. And thank you for the day of not work on the mine of many hard rocks. It is of your generous to think of it in the day to now." Roshan wiped his nose again with the other sleeve.

Gustus looked down at the slimy gob of snot and then up at the three men sitting together on the wagon seat. The mongrel of a dog sat by his side and appeared to study the gob of snot with peculiar fascination. "I see. The three of you are leaving me to do all the work while you go gallivanting off to some trial of a fellow you don't hardly know. I must've been plumb out of my mind when I agreed to give the three of you the day off. And now you're telling me you might not come back for two days. Well, I'm not going to pay you a darn cent for the days you're gone. That's for darn sure."

Sitting to Roshan's right, John Smith wiggled on the wagon seat when a splinter poked him in the butt. "The preacher asked us to go to the trial for this Indian fellow. I'd rather stay here with you and look for gold, but the preacher asked us. I swear it's true."

Roshan tugged on the reins to hold the horses when they started to move forward. "Yes, John Smith speaks of the most truth of it. We want to stay with you at the Mahogany Gulch and look for the gold to get the rich, but the man of black asked of each of us to go to the trial on this of all days. We cannot try to help of it. I know you can see it, if you think of what I say."

Gustus puzzled, "The man of black? Who you talking about?"

Longwei clarified, "Roshan is speaking of the Lutheran, Manfred Herrmann. Roshan calls him the man of black because he always wears a black suit and black shoes. I know it is confusing."

Gustus kicked some dirt over the gob of snot and scoffed, "Well if you ask me, it's downright confusing. He should learn to call him the preacher man like everyone else."

Longwei considered this before answering, "There are many more important things Roshan should learn first, but I will suggest this to him when we get to town."

Roshan did not consider anything before declaring, "Yes, what Longwei speaks is of very true, to be sure of it. There are the many things for Roshan to learn of, and if you can believe me when I say he is doing it every day and on the Friday too, if you hear my lips speak to you of it."

John Smith slid forward on the wagon seat to get off the splinter that was still poking him in the butt. "I can swear to that. Roshan … he's learning new things each and every day." He scratched an itch on his ear. "Come to think of it, I think he's also learning a few things he needs to unlearn when he gets the chance, afore he gets himself in trouble. But it's really none of my business to tell anyone what to do."

The horses skittered and Roshan pulled hard on the reins. The axles creaked and the wagon rolled forward a few inches. "Yes, it is of the trouble who is much worry for me. I do not always know of the trouble when it walks big inside the room. But soon I find out of the trouble before it is too late, if I am of the lucky in the same day."

Gustus clapped his hands together. "I think I've heard just about enough for one day. Get yourselves out of here before I change my mind and fire the worthless bunch of you." He turned to walk away, but then spun around and glared at the three men sitting in the wagon. "And one more thing. If'n you run into the preacher man, tell him I couldn't come to the trial 'cause I got too many things to get done with the three of you gone. I'm sure he'll understand my meaning."

Roshan grinned. "Yes, we be of the sure to tell to him you work too hard to come if the three of us do not come to it in the same. You can count of it." Roshan snapped the reins and the horses plodded off. As the wagon pulled away, he yelled, "Thank you Mister Gustus! We return when it is soonest the possible. But do not surprise of yourself if we do not arrive in Mahogany Gulch for two days from when is the now." And then he twisted his head and shouted in a fading voice, "Thank you once more for the wagon to use, and the horses too. It is much the hard to drive the wagon when the horses are not, if you ask me of it." And although Gustus did not hear it, he finished with, "We more appreciate of it more of you can think to say!"

Gustus shook his head in disgust, cursed, and spit. He trudged back to the cabin with the mangy mongrel of a dog prancing by his side and bumping his hand with its nose. Without looking down at the excited animal, Gustus observed, "Well, at least one person has some loyalty around here." Without breaking stride, he glanced at the animal's bouncing nose and offered an apology. "Sorry. I didn't mean to call you a person. Won't happen again."

After the early morning departure of Roshan, Longwei, and John Smith, Gustus decided to busy himself with a number of tedious chores before beginning the real work of mining for gold. He sat at the small table and used a blunt pencil to make a list on a wrinkled square of paper. Then he got to work, checking off each task after he completed it. He swept a choking storm of dirt out of the cabin using a badly-frayed broom that had seen better days. He cleaned the breakfast dishes and the cooking skillet by wiping them with a greasy cloth. He split a few seasoned rounds with a heavy axe, carried three armfuls of split wood into the cabin, and stacked the wood next to the potbelly stove. After stirring up the glowing embers and feeding two chunks of split wood into the stove, he filled the coffee pot with fresh water and threw in a handful of coffee grounds and set the pot on top of the potbelly stove. He fixed a loose hinge on the front door while the coffee brewed, and then sat at the table and enjoyed a hot cup of coffee. The mongrel of a dog crouched in front of Gustus and rested his chin on the table. After Gustus had thrown back the last swallow of coffee, he heard horses outside the cabin. The mongrel of a dog heard them too and rushed to the front door and whimpered. Gustus opened the door and stepped outside. He held his hand up and shielded his eyes from the morning sun streaming around the outlines of three dark horsemen. The mongrel of a dog sat next to Gustus and tilted his head.

Gustus spoke to the three horsemen without lowering his hand. "Can I help you gentlemen with something?" The horsemen did not immediately reply. Gustus continued brusquely, "I'd like to stand here and chat with you fellows, but I've got a lot of work to get done today. If you got something to say then say it now or move along down the road."

The middle horseman pushed forward on his stirrups. The mongrel of a dog heard the squeak of leather when the man's chaps rubbed against the saddle. "Good morning to you. We're here to offer you protection from them Indians, the ones roaming around the countryside killing people. You probably heard about the massacre of that wagon family. A terrible business it was. A terrible business. We wouldn't want the same thing to happen here, if you get my drift."

Gustus lowered his hand and squinted suspiciously. "Yeah, I heard about it. But if you ask me, the story I heard don't make any sense at all. I ain't afraid of any Indians anyway. None here at Mahogany Gulch, nor in Silver City, nor anywhere in these parts. I appreciate the offer, but I won't be a needing any protection from you or anyone else. So, if you don't mind, you can move along and I'll get back to work."

The middle horseman eased back and snorted. "I don't think you're following my meaning. We're here to offer you protection and we're not leaving until you agree to it." He twisted left and right to assess the property. "Nice piece of land you got here. I'd say for a claim this size, and with a well-built cabin and all, we could guarantee them Indians will never bother you for three hundred dollars a month. If you ask me, we're offering you a downright bargain. You'd be a fool not to accept it."

Gustus reached back until his hand touched the axe handle by the door. He hoisted the axe up and scowled at the dark horseman in the middle. "You're plumb loco if you're a thinking I'm going to pay three hundred dollars a month for protection I don't need, especially from the likes of you." His hand squeezed the ax handle. "I'll tell you what I'm a willing to do. I'm not going to pay you three hundred dollars. I'm not going to pay you one hundred dollars. I'm not going to pay you ten dollars. I'm not going to pay you one peppercorn for your protection." Gustus brandished the axe in both hands. "Now get off my property before you regret you ever came here."

The middle horseman yanked a pistol from his belt and fired. The mongrel of a dog jumped at the sound. Gustus stumbled to his knees when the bullet struck him in the chest. His hands twitched and released the axe when he fell forward into the dry ground.

Surprised, the horseman to the left screamed, "Why'd you have to go and shoot the old coot? Now we're not going to collect any money at all from him."

The middle horseman shoved the pistol behind his belt. "He wasn't going to pay anyway. Now scatter a few arrows around here so folks think the Indians did it. When the town finds out there's been another massacre up here at Mahogany Gulch, people will surely want to pay whatever we ask for our protection."

The third horseman, who had not said a word during the entire affair, finally asked, "Should I scalp him? That's what Csongor wanted us to do last time. Just say the word and I'll scalp him clean."

The middle horseman glanced down at the body. He thought about shooting the old coot in the back, but decided not to waste a bullet on someone who already looked pretty dead. "No, leave him be. Scatter them arrows and let's get out of here. Who knows who might show up after hearing that gun shot."

Without dismounting, the three horsemen scattered a few arrows around the front of the cabin and rode away. The mongrel of a dog did not chase after them, but stayed by Gustus De Angeles to protect him from further injury.

His chest throbbed unbearably and he felt woozy from pain and loss of blood, but Gustus still managed to push himself up to his hands and knees. The bullet had missed his heart, but not the left lung before lodging against a rib in his back. Gustus licked his lips and tasted blood oozing around the sides of his swollen tongue. The mongrel of a dog slapped its tail against the ground when Gustus rose up after a good quarter-hour face down in the dirt. Gustus spoke to the dog with difficulty. "I don't think I'm a gonna make it much longer. I got one more chore to do before I die."

The mongrel of a dog panted at the sound of Gustus's voice and barked twice. Gustus tried to raise his hand to touch the dog, but the pain in his chest prevented it. He smiled weakly before crawling to the front door. With heroic effort he reached up and opened the door. He bumped both knees on the weathered threshold when he maneuvered into the cabin. He paused to rest, but after nearly fainting decided to crawl to the small table. He pulled himself onto a chair. He found the wrinkled square of paper with the list of work tasks, flipped it over, and began writing with the blunt pencil.

LAST WILL AND TESTMONEE

MY NAME IS GUSTUS DE ANGELES AND I LEVE THIS WORTHLESS CLAIM AT MAHOGINEE GULCH TO THAT GOOD FOR NUTHING UNGRATEUL VODKA SWILL-ING FURTRAPING SCOUNDRIL ROSHAN KUZNETSOV BECUS THERS JUST NO WAY ID LEEVE IT TO A DAM CHINAMAN OR A NEGRO WHO CAINT EVEN REMEMBER HIS NAME ROSHAN CAN DO WHAT HE PLEESES WITH THE CLAIM BECUS I DONT GIVE A DAM.

Gustus twisted the blunt pencil to drill the final period in, hastily scanned the words he had written—to check the spelling and punctuation—and signed his name. He set the pencil next to the wrinkled square of paper. A spasm of pain shot through his neck. The mangy mongrel of a dog whimpered. Gustus felt the dog's nose touch his blood-soaked thigh. He looked down at the dog and imagined a glistening sadness in the animal's eyes. Gustus stroked the dog's head three times before slumping over the table. A dark stain of lumpy blood spurted from the wound before smearing across the lower corner of the wrinkled square of paper. The stain nearly reached his cramped signature. The pencil rolled off the table and clattered when it hit the floor. The mangy mongrel of a dog sat patiently and waited for Gustus to finish his nap.

CHAPTER EIGHT

The first day of the trial of Joshua Hotah
May 17, 1872

H is cropped black hair neatly parted down the middle and slicked down with Rowland's Macassar Oil,[6] the prosecuting attorney strutted back and forth in front of the jury. He suddenly faced the ten men sitting in two rows of uncomfortable hardwood chairs near the front of the courtroom. While maintaining visual contact with a bearded miner sitting in the second row, he aggressively pointed at the two men seated behind the small defendant's table. He waited histrionically before issuing his final and most important accusation. "And thirdly, the evidence will prove without any doubt that the defendant coldly and brutally murdered an innocent family when they were simply minding their own business, and…" the prosecuting attorney folded his hands in front of his belt, gazed down at the floor, and reduced his voice to a whisper, "…in an unspeakable act of monstrous cruelty, scalped the children while they were still alive." When he had finished these scintillating words, a woman sitting in the front row right behind the defendant pressed a hand against her lips, sucked in a ragged breath, and nearly swooned. When she pitched forward the bearded man sitting to her right

---

[6] A magazine advertisement published in 1863 London declares the following: "Rowland's Macassar Oil, a delightfully fragrant and transparent preparation for the hair, and as an Invigorator and Beautifier beyond all precedent." The primary ingredients included coconut or palm oil, ylang-ylang oil, and other fragrant oils.

clutched a handful of dress between her shoulder blades and skillfully jerked her upright.

Joshua Hotah whispered in Csongor Toth's ear. "The children were already scalped when I found them. You must tell them."

Csongor answered flatly, "Not to worry. He still has to prove his accusations."

Joshua persisted. "But the children were not alive when I found them. He said they were scalped alive. How can he say this when it is not true?"

Csongor raised his voice. "Patience. We will have our chance to refute everything."

Judge Roy Parker pounded a large gavel on the surface of the dark wood judge's bench. "I'll have no more distractions from the defendant or his attorney while the prosecutor is delivering his opening statement. I'll hold the both of you in contempt if I have to. Do I make myself clear?"

Csongor rose up from his chair and bowed slightly from the waist. "Your meaning is quite clear, your honor. We apologize for this unfortunate interruption of the prosecutor's wild and unsubstantiated accusations. We did not intend for our private conversation to distract the court and only wished to—"

A stocky man standing at the back of the crowded courtroom shook his fist in the air and yelled, "Hang the both of 'em, that's what I say. Hang the pretty Indian-loving lawyer first."

Several men grunted their agreement with this idea, and then a crescendo of incoherent voices cascaded across the courtroom. Judge Parker pounded the gavel. "That'll be enough out of you. Now sit down before I lose my temper." He pounded the gavel a few more times. "Everyone hush up, or I'll clear the whole lot of you out of this courtroom. Do I make myself clear?" Within seconds the incoherent voices faded away to a vague murmur.

Confused, the man who shook his fist blurted, "But your honor, I'm standing 'cause I got no chair to sit on. Did you mean for me to sit down on the floor, or did you want me to go find a chair to sit on, 'cause I can go look for one if—"

Judge Parker hissed, "Of course I didn't mean for you to sit on the floor. I wasn't talking to you. I was talking to the defense attorney. But if you don't stop interrupting these legal proceedings, I *will* order you to sit on the floor. Is that as clear as I can make it for you?"

The man who shook his fist looked down at the floor and murmured, "Yes, your honor. I'll just keep standing, like you say."

Judge Parker pointed at the prosecutor. "What are you waiting for, a personal invitation to start talking again? Get on with it."

The prosecutor, a local man named Reginald Simpson (and a competitor of Csongor's in the business of mining claims), unbuttoned the front of his black frock coat and hooked both thumbs behind the top of his gray pinstripe pants. Although he did not have any particular opinion about Indians, he viewed this trial as an opportunity to elevate his standing in the community and thereby improve his business prospects. He cleared his throat. "Thank you, your honor, for setting the defense attorney straight on that particular point. Now, as I was explaining, the evidence will clearly show that the children were brutally scalped while they still lived—an act of unspeakable horror by any standard of civility. You may be asking yourself, who could possibly commit such a heinous crime?" The prosecutor pointed stiffly at Joshua Hotah. "I shall answer this question for you, my fellow Silver City citizens. It is him, the Indian sitting directly in front of you inside this very courtroom, the Indian they call Joshoway Hotah." And then raising his voice until it nearly cracked, "Have no doubt my fellow citizens. He is the one who did it! He is the one!"

A scruffy juror sitting in the front row asked the man to his right, "What's a *hay nest* crime? Is it something really bad?"

Without moving, the man replied, "Darned if I know, but if you ask me it sounds real bad the way he tells it."

Csongor shot up from his seat. "Objection, your honor. My client's name is Joshua. Please instruct the prosecutor to pronounce his name correctly."

A juror wearing a red flannel shirt and sitting near the middle of the back row chuckled. Judge Roy Parker pounded his gavel. "Do I have to give you another warning, counselor? You can't be objecting during the prosecutor's opening statement. Now sit down and shut up or I'll have the sheriff and his deputies do it for you."

As he lowered into his chair, Csongor intoned, "My deepest apologies, your honor. I meant no insult to my illustrious adversary."

The scruffy juror asked the man to his right again, "What's an *ill ustrous ad versary*?"

The man grumbled, "I have no idea, but you're going to get the both of us in trouble with the judge if you keep asking questions."

Joshua tugged on the sleeve of Csongor's coat. "They were already scalped when I found them."

Csongor pulled the sleeve away. "I believe you, now be quiet."

Roshan, Longwei, and John Smith rumbled up the outside stairs to the second floor of the courthouse and tumbled noisily through the only door at the rear of the courtroom. After scanning the room for an empty chair, Longwei admonished Roshan when he realized he would have to stand at the back. "I told you we should not have taken an unknown shortcut. Now we are too late to find a place to sit."

Roshan waved his arms and exclaimed in a boisterous voice, "It is not the fault of Roshan to take the shortcut to the end of the road and find the wagon stuck before the horses can turn around in the way of right."

Several people in the courtroom laughed, and the scruffy juror stomped his foot and guffawed. Judge Parker pounded the gavel before pointing it at Roshan. "I don't know who you think you are to come in here like that, but if you don't quiet down right this minute, I'll have you and your two friends removed from this courtroom faster than you can shake a stick."

Roshan doffed his hat in the manner Nadia had taught him. "My name is Roshan, and my friends are of the name Tseng Longwei and John Smith, who is not his really name because his remember is not the good. We are of the late when the wagon took the shortcut and the horses found it of the difficulty—"

Judge Parker pounded the gavel. "I don't give a darn who you are. I don't care about your friends or your wagon or your horses neither. Now don't say another word or I'll have the three of you tossed into the street. Do I make myself clear?" Roshan opened his mouth, but Longwei punched him in the ribs before he could say a single word. Longwei faced the judge and bowed. John Smith nodded and grinned apologetically.

Judge Parker eyed Roshan one more time before speaking to the prosecutor. "You got anything more to say before we give the defense attorney a chance to say a few words?"

Reginald Simpson unhooked his thumbs from the top of his pants. "No, your honor. I think I'm pretty much finished." He glided across the front of the courtroom and sat in a hardwood chair behind the prosecutor's table, next to the witness stand.

Judge Parker gestured at Csongor with the heavy gavel. "You have an opening statement, counselor? If you don't want to say anything, that's fine with me."

Csongor stood and his perception drifted to one of the three double-hung windows puncturing the wall behind the judge's bench. The morning light beamed through the windows and sparkled on the myriad dust particles floating in the courtroom. Csongor held out his hand and tried to touch the floating particles. "Yes, your honor. And I will not take as much of the court's precious time as did my rambling opponent." He lowered his hand and faced the ten men of the jury. "Contrary to what the prosecutor has told you this morning, I have no doubt the evidence will demonstrate that my client is innocent of brutally murdering said family on the road outside of Silver City. In fact, gentlemen, I believe the evidence will show that this man, Joshua Hotah, is a peace-loving man who was merely discovered in the wrong place at the wrong time: nothing more, nothing less. True, he was purportedly apprehended while attempting to conceal the bodies of the family..." dozens of whispers flitted around the courtroom, "...and was allegedly covered in the blood of the innocent children..." the crescendo of incoherent voices returned, "...but because the evidence is circumstantial and not a single man actually saw my client commit these monstrous crimes, I have no doubt..." the voices grew into an angry cacophony and Csongor's final words were covered up.

Judge Roy Parker pounded the gavel and shouted, "Order! Order in my courtroom. Order!" When the unruly mob had settled down, Judge Parker sighed and announced: "This trial is adjourned until two o'clock so I can get some lunch."

As dozens of people headed for the only exit door, Manfred Herrmann pushed his way through the crowd until he arrived at the defendant's table. He nodded to Joshua before speaking to Csongor. "How do you think the trial is going? Do you think we have a chance of winning?"

Csongor stood and stretched his back, but did not offer his hand. "I think the trial is proceeding splendidly, but it is too early to predict either success or failure. I will have a better sense of our chances by the end of the day."

Manfred spoke to Joshua. "How are you holding up? This must be very difficult."

Joshua remained seated. "I do not understand anything we have heard this morning. The children were already scalped when I found them. I did not kill the family. I do not understand why people say I did these things when it is not true."

Csongor offered a small measure of encouragement. "Not to worry. It is only the beginning. Things will become clearer when the trial continues."

Sheriff Boyle appeared with a set of leg irons dangling from his hand. "Time to head back to the jail where you belong until the trial starts up again." Joshua moved to the side of the defendant's table and stared dreamily through one of the windows behind the judge's bench while Sheriff Boyle locked the leg irons around his ankles.

After calling several witnesses, including a young woman who testified she had seen the posse and defendant arrive with the dead mother and scalped children tied to a travois, Reginald Simpson prepared to question his star witness. He stood casually in front of the modest desk that served as a witness stand. "For the benefit of the jury, please state your full name and occupation."

The man in the witness stand nodded, but did not remove his hat. "Occupation?"

Reginald Simpson replied, rather brusquely, "Yes. Occupation. What is your livelihood?" Hearing no answer, he asked, "What is your job?"

The man grinned. "Oh, my job. Why didn't you say that in the first place instead of using all them fancy words?"

Csongor Toth shot to his feet. "Objection, your honor. Please inform the witness he is not allowed to ask any questions."

Judge Parker barked, "Overruled." Then he spoke to the witness. "Stop asking questions. It upsets the defense attorney."

The witness removed his hat. "Sorry your honor. I didn't know you had a rule about asking questions. Name's Wendell Boyle. I'm the

Sheriff of Silver City. Been doing it for quite a long time. At least ten, maybe eleven years."

Reginald Simpson sashayed around with one hand behind his back. "And, if you do not mind Sheriff Boyle, please tell the jury what you were doing the day of the massacre of an innocent family, which, I might add, included two young children who were scalped alive."

Sheriff Boyle fiddled with his hat beneath the desk. "Why, I'd be glad to. I was sweeping the floor when these two hombres showed up and told me about an Indian massacre on the road outside of town. I got angry at first, 'cause they tracked a bunch of dirt into my office and I was going to have to sweep the whole thing again. I'm sure you understand I got better things to do with my time than sweep up the same floor twice in one day."

Reginald pulled his left earlobe. "I do understand, Sheriff Boyle. But tell me, is that all they said to you?"

"Why no, it sure isn't. They said they'd seen the whole thing. They said the Indian who killed the family was digging graves to bury the evidence."

"And you trusted these honorable men enough... to do what?"

"I deputized them on the spot."

"I see. Then what did you do?"

"We went out and formed a posse. Found a bunch of good men in the saloon across the street and a few other places. Gave everyone instructions about what we were doing and rode out of town as fast as we could because I was worried the Indian would finish burying the family and get away before we could catch him."

Reginald winked at the jury. "Of course. And what these newly-appointed deputies told you in your office... did it turn out to be true?"

Sheriff Boyle squirmed in the chair. "Why, it sure did. Every word of it. We caught that Indian red-handed trying to hide the bodies, just like they said."

Reginald pivoted around on the heels of his polished shoes and pressed both hands down on the surface of the witness desk. "And is this Indian— the one you caught red-handed trying to hide the bodies of the murdered family—in this courtroom today?"

Sheriff Boyle slowly raised his arm and pointed at Joshua Hotah. "Sure is. He's sitting over there next to his lawyer. Except he's not wearing bloody clothes now. Someone must have cleaned him up this morning before the trial got started. Don't seem right if you ask me."

Csongor Toth tapped a pencil on the table. "Objection, your honor. Whether or not someone cleaned my client up before the trial is pure speculation on the part of the witness."

Judge Parker frowned, but he could not bring himself to disagree because he had already overruled every single one of Csongor's previous objections and thought it was probably about time to rule in his favor. "Sustained. The witness will please not speculate on things he has no idea about. And the jury will forget they ever heard the comment about bloody clothes and getting cleaned up before the trial."

The scruffy juror muttered to the man to his right, "How's he 'spect us to forget something we just heard with our own ears? Don't seem possible."

The man hissed in a low voice, "How you 'spect me to know?"

Reginald smiled at the members of the jury. "No further questions, your honor."

Judge Parker sniffed and glared at Csongor. "You got any questions for the witness? Because if you do, I'd appreciate it if you'd get to it."

Csongor stood crisply and tapped a pencil three times on the defendant's table. "I certainly do, your honor." He walked to the front of the witness desk and pointed back at Joshua. "Tell me, Sheriff. Are you absolutely sure this is the man who murdered that unfortunate family and, as you claim, scalped those innocent children? Please take a good look at him before you answer. I wouldn't want you to make an unfortunate mistake."

Sheriff Boyle spoke promptly. "Well there's a dang fool question if I ever heard one, but if I have to say it again, I will. I'm absolutely sure. Why wouldn't I be?"

Csongor ignored the fact that he had asked another question. "And why, pray tell, are you absolutely sure?"

"I'm sure 'cause we caught him at the massacre. He was wearing those bloody clothes and trying to bury the family so no one would ever find them again."

Csongor ignored the fact that he had mentioned the bloody clothes again. He raised his chin in a presumptuous manner before continuing. "I see. Then you didn't actually see the defendant kill anyone or scalp any children. He just happened to be at the scene when you arrived?"

Sheriff Boyle squirmed. "I guess that's one way of looking at it, more or less, but he confessed he's the one who killed the mother. He said he found her tied to a wagon wheel shot full of arrows. Had to be the work of Indians, which he is one of them. A white man would never shoot a white woman with arrows." Myriad whispers cascaded around the room. The woman who had nearly swooned during the morning session pressed the back of her hand against her forehead, looked to the ceiling, and nearly swooned again.

Csongor lowered his gaze to Sheriff Boyle. "And when my client offered this so-called confession, did he tell you why he killed the mother?"

"Sure did. He said she asked him to." Laughter erupted from all corners of the room.

Judge Parker pounded his gavel with both hands. "Order! Order in my courtroom. Order!" The laughter died down until only a few giggles popped up here and there.

Csongor bowed. "Thank you, your honor." He spoke to Sheriff Boyle. "Did my client tell you how he killed the mother?"

Sheriff Boyle squeezed his hands together. "No, he didn't exactly, but I could see she was shot full of arrows, so that's how he must have done it." To strengthen his point, he offered more evidence. "Someone broke off the shafts, but I could still see the arrows sticking out. It was not a pretty sight."

"Very interesting. You didn't actually see anything, but are now speculating that he must have shot her full of arrows because he confessed to killing her. Did you examine the body to determine if there were other wounds?"

"Why would I do a fool thing like that when I could plainly see she was shot full of arrows?" Feeling a little uneasy, he exaggerated, "I'm not the only one. The whole posse saw it."

Csongor gazed across the faces of the jurors. "But still, you did not see who shot her full of arrows. And when my client offered a confession, he did not say he had killed her with arrows. He only said he had killed her because she asked him to. And you never examined the body to determine how she actually died. Would you agree, Sheriff Boyle, that this is a reasonably accurate description of the facts?"

Sheriff Boyle sputtered, "Well, I would, but there's a lot more to—"

Csongor held up his hand. "No further questions, your honor."

Sheriff Boyle sputtered some more, "But... I think—"

Judge Parker interrupted, "That's enough, Sheriff Boyle. You can step down now because he's finished talking to you and you don't have to answer any more questions." He pointed the gavel at the prosecuting attorney. "You got any more witnesses?"

Without standing, Reginald Simpson announced loudly, "The prosecution calls Deputy Bill Jackson to the stand." Jackson worked his way along the front of the second row, swaggered up to the witness stand, and slumped into the chair with an insolent scowl stretched across his freshly-shaved face. Reginald strutted in front of the witness stand. "Mister Jackson, please state your full name and occupation, for the record."

Jackson immediately removed his hat. "Name's Jackson. I'm an official deputy of this here town of Silver City." He touched the badge hanging from the left side of his leather vest. "Got the badge to prove it, too. Sheriff Boyle, he gave it to me." Jackson pointed at Sheriff Boyle.

Reginald Simpson ignored the badge. "Just so. Your first name is Bill?"

Jackson glowered at the prosecutor. "Bill's my first name, but everyone calls me Jackson, so I don't use it much. Never cared for the name in the first place."

"I see. Mister Jackson, would you—"

"Nobody calls me Mister Jackson. It's just Jackson."

"As you prefer. Then... Jackson... is it true you told Sheriff Boyle you had witnessed the entire massacre when you reported to the jail on that fateful day?"

Jackson snorted, "I don't know about witnessing anything, but I saw the whole thing. And I don't mind telling you... I never seen anything like it. Woman shot full of arrows. Children scalped while they was still alive. Blood all over the place. I never seen anything like it."

Joshua Hotah cupped his hand and whispered into Csongor's ear. "Shouldn't you be objecting or something?"

Csongor murmured indifferently, "No valid reason to object at this time. Patience."

Joshua risked the wrath of Judge Parker and whispered a bit louder. "How did he see the whole thing when there was nothing to see?"

Csongor raised his hand and repeated his earlier counsel. "Patience."

Reginald Simpson droned on. "And, for the benefit of the jury, would you please describe what you saw on that terrible day in more detail?"

Jackson grinned with pleasure. "Why, sure I'll tell ya. I saw an Indian tying a woman to the wagon wheel and tearing her clothes off until she was half-naked and shooting her full of arrows. Then I saw him run these two children down and scalp the both of 'em while they was still alive and squirming around on the ground begging for mercy while he did it. Like I told you, I saw the whole thing. My partner saw the whole thing too."

Reginald marched to the front of the jury in triumph. "And, Deputy Jackson, can you tell me if the Indian you saw on that day—the one who committed these terrible murders and scalped innocent children while they were still alive—is sitting in this courtroom today?"

Jackson smirked. "I sure can." He pointed at Joshua. "That's him, sitting right there. I'm sure of it. He's the one I saw do it. He's the one who shot the woman full of arrows and scalped her children while they was still alive."

Reginald spun around and hissed, "You are absolutely sure?"

The scowl returned to Jackson's face and he leaned forward menacingly. "I already said I was sure. How many times do I have to tell ya?"

Reginald strolled to his chair and quipped to Csongor, "Your witness."

Csongor arose deliberately, but didn't move away from the table. "Please tell me, Jackson, if you were alone when you witnessed the massacre."

"I already said I wasn't alone. How many times do I have to keep on explaining the same darn thing? Seth was with me. He saw the whole thing too."

"And who is this ... Seth?"

"He's a deputy too, just like me."

"Then please explain to me why the two of you did not ride down to the wagon and help the family? After all, you have stated you saw only one Indian. Surely the two of you could have overpowered him with relative ease."

Jackson perked up at this rehearsed cue. "We thought about it really hard, but when we thought about it some more we was terrible afraid them Indians might still be around. We decided it was best to go fetch the sheriff and bring back more men." Then he offered an improvised addition to his prepared testimony: "No reason to add two more scalps to the massacre."

Csongor sat in his chair. "Quite so. No further questions."

Joshua poked Csongor in the arm. "Aren't you going to ask him to explain why he isn't telling the truth?"

Csongor scribbled an illegible note on a sheet of paper. "Do not be afraid. I know what I'm doing. We'll have our chance when the time is right."

After excusing Jackson, Judge Parker asked the prosecutor, "You got any more witness to call, or are you finished? It's getting late in the day and I'm getting real hungry."

Reginald Simpson stood. "No further witnesses, your honor."

"I was hoping you'd say that." Judge parker stroked the heavy gavel against the top of the bench. "This court is hereby adjourned until tomorrow morning at ten o'clock when we will start the proceedings all over again. Now, where can a fellow get a decent steak and a good beer in this two-bit town?"

The leg irons rattled ominously as Sheriff Boyle approached the defendant's table.

CHAPTER NINE

The second day of the trial of Joshua Hotah
May 18, 1872

T he second day of the trial began precisely at ten o'clock—give or take a few minutes—but the formal proceedings did not technically commence until fifteen minutes after the hour. This was because moments after he pounded the heavy gavel on the judge's bench and called the court to order, Judge Parker scanned the jury and noticed two empty seats. When he asked what happened to the missing jurors, Sheriff Boyle said he thought the two fellows looked kind of familiar when he arrested them for disorderly conduct last night at one of the local brothels. When he offered to fetch the men, Judge Parker said not to bother and ruled that the remaining eight jurors were good enough for the legal purposes of this here trial. The sheriff said the two men were probably still drunk anyway, and likely would have trouble staying upright in their chairs. When this issue had resolved itself, the woman who had nearly swooned twice the day before actually did swoon for no apparent reason anyone could discern. After a local dandy (and notorious gambler, womanizer, and purveyor of half-truths) failed to revive the unfortunate woman by patting her hands and fanning her face, two husky men with scruffy beards and dirty boots agreed to carry her to the doctor's office. The courtroom giggled when she suddenly woke up in the hairy grasp of the two strange men and started whacking them on the heads with an umbrella. The courtroom exploded in boisterous laughter when the umbrella opened and the two men dropped the woman neatly into her chair. And finally, just when Judge Parker thought he had everything under control, the same three men who had arrived late the morning of the first day rumbled noisily up the exterior stairs and slammed the door twice after they stumbled comically into the courtroom. Although he was tempted to have the three men arrested on the spot, he decided this would only add to the chaos and instead glared at Csongor Toth and asked, "Are you ready to call some witnesses, counselor? I think it's high time we got started before something else goes wrong." With this simple question, the defense of Joshua Hotah began.

After stroking his fingers provocatively along the border of the defendant's table, Csongor Toth pushed himself up using the armrests of his chair and stood erectly. He sniffed, and announced, "The defense calls as its first witness, Miss Priscilla Kimball."

Whispers cascaded incoherently around the courtroom when a young girl sitting in the third row, next to Manfred Herrmann, stood. Her brown pigtails bounced as she worked her way down the row over feet and across knees and walked to the front of the courtroom. She slid into the witness chair after Judge Parker made her swear to tell the truth, the whole truth, and nothing but the darn truth. The size of the chair diminished her apparent age. At least five of the jurors recognized her from the saloon on the corner of Washington and Avalanche. It is likely that the two missing jurors would have recognized her too (if they'd had the chance).

Csongor Toth clasped his hands behind his back and approached the witness stand. After offering the young girl a comforting wink and a soft smile, he said, "Miss Kimball, please state your name and occupation for the benefit of the court."

Priscilla folder her dainty hands and swung her feet back and forth, which further diminished her apparent age. "My name's Priscilla Kimball. I work at the establishment on the corner of Washington and Avalanche."

"And what exactly, might I ask, do you do at the establishment on the corner of Washington and Avalanche?"

"Oh…mostly clean the rooms upstairs. Sometimes I clean up messes in the saloon, but usually only a couple of times a day." A man seated a few chairs away from the woman who had swooned sniggered, but quickly stifled his derisive laugh when his friend punched him in the arm.

Without looking back at the sniggering man, Csongor waited patiently for the interruption to cease. "Is this all you do at this particular establishment, Miss Kimball? Have you been asked to do other tasks, particularly during the last several weeks?" The man sniggered again.

Priscilla answered cheerfully, "Oh, yes. Margaret—she's the one who runs the place—she asked me to take meals over to the jail. I've been doing it for a couple of weeks now. That's where I met the—"

Csongor interrupted Priscilla before she could complete her statement. "All in good time, Miss Kimball. All in good time. Now, when this Margaret, the one you say runs the saloon, asked you to take meals to the jail, was Sheriff Boyle sitting at the same table." Csongor pointed at Sheriff Boyle.

Priscilla shifted forward in the overlarge chair and stopped swinging her feet. "Oh, yes. He was sitting at the same table as Margaret. They were talking about all sorts of things."

Csongor tilted his head. "Things? What sorts of things were they talking about?"

Priscilla slid back in the chair and squeezed the armrests. "Sheriff Boyle was talking about how he couldn't find anyone in town who was willing to feed the Indian who killed the family, and he didn't want him to starve to death before he got a fair trial and hanged."

Csongor offered a countenance of astonishment for the benefit of the jury. "You appear to have a very good memory, Miss Kimball. Are you sure you heard Sheriff Boyle correctly? Are you absolutely certain Sheriff Boyle publicly declared the guilt of my client nearly two weeks ago?"

Priscilla slid to the front of the chair again. "That's what I heard him say. I was standing right there by the table when he said it." The whispers rose and fell. Two men standing near the back of the courtroom next to Roshan offered audible praise for Sheriff Boyle. At the same time, the double-hung windows behind Judge Parker rattled when muffled thunder rumbled down the Jordan Creek Valley.

Csongor looked through one of the windows when he heard the thunder, and noted the darkening skies. "Then tell me, Miss Kimball… why did you agree to deliver food to the defendant after Sheriff Boyle told you the man had killed the family? Were you not frightened that he might try to kill you as well?"

Priscilla swung her legs. "I was frightened at first, but Margaret said I had to do it. I had no say in it. I just had to do it."

"You had no choice?"

"I had no choice."

Csongor approached the jurors. "Then can you tell me what happened when you delivered the first meal that night?"

Priscilla glanced at Sheriff Boyle. "Sure can. I got to the jail late because nobody told me how to find it until a nice man wearing a black suit told me where to go and two big dogs ran out of an alley and chased me down the street and I nearly dropped the bacon and eggs but I managed to hang onto them by holding the plate against my chest."

"Did you manage to deliver the meal?"

"I did."

"And then what happened?"

"Sheriff Boyle took me back to see the Indian right away, but he wouldn't open the door to the cell because he said the deputies were gone. He told me the murdering redskin could eat his food through the bars if he was hungry enough. Then he left me there alone waiting for the plate and locked the door so I couldn't get out."

"Sheriff Boyle called my client a 'murdering redskin'? He used those exact words?"

"That's what I heard him say."

"Did you speak with this Indian? Or, to use Sheriff Boyle's own words, this murdering redskin?"

"Sure did, but not for three or four days. He didn't say anything until then. It was the night I gave him some carrots when he finally talked to me. I think he liked the carrots."

"And what did he tell you on the night you gave him the carrots?"

Priscilla straightened. "He told me he didn't kill the family."

Csongor waited for the whispers to die down. "Now, this is important, Miss Kimball. Did he tell you who *did* kill the family?"

"Sure did. He told me white men dressed like Indians killed the family."

"And how did he know this?"

"He said the mother told him."

"The mother told him? And when did she tell him?"

Priscilla hesitated as she thought of the best way to answer. "She told him right before he shot her … with his rifle." Priscilla quickly explained, "But she asked him to do it."

Chaos erupted throughout the courtroom. A slender man cupped his hands around his mouth and yelled, "Hang the murdering varmint! Hang him right now!" A juror in the back row stood and pointed angrily at Priscilla and announced, "I remember her now. She's the thirteen-year-old whore Margaret's been peddling. She's not old enough to know a darn thing about anything!" A pious woman sitting four rows behind the defendant's table pointed at the back of Joshua's head and declared, "Shame. Shame. Your eternal soul shall burn in everlasting hell for this outrage!"

Judge Parker stood and pounded the heavy gavel with both hands. "Order. Order. I said. Order in my courtroom or I'll have the whole lot of you cleared out. Order!"

Csongor waited to ask his final questions until everyone had found their seats and an unnatural silence pervaded the courtroom. "Thank you, your honor. Miss Kimball, did he tell you why he shot the mother?"

"Yes, he did. He shot her because she was going to die anyway and she asked him to."

"And is the man you spoke to at the jail about these unfortunate events sitting in this courtroom today?"

Priscilla pointed cutely at Joshua Hotah. "Sure is. He's sitting right there."

"One last question. How old are you Miss Kimball?"

"Almost sixteen."

"You're not thirteen as was claimed by someone in the courtroom during the unlawful outburst that occurred just minutes ago?"

"No. I've been fifteen for a long time."

"Thank you, Miss Kimball. No further questions."

Judge Parker addressed the prosecuting attorney. "You got any questions for this little gal?"

Reginald Simpson remained seated. "Only one, your honor." He shifted in his chair to face Priscilla and smiled pleasantly. "Tell me, Miss Kimball. How old did you say you were?"

Priscilla smiled. "Almost sixteen."

The smile vanished. "In other words, you are only a fifteen-year-old girl with very little real experience in the world and therefore limited capacity to understand the complex issues before this court." Before Priscilla could protest, Reginald concluded, "No further questions."

Judge Parker tried to scowl at Priscilla, but found it impossible. "You're excused, little miss. Thank you for your testimony." He slammed the heavy gavel on top of the bench. "This court is hereby adjourned until two o'clock this afternoon, so I can take a nap."

Manfred hustled to the witness stand. He took Priscilla's hand and guided her to the front of the courtroom where they stood by one of the double-hung windows and watched people spill into the street. They waited until the street had mostly cleared before leaving.

After the court reconvened at precisely two o'clock—give or take a few minutes—Csongor called Manfred Herrmann to the witness stand to confirm Priscilla Kimball's testimony and to attest to Joshua Hotah's character. When Manfred expressed his belief that Joshua was an honest man who would never think of lying, the chaos of the morning repeated itself and Judge Parker nearly broke the shaft of the heavy gavel trying to pound the unruly crowd into submission. The prosecutor followed up with a few awkward questions about Manfred's lack of experience with Indians and his impressive experience with the prostitutes working at the saloon on the corner of Washington and Avalanche. Manfred did not answer the questions particularly well, mostly because Reginald Simpson cut him off before he could finish any of his sentences. Before Manfred had a chance to clear up any misunderstandings, Judge Parker asked him to return to his seat.

Judge Parker glared at Csongor. "Are you finished, counselor?"

Csongor inhaled a deep breath. "Nearly, your honor. I have one last witness to call."

Judge Parker pushed his ample stomach against the edge of the bench and scowled. "Then you'd better get on with it. Time's a wasting and I've got other business to attend to."

Csongor arose and, his voice imbued with confidence, announced to the court, "The defense calls Joshua Hotah."

A wave of astonishment gurgled across the courtroom. Csongor's statement surprised even Joshua, who twitched in disbelief. "You want me to go up there?" Joshua pointed innocently toward the witness stand.

Csongor motioned toward the stand. "Yes, my dear fellow. I want you to take a seat at the witness stand. Do not be afraid. I only want to ask you a few questions."

Joshua rose unhurriedly from his chair and methodically worked his way to the witness stand. When he arrived, he lowered himself into the chair so slowly that everyone's chin lowered in unison as they watch him descend.

Csongor strode confidently to the front of the courtroom. "Please state your name for the benefit of the court."

Joshua replied innocently, "I think everyone already knows my name."

Csongor waved his hand in the air. "It's just a formality. I can't ask you any questions until you state your name."

Joshua squirmed in the uncomfortable chair. "Joshua Hotah."

Csongor crossed his arms and pressed his left fist beneath his chin. "And please, Mister Hotah, tell the court what you have been doing during the last several years."

"I have been looking for my father and my mother."

"I see. And was it this search for your parents that brought you to Silver City?"

Joshua looked over at the jury, and one of the men ran his index finger across his neck. "Yes, it is what brought me to Silver City."

"Now, are both of your parents Indians?"

"No. My father is English. He came here to hunt the buffalo. My mother is Sioux."

"I see. You are only half Indian—what men sometimes call a half-breed. Is this correct?"

Joshua clarified, "Only white men have called me this."

Csongor nodded. "Nonetheless, the fact remains: you are not a full-blooded Indian. Half of you is English. Is this a fair thing to say?"

"I suppose it is. But I do not know what difference it makes."

Judge Parker interrupted, "I don't know what difference it makes either, counselor. Do you plan to end up somewhere that makes any sense, or are you just wasting the court's time with more useless questions?"

Csongor explained, "I am merely pointing out to the jury that my client is not technically an Indian. He is half English."

Reginald Simpson perked up. "Objection. As far as I'm concerned, half an Indian is a full-blooded Indian. It doesn't make a bit of difference if his father was English or Portuguese or anything else."

Judge Parker thought about this before announcing, "Sustained." He glared at Csongor. "Now stop wasting my time and stop asking silly questions."

Csongor shrugged indifferently and turned back to Joshua. "Since the court finds this line of questioning abhorrent, I will try something else." He raised his chin and exhaled. "Mister Hotah...Priscilla Kimball has testified that you told her you killed the mother. Can you please confirm that her testimony is accurate and explain the circumstances of the event?"

"Circumstances?"

"Yes. Simply explain what happened in your own words."

Joshua relaxed, but only a little. "There is not much to explain. I heard shots and rode to the sound of the shots. When I arrived, I found the wagon with a woman tied to a wheel and a dead man sitting in the front. The woman was shot with many arrows. She asked me to find her children. When I found them, they were both dead and someone had scalped them, even the little girl."

When Joshua did not immediately continue, Csongor asked, "Did you return to the wagon after you found the dead children?"

"I went back to the wagon and told the mother her children were safe. This made her very happy. Then she asked me to kill her."

Csongor lowered his voice. "And did you honor her request?"

"Honor her request?"

"Yes. Did you kill her like she asked you to?"

Joshua remembered the deafening sound when he squeezed the trigger. "I shot her in the heart with my Henry rifle."

"Then what did you do?"

"I cut the mother down from the wheel and wrapped her in her dress. I carried the two children down the road and laid them next to their mother. I found a shovel in the wagon and walked to the creek and started digging graves. The shovel broke before I finished the first grave. I buried the father in this grave because he was a small man and it was not big enough for two and I did not have another shovel."

"Interesting. You abandoned the idea of digging graves for the mother and children after the shovel broke. What did you do then?"

"I decided the mother and children would be happy in the white man's cemetery in Silver City. I cut branches to build a travois, tied the mother and children to it, and pulled the mother and children to town."

Csongor swung around and gazed vaguely into the middle of the jury. "But you never arrived in Silver City, did you?"

"No. I never arrived."

"And why did you not arrive?"

"The sheriff and his men stopped me on the road."

"Just to be clear, you were riding on the road toward Silver City when Sheriff Boyle and his posse stopped you?"

"Yes. I was riding to Silver City."

Csongor walked back to the defendant's table. "No further questions, your honor." After sitting, he said, "Your witness."

Reginald Simpson appeared quite bored as he strolled toward Joshua Hotah. After arriving in front of the witness stand, he stifled a small yawn. "Good afternoon, Mister Hotah."

Joshua greeted the prosecutor suspiciously. "Good afternoon."

Reginald patted his lips before dropping his hand. "I must say… I found your story quite compelling. But if you don't mind, there is one aspect of your testimony that troubles me."

"I do not mind."

"Good. Then we agree with one another. Will you please explain to the jury why the mother asked you to kill her after you said the children were safe? I just can't seem to understand why she would not have wanted to see the children one last time before she died."

Joshua thought about this question for at least five seconds. His prolonged indecision did not look good to many members of the jury because they assumed he was trying to concoct a lie to conceal his misdeeds. "I told her I did not bring the children because I did not want them to see her in such a terrible way."

"Mister Hotah, this strikes me as very important information. Why did you not tell us about this before now?"

"Because the question was not asked before now."

Reginald sneered, "How convenient. The moment I point out a serious flaw in your story, you offer up new information in an attempt to explain away the flaw. Do you really expect me to believe any of this constantly changing story?"

Csongor stood. "Objection. The assertion that the story is constantly changing has not been proven. The witness has simply offered new information."

Judge Parker did not hesitate. "Overruled. Answer the question."

Joshua felt a rivulet of cold sweat dribble down his back. "What is the question?"

Emboldened, Reginald Simpson expanded the scope of his inquisition. "Do you really expect the jury to believe this fairy tale when it changes whenever I ask a new question?"

Without thinking too much, Joshua answered directly, "I do."

Reginald scoffed, "I have no further questions," before slithering back to his seat.

Exhausted. Judge Parker slumped back. "You got any more witnesses, counselor? It's almost four and I want to finish this before dinner."

Csongor stood. "No further questions."

Judge Parker straightened up and slammed the gavel down. "Then this court is hereby adjourned until five o'clock when I expect the jury to return with a verdict because I have no intention of staying in Silver City through the weekend." He glared at the jury. "Is that understood?" Seven of the men nodded in unison, but the juror who had fallen asleep halfway through Joshua's testimony just slouched to the side a little.

When the eight jurors wandered back to the courtroom (at precisely seven minutes before five), Manfred Herrmann attempted to discern the temperament of each man. The jurors crossed the front of the courtroom in a ragged line and dispersed to their seats. A grizzled miner standing near the back opened the door and yelled down to the street that the trial was starting up again and dozens thundered up the wood stairs and piled noisily into the courtroom. Having decided it was just too much trouble to take Joshua Hotah back to jail when Judge Parker had ordered the jury to return with a verdict in an hour, Sheriff Boyle had locked him into the leg irons and ordered him to stay put. After complaining of the stifling air in the courtroom and promising to return before five, Csongor Toth had taken the opportunity to go for a walk. Roshan, Longwei, and John Smith stayed in the courtroom during the recess and—after standing in the back for two days—had taken the opportunity to procure three seats in the fourth row. It turned out they really didn't need the seats because a little after five the jury announced a unanimous verdict of guilty of murdering the mother and two children. They evidently could not come to any agreement on the father because one juror, the one who had fallen asleep during Joshua's testimony, had somehow convinced himself that the father might have died of natural causes before the massacre started. Judge Parker quickly announced that it didn't really matter anyway, and sentenced Joshua Hotah to hang by the neck until dead. He set the date of the hanging for one week from Monday because he wanted to give the town enough time to build a proper hanging scaffold to avoid the appearance of vigilante justice. He pounded the heavy gavel one last time and the trial was over. Sheriff Boyle had to fight his way through an angry mob to get Joshua out of the courtroom. Then he had to fight his way down the crowded stairs. And then he had to fight his way into the ground-floor jail where he locked Joshua up. Manfred had hoped to speak with Csongor about any possible legal recourse, but Csongor never returned from his walk. Manfred assumed that he must have had a good reason to miss the jury verdict and sentencing.

CHAPTER TEN

Alexandra implores Manfred to intervene
May 19-20, 1872

T he weather had improved considerably: tattered clouds and broad
stretches of crystal blue and the pleasant chatter of birds displaced
the darkly overcast skies and faraway thunder of the day before. Manfred
Herrmann sat on one of two rickety chairs on the small covered porch
of his modest shack, reading a chapter from the *Book of Romans* in his
dogeared Bible. The afternoon sun had swept across the porch a few
hours earlier and would soon begin its descent behind the mountains to
the northwest. Manfred enjoyed the comforting warmth of the sun on his
face as he read. Jordan Creek gurgled pleasantly to the east. A peaceful
breeze swayed the willows along the muddy banks of the creek. His cat—
the one with black fur, white paws and chest with a flash of gold around
the margins, blue lizard eyes (a bit crossed), and a small chunk missing
from the left ear who he had told several times to never come back—had
curled up in the other chair soon after the appearance of the afternoon
sun. The cat purred from time to time (for no apparent reason Manfred
could discern) and occasionally shifted in the chair to alternately warm
his tummy or back.

Manfred turned the page and began reading a new verse, but the sound
of hooves clicking randomly over the rocks littering the meandering trail
to Silver City interrupted his reverie. He lowered the Bible and positioned his hand to shade his eyes. He glimpsed a fleeting image of an
approaching horse and rider through the scattered trees. The clicking

grew louder. Manfred pushed himself up from the rickety chair and walked a dozen paces toward the clicking hooves. When the rider and horse cleared the last tree and arrived fully in Manfred's view, the cat raised its head and meowed.

Manfred lowered his hand and smiled when the rider stopped in front of him. "If I'd known you were planning to visit me today, I would have brewed some tea and donned a proper coat and tie." He began rolling his sleeves down and buttoning the cuffs.

Alexandra Smythe clutched her dark olive skirt with a gloved hand and repositioned her right leg around the horn of the sidesaddle. "I didn't know I would be visiting you until an hour ago. I hope you can spare a few minutes to talk. I apologize if this is not a convenient time."

Manfred shifted the Bible to his left hand. "No problem at all. I was just sitting on the porch reading." Manfred's eyes descended from Alexandra's dark olive vest, and he noticed that both of her legs dangled to the left of the saddle. "It's none of my business, but how are you managing to stay up on your saddle with both legs on the same side?" He noted the contour of her legs through the fabric of the skirt. "Looks a little precarious to me."

Alexandra lifted her right knee above the upper horn of the sidesaddle, lowered her right foot to the ground, and pulled her left foot from the stirrup. "It's called a sidesaddle. Have you never seen one before?"[7]

Manfred rubbed the back of his neck. "Can't say if I have or not, but my knowledge of horses is very limited." The double horn at the front of the saddle baffled Manfred. "Why not use a regular saddle? If you ask me, this sidesaddle looks sort of dangerous."

Alexandra patted the wrinkles from her skirt. "Because it would require me to wear trousers, which I think you would agree is not very ladylike."

"Trousers?"

"Yes. The sidesaddle allows me to ride in a skirt." Alexandra pulled the front of her skirt up until the hem lifted several inches off the ground. Although tempted, Manfred avoided looking down at her exposed ankles. "I'm sure you must see how difficult it would be to ride a regular saddle dressed like this."

---

[7] Alexandra is using a western sidesaddle based on a design Texas cattleman Charles Goodnight originally developed for his first wife, Mary Dyer Goodnight.

"I guess that makes sense, if one were to assume I have the slightest interest in horses or how to ride them." Manfred motioned back at his modest shack with an upturned palm. "Would you like to sit on the porch? I'll have to ask the cat to move off the chair, but I don't think he'll mind too much."

Alexandra nodded and stepped toward the porch with the reins in her hand and the horse following behind. "I'd love to sit with you on such a pleasant afternoon. Should I ask the cat to move, or will you do it?"

Manfred moved to Alexandra's side but did not take her arm. "No, I'll do it, because I might have to shoo him off the chair with a broom."

When they arrived at the front of the deck, Manfred disappeared into the shack to find the broom. Alexandra apologized to the cat as she tied the reins off to the corner post of the porch roof. "I'm sorry to make you move, but there are only two chairs. I'm sure you can find another place in the sun, if you don't mind."

Manfred came out of the shack and instantly nudged the cat off the chair with the bristled end of the broom. "Shoo, you nasty little varmint. And don't be dragging any mice or birds onto my porch while Miss Smythe is visiting." The cat protested with a gravelly whine and jumped off the chair and sprinted around the side of the shack. Manfred swept the chair and balanced the broom handle against the door jamb.

Alexandra stepped onto the porch and sat in the chair. "Thank you, but it's a shame you had to use a broom on such a lovely animal. Do you think he's upset?"

Manfred chuckled. "I've never called him lovely, but I have learned if you want the best seat in the house you have to move the cat." After settling into the other chair, he continued, "He'll get over it. What did you want to talk about?"

Alexandra folded her hands above her knees. "As you may know, I did not attend the trial. This morning I spoke to Mr. Sommercamp at the general store; he said you attended both days of the trial. He also told me something quite curious. This is the reason I have come to visit you."

Manfred shifted his feet against the weathered boards beneath his feet. "Curious?"

"Yes. He told me he spoke with you the other day, and said you were convinced of this man's innocence."

Manfred squirmed in the hard chair. "His name is Joshua Hotah. And yes, I believe he had nothing to do with the massacre." He squirmed again, but could not find a comfortable position. "They sentenced him to hang. Almost everyone in the courtroom cheered when the judge announced the verdict, but it made me feel sick."

Alexandra shifted her knees closer to Manfred's and softened her voice. "Quite unfortunate, but I'm not really here to discuss the details of the trial."

"Why are you here, then?"

"I'm here to ask if you intend to do something about it."

With a noticeably prickly tone, Manfred answered, "Do something about it? What do you mean?" He thought of everything he had already done in his failed struggle to save Joshua Hotah. He was astonished to hear that Alexandra thought he should do more.

"Do something to save an innocent man from hanging."

"Not to be argumentative, but I don't think there's anything I could possibly do to save him … at this point."

Alexandra twitched her nose. "But there must be something more you can do. Are you really willing to give up so easily? Are you not willing to even try? Especially if you truly believe in his innocence."

A sour taste spilled across the back of Manfred's tongue. He answered defensively, "I visited him in jail three times before the trial. After hearing his side of the story, I believed he was innocent. That's why I collected money and hired Csongor to defend him. If it wasn't for me, he wouldn't have had any defense at all. I attended both days of the trial and offered him as much support as I could. I can't imagine what more I can do."

Alexandra attempted to cajole Manfred with praise. "But you are a clever man. I know you would think of something … " but then she drove the dagger in, " … if you would only try."

Manfred's previous admiration of Alexandra abruptly turned to exasperation. "There's nothing more to do. It is finished."

"I see. You're satisfied that you've already done enough. You intend to do nothing more to save the life of a man who you believe is innocent." She brushed a fleck of dust from her knee. "I must admit to you … I am a little disappointed."

Manfred abruptly stood. A wave of searing heat flashed down his back. "I think we have nothing more to discuss on this subject, Miss Smythe.

Thank you for visiting me today." He held out his hand. "I hope we have the chance to visit again soon."

Alexandra stood but did not take Manfred's hand. "I will leave then, since it appears you have made up your mind to do nothing. Goodbye then." She stomped brusquely off the porch, untied the reins, mounted the sidesaddle, and rode away.

Manfred swallowed hard as he watched her amble down the trail. The sour taste returned to augment his regret.

The next morning, Monday the twentieth of May, Manfred ruminated while eating a meager breakfast of hard biscuits and strong coffee. The weather had fluctuated again; the gray skies and irregular sprinkles mimicked his dark mood. A sporadic gust of cool air sent the branches of a young cottonwood scratching against the glass and mullions of a small window on the side of his shack. Earlier the wind had gusted sufficiently to rattle the front door and creak the hinges. The cat had curled up on the floor in front of the fading warmth of the potbelly stove even though Manfred had not bothered to stoke the fire for nearly an hour. He tried to think of other things while he finished his last biscuit, but Alexandra's harsh words constantly pushed his thoughts aside and consumed any pretense of contentment. At first, he had attempted to disparage her words by condemning her audacity. This strategy worked initially, but when he finally admitted his love for her, and that he trusted the integrity of her words and the purity of her intentions, he slumped into the chair in emotional defeat. After sulking a few minutes, he straightened up and began earnestly thinking of how he might still save Joshua Hotah from the hangman's noose—in only four days. At first nothing practical emerged from his jumbled mind, but when the cat sauntered away from the stove and jumped up on his bed to snuggle against his lumpy pillow, a worthy idea presented itself.

Manfred retrieved a sheet of paper and a pencil from a small wood box. He sharpened the pencil with a pocket knife and began writing. After filling the page, he wrote the words "Best Regards" at the bottom and signed his name with a satisfying flourish. He folded the sheet neatly and slid it into one of his last two envelopes. The cat raised its head when he tromped across the wood floor, and jumped when he slammed the front door. Manfred hiked along the meandering rock-littered trail to the southern border of Silver City, then veered onto Jordan Avenue and marched north. After passing several dwellings and businesses, he arrived at the livery where the blacksmith was willing to loan him the use of an old mare and carriage without charge. He stopped briefly at the Sommercamp Emporium & General Store before resuming his journey. Over an hour and four miles later, he arrived at a well-maintained cabin set into a yellowed hillside bristling with juniper trees. Three horses pranced to the side of a circular corral located next to the cabin when Manfred dismounted from the carriage. He crossed the open area fronting the cabin and knocked three times on the small door. He thought he heard someone moving around inside, but no one answered. He waited half-a-minute and knocked again. Still no answer. He waited a minute more and knocked a third time. Something scraped along the floor. He knocked a fourth time and the door did not open. He tried to peek through a small window, but a gauzy curtain obscured the clarity of his view. At the moment he cursed his bad luck and prepared to leave, the door creaked open and a small face appeared though the crack.

Manfred spun around. "Mr. Airingsail! Please accept my apology for arriving without invitation, but I have something of great urgency to discuss with you and could not wait for a chance meeting in town."

Conrad Airingsail tugged his bandana a little higher, pulled his hat a little lower, and adjusted his glasses.

Manfred removed the envelope from his coat pocket. "You are probably wondering how I found you. William Sommercamp gave me directions to your ranch. I trust you will not hold this disturbance of your privacy against him."

Conrad Airingsail opened the door a little more and shook his head slowly from side to side.

"Thank you, Mr. Airingsail. Now, to business. I must ask a favor, which you may choose not to grant. I am in need of an expert horseman to deliver an urgent message to Captain Ethan Plantagenet at Fort Boise." Manfred pointed at the front of the envelope. "I've written his name on the front so you will not forget. The person who delivers this letter must be someone I can trust; someone who will not fail to complete the delivery by tonight." Manfred lowered the envelope to his side. "I realize this is a daunting task. If I had made this decision even a day ago, I would have made the trip to Boise myself to speak directly with Captain Plantagenet." After licking his lips, Manfred explained, "Because of my regrettable indecision—which was recently pointed out to me by a dear friend—I have already missed the morning stage and cannot wait another day."

Conrad Airingsail open the door another inch and the hinges squeaked.

Manfred tried to glance inside the cabin, but the darkness prevented him from seeing its contents. "Before you answer, I must warn you that it involves the man named Joshua Hotah, the Indian who was sentenced to hang this week. I saw you at the trial. I believe you will therefore understand what you are getting into."

Conrad Airingsail nodded.

"I believe to the depth of my soul in Joshua Hotah's innocence. This letter is my pathetic last attempt to save him. Consequently, I must give you a stern warning: if you agree to deliver the letter, you may invoke the wrath of the town. Many have turned against him. It is a dangerous task, Mr. Airingsail, but I could think of no better man to do it."

Conrad Airingsail nodded.

Manfred presented the envelope. "What do you say, Mr. Airingsail? Will you deliver the letter to Captain Plantagenet? And if your answer is yes, can you leave immediately? There is no longer any time to waste."

To Manfred's surprise, Conrad Airingsail reached out and snatched the envelope and shut the door. Although this astonishing maneuver startled Manfred, he waited a few minutes before knocking. No answer. He waited a few more minutes and knocked again. Still no answer. He waited one more minute before pounding vigorously on the door and pleading in a loud voice. "Mr. Airingsail, please open the door. I must speak with you immediately. I fear you have not understood my intentions. Mr. Airingsail!"

The door swung open and Conrad Airingsail strode into the morning light wearing mud-splattered boots and riding chaps. He shouldered his way past Manfred and spur-jingled to the corral. Manfred followed him, and then watched Conrad saddle up a muscular horse with scattered white splotches. Manfred stepped aside when Conrad led the horse out of the corral. After closing the gate and tying it off with a rope, Conrad held the envelope up before shoving it into a saddle bag. He swung his boot into the left stirrup, mounted the horse, and kicked his heels into the horse's haunches.

Manfred waved and yelled, "Thank you, Mr. Airingsail, I really appreciate it!" but Conrad just galloped away. Moments later, a colossal explosion rumbled the southern slopes of War Eagle Mountain. When Manfred looked in the direction of the impressive blast, the front door of Conrad's cabin rattled ominously.

CHAPTER ELEVEN

An unusual incident at Mahogany Gulch
May 20, 1872

Despite the glorious return of the sun, Tseng Longwei and John Smith prepared to work the claim at Mahogany Gulch immersed in gloom. In the days after finding Gustus De Angeles slumped over the bloody table, they had both experienced an unexpected fondness for the cranky old coot and now desperately rued his loss. Roshan likely felt the same, but they did not know for sure because he had refused to talk about it—possibly because of his angry declaration two weeks earlier that everyone would be of the better if Gustus did not live the more of now if you know the meaning of my lips. But they could not talk to Roshan about it this sunny morning because he had driven the wagon into town yesterday to visit Nadia and—or so he had claimed—to drink enough whisky to kill a large horse. Both Longwei and John Smith thought this an odd statement at the time, because neither one of them had ever seen a horse drink even one glass of whisky, let alone enough to cause premature death.

John Smith watched Longwei load a pickaxe, sledgehammer, and two shovels into a rusty wheelbarrow. "What do you figure on us doing this morning, Mister Longwei? No telling when Mister Roshan will get back, 'specially if he drinks enough whisky to kill a large horse like he said. Not that I pay much attention to such things, but I never seen a horse drink any whisky, not even a single sip. But being that a horse is such a large animal, I suppose it would take at least four bottles of whisky to kill it."

Longwei rubbed his hands together then slapped them on the front of his black trousers. "I believe he was making a joke. I do not believe he will drink enough whisky to kill a horse."

John Smith lifted a case of dynamite and muscled it into the wheelbarrow. "Maybe you're right, but if you ask me, he sounded mighty serious when he said it."

Longwei wedged a metal tin of blasting caps and a coil of safety fuse[8] between the case of dynamite and the side of the wheelbarrow. "Is this the last box of dynamite? If it is, I can ask Roshan to buy more when he returns with the wagon."

John Smith snorted, "Nay. There's three more tucked away in the shed down by the new mine shaft. I carried them there myself two days ago. Mister Gustus…he bought them a few…." John Smith's voice trailed away. "Didn't mean to mention Mister Gustus when he's already dead and can't speak for himself. I do apologize."

"It is not a problem to speak of Mister De Angeles after he has died, and there is no reason to apologize. I do not think he would mind."

"Then I'll speak my piece. Mister Gustus bought them cases a few weeks ago 'cause he said we needed an awful lot of dynamite for the new tunnel. Guess he was planning on taking this one real deep."

"Then we should honor his memory by using all of the dynamite on the new tunnel. It appears he would have wished us to do so."

"Shouldn't we ought to wait for Mister Roshan? Since he's the new owner of this worthless claim, he might want to have a say about it."

Longwei pondered the suggestion. "I do not think we should wait for Roshan's return. If he does drink enough whisky to kill a horse, we may not see him for many days to come."

"We might not see him for weeks the way things are going around here. As a matter of fact, maybe we'll never see him again."

---

8   An English leather merchant named William Bickford invented the first practical fuse in 1831, later called the "safety fuse." He fabricated the fuse from jute yarn spun around a core of gunpowder and varnished with tar. Bickford's fuse was supplied as a "rope," and burned at a consistent rate of approximately 30 seconds per foot.

"Then we should work on the new tunnel this very morning. Roshan will surely be impressed with our progress by the time he returns, especially if he does not return, as you say, for many weeks."

John Smith walked to the back of the wheelbarrow and lifted the weathered handles. "Then let's get working. Don't want to waste any more of this nice morning talking about things we can't do anything about."

Longwei followed John Smith and the wheelbarrow to the entrance of the new tunnel. They chatted a little more about the unfortunate demise of Mister Gustus and offered more predictions about when Roshan might return with the wagon after drinking enough whisky to kill a horse and discussed if the weather conditions might change before the end of the day. They rummaged through the shack looking for a couple of good drill bits. After finding a brand-new drill bit, which neither one of them knew about because Gustus had evidently hidden it under several coils of rope, and one used drill bit that was only slightly nicked up, they heard Roshan singing and the sound of the wagon approaching from the west.

Her foot, Oh! Golly! Twas a beauty,
Her shoes were made of Dig-by pine,
Two herring boxes without the tops on
Just made the sandals of Clementine.

Oh! my Nadia, Oh! my Nadia,
Oh! my darling Nadia.
Now you are gone....

John Smith and Tseng Longwei scrambled from the shack and ran across the uneven ground to greet Roshan. He stopped the wagon next to the cabin, tied the reins off to the brake shaft, and hopped down. Roshan smiled broadly as he addressed John Smith and Longwei. "Why do you stand there looking up Roshan like a newly ghost you have not seen in the time before? It is of the beautiful morning, my two lovely friends, and I have of the good news to share with the both of you if you will listen of it in the day."

John Smith spoke first. "We're surprised to see you. The two of us were just saying we didn't think you'd come back for at least a week or two."

Longwei spoke second. "It is good to see you only one day after you departed to drink enough whisky to kill a horse. Did you ever find such a horse?"

Roshan reached out and squeezed Longwei's shoulder. "No, I did not drink as you say of the horse for to kill it. Miss Nadia told of me in many uncertain words I could not speak to her over again for the ever if I did of such a foolish thing to the horse."

Longwei slid each hand into the opposite sleeve of his black tunic. "It is good there is someone on the face of the earth who you will listen to. Until this day, I did not think there existed such a person."

Roshan reached out with his other hand and squeezed John Smith's shoulder. "This is of the truth. And because of truth, I do not drink of the horse and came the back sooner before the week and will please help you dig in the new tunnel this morning of the nice sky to be sure." He snapped both hands away. "But now I must tell you of the important news before we begin of the work you must know."

Longwei squinted. "What important news do you have?"

Roshan hesitated before announcing, "I have change of the mind. I will surprise the both of you too on the time of dinner. Then you can look to enjoy the forward it."

John Smith slapped his hands then rubbed them together. "Then let's get started. What do you want me to do first?"

Roshan thought for a moment, then answered, "Set two humble sticks of dynamite in the deep of the new tunnel. I have the important to speak with my partner of business and will speak it while you do of the work away from the here. I am of the sure you will not mind of it."

John Smith smacked his hands together again. "Sounds good to me. I'll get started right away." He headed to the shack to fetch the dynamite.

Roshan waited until he thought John Smith was out of earshot, then spoke to Longwei in a solemn voice. "I hope you do not mind of it, but I must speak of you lonely before the dinner."

Longwei shrugged. "What is it you must say to me without the presence of John Smith?"

Roshan's tone grew even more serious. "As you may know of it, Miss Nadia talked of many things to Roshan on the night and morning. She told Roshan he is of the fool to drink the horse, and he must share his…

what did she say of it...new-found wealth...yes, this is what she said of it...with my partner of business, Longwei."

"I see. This is a very serious decision for you to make."

"There is more to do of it and you may think to be."

"More?"

"Yes, the more. Miss Nadia told Roshan to share also of the new-found wealth with not my partner of business the man of black John Smith, if you can believe of it."

"I see. But do not be afraid to make this important decision. John Smith has proved himself a good and worthy companion. I will not oppose you if you decide to share the wealth with him. It would be generous of you if you decide to do as Nadia recommends."

Roshan grinned. "Then if you also think of it the good idea, I will do of it. I will tell him of the new-found wealth when he returns. I will not wait until the time of dinner."

Longwei's attention appeared to drift away, but then he said, "But I have another question for you, a question not related to what Nadia has told you."

"I will hear the question if you will speak to Roshan of it in the good time."

"Why did you ask John Smith to set two humble sticks of dynamite in the new tunnel? I did not know dynamite could be humble."

Roshan chuckled. "Oh, it is of the simple. Miss Nadia said to me of the new word 'humble' in the night, and told Roshan to use the new word in the soon to not forget of the new word. I have done what she said of it."

"I see. I would not have used the word in such a way, but it is good for you to improve your English at every opportunity. In truth, I think you have improved since we first met. Maybe not enough for people to always understand what you are saying, but you have improved."

Roshan looked in the direction of the new tunnel. "Thank you, my partner of business, for speaking kind to my English. But I have a question to say of it. Why is John Smith gone for the much too long? We should see of him long before the now."

Longwei also looked in the direction of the new tunnel. "Yes, I agree. He has been gone a very long time. Maybe we should walk to the new tunnel and make sure he is not hurt or having some other problem."

"Yes, maybe we should. Or we could wait of the few minutes, if you agree of it to the wise."

"I do not think we should wait. I think we should walk to the new tunnel now." But before Longwei could take his first step, John Smith appeared from behind a tree and trotted briskly in his direction. Longwei grabbed Roshan's arm. "Look my partner of business. John Smith is returning as we speak. It appears we have worried for no reason."

When John Smith arrived, he lifted his hat and used his grimy fingers to comb his hair. "Never done that before. I guess there's a first time for everything."

Roshan coughed and spit from the dust and asked, "Never done what in the before?"

John Smith dropped the hat onto his head and pulled the brim down. "Never set two-hundred sticks of dynamite. I thought it was an awful lot of explosives, but you're the boss now, Mister Roshan. I guess you know what you're doing."

Longwei gulped and his eyes bulged. "You set two-hundred sticks of dynamite? How long did you cut the fuse?"

John Smith counted the fingers on both of his hands. "Ten feet, just like I always do."

Longwei quickly calculated: "Ten feet times 30 seconds per foot divided by 60 seconds per minute is … is … five minutes. I will run back and cut the fuse. I think there is time to do it."

John Smith held out his arm to block Longwei. "No you won't. I stopped on the way back to take a pee next to the big tree over there. Probably took at least two minutes by the time I was finished."

Longwei did not reveal any particular concern when he advised, "Then I suggest we all take refuge in the cabin before it is too late."

Without further discussion, the three men sprinted to the cabin. John Smith yanked the front door open and the three men tumbled inside. When Roshan hit the floor next to the potbelly stove, a colossal explosion ripped open the rugged face of the mountain around the entrance to the new tunnel. Moments later, an immense shock wave overturned the wagon, knocked the horses to the ground, and peeled back the cabin roof and tossed it over by a pile of split wood. By sheer coincidence, all three men rolled to their backs and peered up at the blue sky, now visible because of the missing roof.

Roshan hacked up some dust and offered an observation. "I believe it is true to speak the worst of it is on the end, and we are not the dead because of it."

Longwei agreed. "Yes, we are fortunate to be alive. Surely no more trouble could possibly befall us on the same day."

John Smith added, "I say amen to that."

The sky darkened above as dust whooshed over the cabin and settled thickly on the upturned faces of the three survivors. Wedged between the other two men, Longwei sat up and wiped some of the chalky debris from his eyes. "It is possible I have spoken wrongly about this day." When he finished his sentence, the four sides of the cabin creaked horribly as the four corners unzipped from top to bottom and the walls fell away and crashed to the ground, causing a second wave of dust to swirl over the men.

John Smith, the thick layer of dust giving him the guise of an albino, lurched up at the sound of the collapsing walls. He stared straight ahead and unexpectedly blurted out, "Halleluiah! I just remembered my name!"

Afraid to open his eyes or sit up because he was worried of what he might see, Roshan remained perfectly still. "And what is this name you will tell us about it to remember?"

John Smith opened his eyes wide and grinned. "My name is Elijah. Elijah Brown."

Roshan sat up, but still did not open his eyes. "Elijah Brown. This is of the good you have the name. You must of the happy be much for now."

Elijah closed his powdered lips and the toothy grin vanished. "Not all that happy, I'm afraid to say."

Longwei offered some encouragement. "But you must be happy to remember your name. How could you not feel much gladness in your heart at such an event?"

A poignant darkness tainted Elijah's voice. "Because I also remember what I did for a living before I met the two of you."

CHAPTER TWELVE

A mysterious nocturnal rendezvous
May 21, 1872

T he pleasant warmth of the previous day grew a little warmer the next afternoon. Still wounded by his regrettable conversation with Alexandra, Manfred Herrmann attempted to distract his troubled thoughts by cleaning and organizing the small shack. Curled up on the bed next to the pillow, the cat followed him with slightly-crossed lizard eyes while Manfred shoved his meager furnishings out of the way and coaxed little piles of dirt and debris across the wood floor with a shabby broom. After much thrashing about, he managed to accumulate one large pile near the threshold of the front door. Manfred opened the door and stroked the pile outside. After creating a great billowing cloud of choking dust, he blundered through the door and swept dirt off the porch. When he had finished spitting and coughing, he shoved the two chairs around and swept the rest of the porch. He restored the chairs to their original positions, then waved the broom overhead and knocked down the countless spider webs and egg sacs that had already accumulated since the end of winter. He slapped the broom against a roof post to clean the bristles before backing into the cabin and closing the door. After storing the broom in a corner next to a gardening spade he never used, he retrieved a metal bucket from beneath the bed and hiked down to Jordan Creek to collect some water. He managed to smear the toes of both shoes with mud when he slipped near the edge of the creek. Water sloshed against his leg when he hauled the heavy bucket back to the cabin. He used half the water to clean the small table, make a fresh pot of coffee, and wash his face and hands. He saved the remaining water for later use in the preparation of supper.

After pouring black coffee into a metal cup, he sat at the small table to work on his sermon for Sunday. He had decided a few days earlier to preach on the *Book of Romans, Chapter 8, Verses 38 and 39*. At the time he had also prayed for the Lord to grant him inspiration; thus far divine encouragement eluded him. He tapped the pencil on the table. The unfortunate argument with Alexandra replayed in his head. He rubbed the back of his neck and diverted his thoughts to the letter he had written to Ethan Plantagenet. He did not know if Conrad Airingsail had successfully delivered the message. He decided there was nothing more he could do at this point: the entire tragedy was now in God's hands.

After writing the opening paragraph to the sermon four times and crossing off the words four times, he finished the last swallow of coffee and retired outside to clear his jumbled thoughts. He considered taking a nap in one of the chairs, but instead walked around the side of the shack and headed south with vigorous strides. The cat following him briefly, but soon scurried down to the creek to hunt for a small rodent or bird to kill. Manfred walked a long time. He did not return to his small shack until the color of the western skies had drifted to the purple hues of dusk. Still lacking the inspiration he had hoped would appear during the walk, he ignited the charred wick of a kerosene lamp and stoked the potbelly stove. He fried a wedge of bacon and boiled the last potato and a few carrots for his evening meal. When he had finished eating, he pulled out his watch and held it close to the lamp to read the time.

He spoke to the cat—who had completed a successful hunt before dinner and now sprawled comfortably on the warm floorboards near the potbelly stove. "Not even seven-thirty yet. I'm starting to regret agreeing to this midnight meeting. I can't imagine why he chose such an unusual time. But you know how he is. Always a penchant for the theatrical." He moved to the table and browsed through a week-old copy of the local newspaper. After reading a few tedious articles about local mining issues and the weather, he stood and yawned. The cat had not moved. "I guess I'll just take a little nap before the meeting. Wake me around eleven, if you don't mind. You know I don't like arriving late to my appointments."

He pried off the heels of the muddy shoes with his toes, kicked the shoes to the floor, and stretched out on the bed.

He slept fitfully until a little after ten, then arose stiffly from the lumpy bed. He poured himself a cup of burnt coffee and sat at the table. When he had finished the bitter dregs, he donned his coat, stepped outside, sprawled on one of the porch chairs, and listened to the night songs of the crickets and frogs. He dozed off and did not awaken until a few minutes before midnight. When he realized the time, he hurried into the shack and pulled on the muddy shoes. He rushed through the front door without closing it. The cat following him briefly before sauntering back to the residual warmth of the potbelly stove.

Manfred worked his way down the centerline of the meandering trail with only the scattered light of the gibbous moon to guide his steps. Because of his accelerated pace he tripped several times, but luckily did not fall to the rocky ground. When he neared the first dwellings of Silver City, the light of oil lamps glowing behind the sooty glass of several windows flickered into view. His eyes had long adjusted to the darkness, and he easily found the way to the southern end of Jordan Avenue. He moved quickly down the moonlit street until he arrived at the front of a two-story livery stable, a few hundred feet south of the Idaho Hotel. Someone had pulled the large sliding door open a few feet, and light glowed on the dirt floor inside the livery.

He waited until his breathing slowed, then sidestepped through the narrow opening into the building. Someone had left a lighted kerosene lantern hanging on a shiny nail pounded into the wall next to the sliding door. Manfred walked over to the lantern and noticed a piece of paper impaled on the nail. He tilted his head to read the note.

TAKE THE LAMP
AND WALK TO THE
FAR END OF THE LIVERY

Manfred lifted the lamp from the shiny nail and began walking. The muggy air of the livery reeked sweetly of fresh manure, animal sweat, and cut hay. The roughhewn timber beams above (supporting the wood decking of the hayloft) were individually revealed in the light of the moving lamp before receding again into the gloom. Except for the muffled sound of Manfred's footfalls, the rhythmic squeak of the lantern bail, and the faraway barking of a lonely dog, the stillness of the livery belied the intensity of the moment. From time to time Manfred raised the lantern and illuminated one of the murky stables lining the right side of the long building, but he observed only the occasional horse or mule. Once he swerved to the left and held the lantern above a blacksmith's anvil and then over a long workbench piled with unusual tools, but after a large rat scurried across the dingy floor in front of the bench he continued on his way. When he arrived at the end of the livery, the second floor terminated above the last stall and the space opened up to the roof. He raised the lantern above his head and the light shined dimly on the underside of the high rafters. Manfred slowly rotated in a full circle, sat on a bale of hay located conveniently near the last stall, and lowered the lantern to the dusty ground. He waited patiently for five or six minutes, but nothing happened. After waiting five minutes more, he picked up the lantern and pulled out his watch to check the time. Nearly half-past-twelve. He dropped the watch into his coat pocket and prepared to leave.

A solemn voice spoke to him out of the darkness above. "Don't leave."

Manfred's eyes popped up, but he could not see anything in the inadequate light of the lantern. "Who's there?" Hearing no answer, he asked, "Csongor, is that you?"

"Yes, it is me. Did you expect to find someone else waiting for you in a deserted livery stable at the midnight hour?"

Manfred lowered the lamp, but took care to hold it away from his leg. "I suppose not. I just didn't recognize your voice at first."

"I understand. But it is good that you have kept our appointment, although you did arrive quite late. It is good because I have something of great importance to tell you."

Manfred replied with perceptible irritation. "Could we not have met at your office during the day? Why have you invited me to such an unusual meeting place in the middle of the night? And why are you hiding up there in the hayloft?"

Csongor paced across the floor of the hayloft, the creak of the floor boards revealing his path. "No, we could not. I chose this place and time for reasons of my own. I am certain you will understand soon enough."

Manfred stared at the lantern. When he looked away, he could still see the glowing wick dancing across his vision. "If it's something important, as you have said, then come down from there and we can talk face to face."

Csongor countered, "If you don't mind, I shall remain here while we speak. And when we have finished our conversation, I would appreciate it if you would leave as you came."

Manfred crossed his ankles and rested his hands on the prickly hay bale. "Alright. We'll do this your way. What do want to talk about?"

The pacing ceased, and what sounded like the legs of a chair scraped along the floor. "Before we begin our little chat, a few preliminaries." Csongor settled into the chair and the floor creaked again. "You must promise me our conversation will remain strictly confidential. As a man of the cloth, I assume this is a standard practice of your profession. But to be sure, I must ask the question. Are you willing to make such a promise?"

A little more impatient, but also more interested, Manfred agreed. "Yes, I promise whatever you tell me will remain a secret." Then he joked, "Maybe you should talk to Father Nero. He could hear your confession up at the Catholic Church. I'm sure he wouldn't mind."

"A provocative suggestion, but I have no desire to speak with Father Nero. It is you who I must confess to."

"I thought we were having a friendly conversation. Now you tell me you are here to confess? Confess what?"

Csongor's voice waxed melodramatic. "A dark secret. A very dark secret you will likely find difficult to believe"

Manfred looked up at the voice emanating from the hayloft. "And why have you decided to tell me this dark secret now?"

Csongor took a few shallow breaths. "The reason is quite simple. Before this week, I did not realize that I have a conscience." He smirked, but Manfred could not see it. "Not much of one, mind you, but sufficient to require our meeting tonight."

Manfred shifted his position on the bale of hay. "I find it hard to believe you don't have a conscience. Even the vilest outlaw must know the difference between right and wrong."

Csongor picked at the creases of his pants. "Then maybe I have chosen the wrong words to describe my feelings. Let me try a different approach. I have always nurtured a keen sense of the difference between right and wrong. But until recent days, I have treated the difference as an amusing observation rather than something to be taken to heart. I've never felt *bad* about anything. In fact, I've actually found it quite comical to observe some poor fool writhe in shame after committing the tiniest of sins when only days before I have committed a monstrous transgression without feeling the slightest hint of guilt." Csongor coughed to clear his throat. "Not to say I am a man without emotions. Quite the contrary is true. I know you cannot even begin to appreciate this, but I have experienced a sense of ecstasy so exquisite that all else fades to nothingness. I doubt I could find the words to adequately describe it to you. You will simply have to believe that what I say is true."

Manfred stood. "Maybe I should come up ... or maybe you should come down. I'm not sure I like talking to someone sitting up in a dark hayloft where I can't see them."

Csongor held up his hand, even though Manfred could not see the gesture. "No, my friend. I will leave if you attempt to climb the ladder. And I will not come down. Please remain where you are if you want to hear my confession."

Manfred found a more comfortable position on the bale of hay. "Then why don't you just tell me what's on your mind? I'm listening."

After a prolonged hesitation, Csongor began decisively. "The half-breed named Joshua Hotah is an innocent man."

This pronouncement did not surprise Manfred. "I'd already come to the same conclusion on my own." He reached down and turned up the wick on the kerosene lantern. The flame blazed with renewed energy. "Is this the dark secret you could not wait to tell me?"

Csongor lowered his voice. "No. There is more."

"More?"

"You believe Joshua Hotah is innocent because of your clean heart and reasoned mind. I believe he is innocent because I know who slaughtered the wagon family."

"You know? How could you possibly know when you didn't say anything about it during the trial? After all, you defended him with great skill."

140

Csongor stretched out his legs and clasped his hands behind his head. "Yes, I defended him with more skill than you could possibly imagine. It is quite simple, really. I know he is innocent because I am the one responsible for the mother's death."

Manfred stood; his hands trembled. "You killed her? That can't be true. You cannot expect me to believe such a farfetched statement."

Without a hint of sentiment, Csongor answered, "But it is true, my friend. And you must believe my words if I am to properly assuage my budding conscience."

Manfred plopped down on the bale. "I still don't believe it."

Csongor raised his right ankle over his left knee and settled back into the chair. "Then I will offer my confession so that you may believe. I ordered my men to remove the woman's outer garments and bind her arms and legs to the wheel. When they had finished these preparations, I shot her with arrows to give the appearance of an Indian massacre. Her death was inevitable. Joshua Hotah merely hastened the process." He lowered his foot and sat up in the chair. "But I must mention an important detail. If it had not been for me, the men surely would have stripped her naked and ravished her with glee. My intent was to recreate the artistry of the martyrdom of Saint Sebastian, not the vile rape of the Sabine Women. She was allowed to perish in a dignified manner only because of my personal intervention."

Manfred tried to swallow, but his tongue had gone dry. "And the children? Would you call their deaths…dignified?"

A glimmer of defensiveness tinged Csongor's accent. "I will agree the children were a messy affair, but I was not the one who did it. One of my men accomplished this unpleasant task."

Manfred chewed the inside of his cheek when he remembered that the boy and girl had been brutally scalped. "Unpleasant indeed. How good of you to point this out."

Csongor sensed Manfred's anger, but continued his confession without concern. "Nor did I shoot the father. This unfortunate incident was not part of my original plan."

Manfred squeezed his hands into fists. "And what was the purpose of your…how did you say it…original plan?"

Csongor patted his lips with his fingertips and yawned. "Quite simple. My plan involved a rather ingenious business venture. Nothing more, nothing less."

Suddenly deflated, Manfred slumped forward, braced his forearms on his knees, and stared into the flame of the lantern. Fearful of hearing more horrific details, he simply asked, "What happens now?"

Csongor sniffed. "Why, nothing happens now. Nothing at all. I have confessed. And as agreed, you will say nothing of it to anyone." He arched his back and extended his arms to the sides. "I must admit…I do feel better now. I did not find much pleasure in my fleeting brush with guilt. It was good to talk."

Manfred rubbed his hands together. "That's all? You have confessed to an unspeakable crime for which an innocent man is about to hang, and now you feel better because you have told me about it? You have nothing more to say?"

The chair scraped the floorboards of the hayloft when Csongor stood. "No, I do not. Adieu, my dear friend. Thank you for listening to me. Your compassion has washed away my guilt. I promise you…I will never speak of this again."

Manfred said nothing. He listened to Csongor's footsteps withdraw into the shadows of the hayloft before diminishing to silence. Manfred remained seated on the bale of hay until the wick of the kerosene lantern burned out. After lingering in the gloom for a long time, he wandered out of the empty building consumed by sorrow.

CHAPTER THIRTEEN

A tricky proposal
May 26, 1872

After a curiously restrained Sunday morning service—featuring an exquisitely distracted sermon on the *Book of Romans, Chapter 8, Verses 38 and 39*—Manfred Herrmann walked briskly from the saloon on the corner of Washington and Avalanche without saying goodbye or, as was his custom, waiting around to greet each of the ragtag parishioners before they escaped the back room. Around the midpoint of the lackluster service, Nadia had tried to encourage more lively participation in the hymns by playing her concertina with added vigor, but none of the attendees followed her cue. Roshan Kuznetsov had certainly bellowed out every hymn a touch out of tune, but this was no surprise to anyone. As usual, Tseng Longwei had eschewed any excessive behavior and purposely maintained a dignified manner throughout the service. The mute Conrad Airingsail did not sing at all, although he clapped his hands during several of the refrains, and once he engaged in a bit of foot stomping when the bellows of the concertina nearly ruptured during a particularly violent crescendo. Elijah Brown's melodic baritone had provided a measure of religiosity to the hymns, but the recollection of his profession after the stunning detonation at Mahogany Gulch subdued his normal enthusiasm. Deeply worried by the impending execution-by-hanging of Joshua Hotah, Priscilla Kimball had nearly skipped the service altogether; the remarkable exuberance of the concertina did not improve her mood. The two strangers (one wearing a rumpled top hat and the other no hat at all) who had wandered in near the end of the first hymn appeared disoriented from the beginning, and neither reacted in any noticeable way to Nadia's musical cues. And finally, Sue—a fragile nymph du prairie who worked upstairs during the weekends (and sometimes on Friday)—had sat quietly in her chair with hands folded and knees pressed together during the entire service because she was not yet convinced that her particular sins were pardonable.

Manfred pitched broodingly into the dusty street and abruptly halted. An overloaded freight wagon pulled by four panting oxen shook the ground only a few feet from his toes, but Manfred did not feel it. A trio of Cousin Jennies, each wearing clean-but-threadbare bonnets and aprons, scurried along the boardwalk behind him loudly chattering away about the best way to bake sourdough bread, but Manfred did not hear them. Across the street, directly in front of the county courthouse, two men argued with Sheriff Boyle about a disputed mining claim and spat on the ground and swore and shook their fists at each other, but Manfred did not see them. Still beleaguered by the troubling thoughts of his nocturnal meeting with Csongor Toth, he did not cross the street as he had originally intended, but instead ambled south. He had nearly reached the main entrance to the War Eagle Hotel when a boisterous voice from behind pierced the muddled shroud of his reverie. The man who owned the voice ran around Manfred and then blocked his way. Because of his distracted thoughts, Manfred did not immediately recognize the man.

Roshan Kuznetsov slapped Manfred on the arm with a grimy hand, leaving a white-fingered imprint on the coat sleeve. "I did not know you left the saloon church of soon before I could speak to you of same I find concern, but now it is of the good I find you before it is too late by the street, if you believe to me when I speak the truth of it in the now."

Manfred glanced at the grimy hand print on his sleeve then refocused on Roshan's annoyingly cheery face. "Roshan, what are you doing here?"

Roshan tried to brush the imprint away. "It is of the way I tell it to you. You walked in the fast from the saloon church too soon before I could speak to you of the…." Roshan faltered. "I do not remember of the rest to say it the best. Did you not hear of my lips before the day?" Having merely smeared the imprint around, Roshan stopped brushing and simply grinned.

Manfred smiled weakly. "I am sorry, Roshan. I should have listened more closely when you first spoke. I'm afraid I've got a few things on my mind today. You may have noticed this during my sermon. I fear it was not one of my better efforts."

Roshan's grin diminished to a mild smirk, and an aura of urgency began spreading across his bearded face. "Yes, the sermon of today did not give you the look of the best. To tell you the truth of it, the sermon gave you the look of not the best, if you will hear of it."

"I know. I appreciate your honest appraisal of my miserable performance this morning. I promise to do better next Sunday."

Roshan's smirk vanished entirely, and he violently scrunched his brows. "This is of the good for you to do the better, but you must listen because Roshan cannot wait for the next Sunday to speak of this. You must listen in the now before it is the late."

Manfred raised his hand to Roshan's shoulder. "Certainly, I will listen. Would you like to go into the War Eagle Hotel? I can buy you a cup of coffee and we can talk of your concerns in a more comfortable setting."

Roshan shook his head. "I would love the coffee cup, but I do not have the time to speak of it in the hotel of the war eagles. I will tell you of it in the street where we are to stand in the now, if you miss the coffee."

"Fair enough. Then tell me what's on your mind. I'd really like to hear about it." Manfred relaxed his hand to his side.

Roshan grinned again, but not as broadly as before. "It is of the simple and not of the simple of the same in time, if you know what I speak. If it is of the simple, Roshan has not the same to speak to you when you do not have the time of it."

Manfred pushed the unsettling thoughts out of the way and concentrated on Roshan's words. "I think I understand what you mean. Keep talking."

"Then I begin with the simple. I love Nadia too the much."

"Nadia? Are you talking about our Nadia, the one who accompanies the hymns on the concertina every Sunday?"

"Yes, of the same one you speak. And the concertina is too of the same."

"And why is your love of Nadia a problem?"

"My problem is of this. Is it the sin to love Nadia who is whore and sleeps in the same with other men I do not know of the all?"

Manfred took a few seconds to consider the best response to this question. "No, it is not a sin to love Nadia. Yes, she has sinned, but so have we all. I would also say this to you: love bears all things, believes all things, hopes all things, and endures all things. There is no sin in loving someone. It is the very opposite of sin."

Roshan sucked in a deep breath and exhaled noisily. "I am the happy to hear of it. It was of the bother to me but you speak in a way to stop the bother in a good time. Then I will ask Nadia to give me to her hands."

"You mean, ask for her hand in marriage?"

"Yes, I will ask for the both hands of the marriage, to be sure."

Manfred's jaw flinched and he rubbed the back of his neck. "All well and good, Roshan, all well and good…but I have heard from Nadia herself that she has dreams of moving to California and buying a house somewhere with a view of the ocean. This dream will require a lot of money. The problem is this: you are a poor man." He segued smoothly. "There is certainly nothing wrong with being poor—some might even say it is a virtue. But do you think there's even a small chance she will say yes when you propose to her?"

Roshan kicked at the ground. "This is the one of the not simple. It is because Elijah Brown set the two humble sticks of dynamite and took the pee behind the tree, we have found the vein of big gold of the bigger you would not believe of it this big. Who would have seen such the luck of it? It is much sorry Mister Gustus did not see the luck after the many years to not see the luck. Roshan is not of the poor today. Roshan is of the rich beyond the woolliest of dreams."

"Two humble sticks of dynamite? I'm not sure I understand what you're talking about."

"No, not the two humble. I told to Elijah to set the two humble sticks because Nadia said to Roshan to practice the newest of words 'humble' in the soon, but Elijah did not hear with two ears and set the two hundred sticks because he did not hear and the two hundred sticks of dynamite did the job in the mine more than you can believe if you see of it. It is of the good Elijah Brown took the pee behind the tree and Longwei did not run away to pull the fuse, if you hear my lips."

Now Manfred grinned and seized Roshan's grimy hand and shook it vigorously. "I guess it doesn't really matter what happened. The main point is, you've been presented with a wonderful opportunity. Why don't you run back to the saloon right now and ask Nadia to marry you? If she wants to move to California and buy a house with a view of the ocean, you can afford to take her there and buy anything she wants."

Roshan dropped his beard against his chest. "It is of the not simple. On the other day I did not ask for both hands because Roshan is poor. On the today I did not ask for both hands because Roshan is rich. It is of the simple and the not simple."

Manfred pulled his elbow with his left hand and stroked his chin with his right. "I see your predicament. Before, you were afraid to ask Nadia to marry you because of your poverty. Now, you are afraid to ask her to marry you because of your wealth. Quite a dilemma."

"Yes and yes to the both. It is of the simple and the not simple. What is it to do? Can you think of it to bring the answer?"

Manfred ceased stroking his chin and focused on the distant mountains above Roshan's shoulder. As he watched a golden eagle soar near a rocky pinnacle, a brilliant idea presented itself. "Like you would say, Roshan, it is of the simple. Ask Nadia to marry you, but do not tell her of your good fortune beforehand. If she says yes to your proposal when she thinks you are poor, then she truly loves you and you have nothing to worry about. On the other hand—"

Roshan interrupted, "I know of this other hand you speak. It makes the simple of the not simple. I will ask to her of the hands—"

Manfred interrupted, "Exactly. If she says no because she thinks you are poor, then she does not truly love you. It absolutely makes simple of the not simple."

"It is the idea of the not to be stupid. I will do of you say, to be sure. I will ask Nadia to give me both hands. I will not tell her Roshan is of the rich beyond the woolliest of dreams."

Manfred corrected, "You will ask for her hand in marriage."

"I will ask for her hands in marriage."

"Just one hand, Roshan. Just one. You will ask for her *hand* in marriage."

"I will ask for just one hand in the marriage, not the both."

Manfred chuckled. "It doesn't matter. I'm sure she'll figure it out whatever you say."

"Yes, she will figure the hand out."

Manfred urged, "You should walk back to the saloon right this moment and ask her before you forget how to do it."

Roshan stroked his lower lip with the tip of his tongue. "Yes, but do not worry of the words to do it. Roshan is not of the ready to ask of the right moment in the now. I think it is the best to sleep for it in the night bed. I will ask for just one hand in the marriage tomorrow... or maybe on the next, if you hear me speak of it."

"Don't wait too long, or you might not find the courage to ask her at all."

"Roshan will not wait in the long for the courage."

A freight wagon rolled by the War Eagle Hotel, the mules and iron-rimmed wheels churning up dust in the fresh morning air. Manfred squinted down the street toward the county courthouse. "I was thinking of going for a walk, but I've just remembered that I had other plans. I think I'll stop by the jail and visit Joshua Hotah. Maybe I can offer him a small measure of comfort before his last day on this earth."

Roshan ignored the freight wagon as it rumbled by. "Yes, it is a good thing to do for you. I will ask Nadia for just the one hand in marriage not long for the courage. Wish me lucky, if you think to do of it."

Manfred grasped Roshan's right hand and shook it again. "Good luck, Roshan. I promise to pray for both you and Nadia... and your new life together in California."

Confused, Roshan asked, "How do I know of it, this promise you pray of the new life in the new California?"

Manfred firmly squeezed both of Roshan's shoulders. "You will know I have kept my promise to pray when Nadia says yes." And then Manfred thought to himself: *and when I finish praying for Roshan and Nadia, I must remember to pray for the lost soul of my friend Csongor Toth—if only I can summon the courage to begin.*

CHAPTER FOURTEEN

An evening gathering at Csongor's office
May 26, 1872

O
n the eve before Joshua Hotah's hanging, the last four bottles of
Old Pulteney waited patiently in a neat row near the front of the
desk. Seth, Jackson, and Miguel waited too, each man slouched awkwardly in a wood chair, each man watching Csongor prepare and light a
fresh cigar, each man growing more agitated with the passing of each tick
of the Seth Thomas clock on the wall behind Csongor's desk. After extin-
guishing the match with a graceful flick of his wrist, Csongor sucked in
three short puffs and exhaled a luxuriant haze of gauzy smoke. The haze
drifted contentedly over the bottles of whisky. Csongor lighted the wick
of a kerosene lamp with the glowing tip of the cigar. When he lowered the
glass chimney and adjusted the wick, the radiance of the lamp shimmered
mystically inside the bottles of Old Pulteney. Csongor settled back in his
chair and puffed the cigar.

Annoyed because he had several important tasks to finish before midnight, Jackson growled, "I got some things to get done. I reckon you must
of called us here for some sort of reason other than just sitting here in
these hard-ass chairs and watching you smoke a cigar."

Csongor puffed a few more times before removing the cigar from his
lips. "This is what I love about you, Jackson. Fearlessly direct and to the
point. Never beating around the bush, as they say in some of the less
sophisticated circles."

Even though he felt no less annoyed, Jackson moderated his tone. "Like I said, I got some things to get done. Unless you got something to say that needs listening to, I need to be moving along soon."

Csongor lowered the cigar and flicked off some ash. "Patience, my dear Jackson. Patience. On the other hand, your utter lack of patience is precisely what makes you useful for certain jobs. If you will allow me a few more seconds to enjoy the delicious bouquet and flavor of this superb cigar, I will tell you why I called the three of you to my office on such a pleasant evening."

"I reckon I can wait a few seconds, but I still got things to do." Jackson squirmed against the back of the chair.

Csongor puffed. "What I have to say concerns our little business venture. But before I begin, I would appreciate a report on recent activities, if you can spare the time."

Jackson spoke first. "Yeah, we got something to report. Finally got that rancher south of town to pay up. He agreed to the amount we was asking for, and he agreed again when we raised the amount 'cause of all the trouble he caused us."

Csongor puffed. "Good. Very good. And how did you finally convince him to pay after so many weeks of resistance?"

Seth broke in. "Turned out pretty simple. We dressed like Indians and visited his place when he was out and found his wife all alone tending to the garden. We chased her down and handcuffed her to a big tree. Then we poured hot tar on her and decorated her with Indian feathers. She screamed something awful and tried to kick us when we poured the hot tar over her head. Never heard anything like it. She yelled even louder with the feathers."

Miguel offered a personal observation. "She screamed so much I thought she was dying. But I heard yesterday she's still alive."

Csongor puffed. "Excellent. And I assume you left the key for the handcuffs?"

Jackson scowled. "The key?"

Csongor lowered the cigar. "Yes, the key. I assume you left the key to allow the poor man to release his wife when he returned."

Seth fidgeted. "I still got the key in my pocket. Didn't even think about leaving it."

Csongor pressed his fingers together without setting the cigar down. "I see. Well, it's not really our problem, is it? I suppose he could have hired one of the local blacksmiths to release his wife. Although in hindsight ...."

Miguel suggested, "Maybe he cut the tree down to let her loose. That's what I would do. Not that I would've married the woman in the first place. She seemed sort of cranky."

Csongor puffed. "Just so. I suppose there are many ingenious ways to have saved the woman from her bondage. But enough of the rancher's hapless wife and her disagreeable personality. What business activities have you planned for the coming months?"

Jackson reported, "Nothing special. Just working our way through the valley like usual. I expect we'll have everyone covered by the end of summer. Some folks take more persuading than others. Some we leave be 'cause they're just too ornery to bother messing with. No reason to take any chances and get killed." He glanced down at the bottles of Old Pulteney when he had finished his report. "What's them bottles for?"

Csongor puffed. "You may each take one of the bottles with you tonight. But not until I have shared something of the utmost importance."

Seth pointed. "Who's the fourth bottle for?"

Csongor noticed Hector Faure standing outside the window next to the front door. Monsieur Faure smiled and touched the brim of his shiny top hat with the eagle-headed grip of his walking cane, then tapped on the window with the cane. "I am saving the fourth bottle to share with a dear friend, someone who's been a confidant of mine for many years. He will join me after we have finished our meeting. This is all you need to know."

Jackson snorted, "Can't decide if I like this here whisky or not. If you ask me, doesn't have much of a kick to it. You sure someone didn't water it down?"

Csongor puffed. "I imagine it does not compare to the rotgut you normally drink. But to each his own. Take it or leave it, as you prefer."

Jackson reached for the nearest bottle, but Csongor chided him. "Please do not touch the Old Pulteney yet. You may each take one of the bottles after I have concluded my remarks. Patience. Patience."

Jackson jerked his hand back. "Like I said, I got things to do. Seth and Miguel, they got things to do too. We can't be sitting here all night for no good reason."

Csongor gestured gracefully with the cigar. "I applaud your enthusiasm for hard work."

Miguel answered innocently, "Why, thank you."

Jackson sneered, "Shut up Miguel. Stop interrupting the man. We need to hear what he has to say so we can get back to work."

Csongor flicked a large ash into a ceramic ash tray with a colorful floral design. He raised his eyes to the ceiling and sucked in a deep breath, then lowered his eyes to the three men as he exhaled. "First of all, I would like to thank each of you for your devotion to our business enterprise. When I first conceived of the idea, I knew that uncommonly ruthless men were required to achieve success. To this end, each of you has excelled in the required skills beyond what even I thought was possible. Because of your many talents and devoted effort, our venture is more lucrative by nearly twice of what I had originally predicted. I applaud you all."

Miguel whispered into the side of Jackson's head. "What's lucrative?"

Jackson mumbled out of the side of his mouth. "I told you to shut up."

Csongor did not appear to notice the spat, and continued smoothly. "But as with all good things, the time has come to incorporate certain modifications into our arrangement."

Seth asked, "Incorporate certain modifications? What do you mean?"

Jackson punched Seth in the shoulder. "Didn't I just finish telling Miguel to shut up?"

Csongor held up his free hand. "Calm yourselves, gentlemen, and I will explain."

Seth rubbed his arm. "Didn't have to hit me. Just asking a question."

Jackson quivered. "Just stop talking, the both of you. I got things to do, and I want to hear what the man has to say so I can get out of here."

Csongor enjoyed several puffs before proceeding. "The simple truth is this, my faithful business associates: I have recently experienced an unexpected moral epiphany and can no longer, in good conscience, participate in the business. After much consideration, I have therefore decided to withdraw as president to allow myself the opportunity to pursue other activities, activities which I believe will be more beneficial to my new-found perspective."

Seth could not help himself, and lurched forward in his chair. "There he goes again. What in Sam Hill is a 'moral epiphany'?" He spoke to Jackson.

"I'm darn sure even you don't know what he's talking about, so don't even think about punching me."

Csongor mediated before Jackson could tell Seth to shut up. "Not to worry, my dear Seth. Your limited vocabulary aside, all will be made clear in due course."

Seth slumped back, folded his arms, and crossed his ankles. "Then I'll just shut up, like Jackson says, and won't worry myself that most of what you're telling me don't make a lick of sense."

Csongor verified that the mysterious gentleman was still standing outside the window and, after a thoughtful silence, nodded. "Let me say it a different way. I have recently experienced an unanticipated change of heart. For reasons I cannot even begin to explain, I sought the council of a local man of the cloth. Only a few days ago, I met with this man and confessed my sins. And, I am pleased to report, this man has completely absolved me of all of my transgressions. This is the moral epiphany I spoke of. This is what has changed everything. This is what has prompted me to pursue a completely different course in life."

Miguel opened his mouth and raised his hand to ask about the word "transgressions," but simply said, "Never mind."

"I have therefore committed myself to a new endeavor. Simply stated, I intend to promote an honest law practice dedicated to the downtrodden of society. Fortunately, the good citizens of Silver City should provide many clients in this regard." When he had finished his sentence, he puffed the cigar and raised his chin in a display of immaculate triumph.

Jackson waited for Csongor to resume, and spoke when he could no longer tolerate the silence. "Are you telling me you're quitting?"

"That's exactly what I'm telling you."

"What about the money. Are we supposed to still give you half of it, like always?"

"Of course not. You keep it. I don't want any of it."

"Then who is going to be the president?"

"I recommend the three of you convene a meeting at a different place and time to elect a new president. When you have completed the task, you should make a formal announcement to the other men. We don't want any unnecessary confusion to permeate the ranks."

Seth inquired, "Then what are you going to do?"

Csongor retorted serenely, "Just as I told you. Help the down-trodden of society."

Seth twitched. "Still don't know what you're talking about."

Csongor's patience thinned. "Downtrodden of society: poor people, prostitutes, miners who have been unfairly treated by the law, and other individuals of similar dispositions."

Jackson finally understood. "How you going to make any money off these people?"

Csongor stood and flicked the end of the cigar into the floral ash tray. "Why, I have more money than I'll ever need. I therefore intend to donate a significant portion of my wealth to charity...and other worthy causes of my choosing."

Jackson smacked his lips. "Then we get to keep all of it? You don't want your fifty-fifty cut anymore?"

Csongor shrugged. "That is correct, my dimwitted former partner. I evidently did not make this perfectly clear during my earlier presentation. But to be sure there is absolutely no confusion, the business now belongs to the three of you, and the three of you now keep one-hundred percent of the profits. As a point of clarification, it is my hope to never see any of you again, although this is likely a false hope given the modest population of Silver City. Nonetheless, I'm sure you understand my meaning."

Not caring a whit about the definition of the word "dimwitted" because of the unexpected increase in personal wealth, Jackson stood and rested his hands on the front of the desk. "What about that half-breed the town's fixing to hang tomorrow. You plan to do something about it?"

Csongor waved his hand in the air. "I am not. This innocent man's conviction by a court of law is the very cornerstone of the successful business enterprise you have just inherited. Although I now regret his sacrifice, I also have no intention of rectifying past events for which I have been forgiven. Rest assured: what's done is done."

Jackson relaxed. "Good. You had me worried there for a moment. Glad to hear you wasn't planning to do something stupid that might ruin everything."

"And now, my former business associates, you may each take your bottle of Old Pulteney and depart in peace. I wish you nothing but success. And if you should ever require legal services, I promise to offer a reasonable discount."

Jackson snatched one of the bottles and announced, "Let's get out of here pronto. We got a lot more work to do than I thought."

When Jackson, Seth, and Miguel had gone, Hector Faure entered through the front door and stood in the shadows near the corner of the room. Without speaking, Csongor fetched two glasses, opened the last bottle of Old Pulteney with a pocket knife, poured the amber liquid into each glass, and slid one of the glasses across the desk toward Monsieur Faure. As he sipped the aromatic beverage, Csongor prayed that Hector would approve of his decision. But then he thought to himself: *Not to worry, I shall find out soon enough.*

CHAPTER FIFTEEN

A day of reckoning
May 27, 1872

The carpenter drove a cut nail into the last board of the scaffold's deck with three decisive hammer strokes. He scooted on his knees to the left, retrieved another nail from the leather pouch slung around his waist, and pounded it in with three quick strokes. When he reached the end of the board at the corner of the scaffold, he stood and wiped a glistening sheen of sweat from above his eyes. After using a calloused thumb to scratch an itch inside his left nostril, he looked at the bottom of the stairs and discovered one of Sheriff Boyle's deputies staring up at him, his faced crumpled into a scowl.

Miguel Cervantes tugged the brim of his hat to shade his face from the morning sun and squinted up at the carpenter. "You finished yet? The hanging's in four hours and it looks like you're still working on it. Sheriff Boyle sent me over to check on how you're doing." To emphasize the urgency of his concern, he added, "He's worried we're gonna have to…" Miguel struggled to recall the exact word the sheriff had used, "…postpone the hanging. We want to hang the Indian today, but it doesn't much look like you're exactly done from where I'm standing."

The carpenter listened to Miguel, then twisted at the waist and gazed across the street. "I don't mind telling you, that's the strangest thing I ever saw. And in my line of work, I've seen plenty of strange things."

Miguel looked in the same direction, but did not see anything that struck him as particularly strange. "What're you talking about? It's just a rundown building with a tin roof. Nothing strange about it at all."

The carpenter pointed with the hammer. "Not the building. You're looking at the wrong thing. I'm talking about that." He jabbed the hammer to clarify what he was pointing at.

Miguel lifted the brim of his hat. "What? I don't see a dang thing that looks strange."

The carpenter pointed more vigorously. "Right there. Standing near the eave of the roof, gawking at us as we speak. The white raven. Never seen anything like it."

Miguel's eyes darted around until he spotted the pale bird. "That's no raven. Ravens are black. That bird's as white as the new moon."

The carpenter stuffed the hammer into the leather pouch so he could gesture with both hands. "I thought the same when I first saw it. But I've been studying it for three days now, and it's a white raven for sure. Don't know where it came from, but it's been watching me build this scaffold for the last three days. Not all the time: it comes and goes. Still, the strangest thing I ever seen. And in my line of work, I've—"

"Yeah, you said that already. I don't see what difference it makes what color the raven is. Don't mean a thing to me or anyone else. Sheriff Boyle still wants to know if you're finished building this scaffold. He thinks it's taking too long, and the hanging's in four hours. People are starting to worry. Maybe you'd best stop gawking at the raven and get cracking on them boards."

The carpenter's words rolled out a little faster. "The white raven has nothing to do with it. The only way I know how to build things is to build them strong and true. It's the way I was taught by a carpenter from the old country. If the sheriff wanted it done fast and crude, he could've hired someone else more to his liking." He pulled the hammer out of the nail pouch and pointed it at Miguel. "You go tell him what I just said."

Miguel lifted his foot up to the first step and pressed his palm down on his knee. "I don't care about how you were taught by someone from the old country. Just tell me if the scaffold will be done in time for the hanging. That's all I need to know."

The carpenter bent down and grasped his knees and glowered at the troublesome deputy. "Tell him it'll be done in time. A few more nails here and there, and I'll start my final inspection."

Miguel sneered, "About time you stopped fussing with it." After he turned and tromped down the street to tell Sheriff Boyle the scaffold would be ready for the hanging, he muttered to himself, "Only going to use it one time to hang one harmless little Indian. Don't see why it has to take so long to build."

The carpenter straightened up to look at the white raven again, but the extraordinary bird had mysteriously vanished without making a sound.

Manfred Herrmann pressed his forehead against the cool iron bars. The air in the jail had become unpleasantly stuffy; a rivulet of sweat rolled down Manfred's cheek, dripped from his chin, and splashed on the dusty toe of his shoe. Priscilla sat primly on a creaky chair with her hands folded on her lap. After noticing that her leg had fallen asleep, she separated her hands and adjusted the position of her knees and feet. Joshua Hotah reclined on the rough-sawn bed with his legs stretched out and the frayed wool blanket folded loosely into a pillow behind his head. He pulled his knees up and the chain of the heavy leg irons clinked. After some meaningless small talk when Manfred and Priscilla had first arrived, no one had offered any further conversation.

Manfred pulled his forehead away from the iron bars and broke the uneasy silence. "I'm sorry I couldn't do more. I believe I did everything I could. I just couldn't think of anything else to try. I'm truly sorry this day had to come."

Joshua repositioned the blanket pillow. "It is not your fault I am still sitting in jail. It is not your fault I will be hanged today. You did what you knew how to do. There is nothing more you could have done. It is finished."

Priscilla tried to change the tone of the discussion. "I sure enjoyed getting to know you, Mister Joshua. I was glad to bring you food and talk to you while you ate it. I will never forget our time together. I promise, I will always remember you."

Joshua attempted a smile. "It is good to know I will be remembered, especially by someone who is young and still has many years to remember."

Manfred pressed his forehead against the iron bars again. "An eloquent sentiment, Miss Kimball. I also promise I will never forget you, Mister Hotah, although the thought of what is about to happen already causes much pain. I wish things would have turned out differently."

Joshua closed his eyes. "You should not be sad about today. I have lived a good life with many good adventures. Today I will die like I have lived, without too much fear or regret." After he said this, he remembered the Nez Perce woman and her son, and worried about what might happen to them after the hanging.

Priscilla squirmed her little derriere against the splintery seat of the creaky chair. "I will never forget you, Joshua Hotah."

Excerpt from
A Concise History of the West
by Muireall Anne Ravenscroft
The U.S. Cavalry: 1865 to 1890

This is a remarkable period in American military history. The year 1865 marks the conclusion of the Civil War, the subsequent emergence of traditional American opposition to a large standing army, and the beginning of a lengthy period of national uncertainty about the primary mission of the U.S. Army. The year 1890 marks the official conclusion of the Indian Wars (defined by the iniquitous Battle of Wounded Knee), the ensuing redeployment of U.S. Army forces more uniformly across the country based on regional rather than local considerations, and the relegation of the cavalry to low-risk assignments such as escorting Indian children to school and supporting the management of the incipient national park system.

At the beginning of the Civil War, the five mounted regiments of the Regular Army comprised the 1st and 2nd Dragoons, 1st Mounted Rifles, and 1st and 2nd Cavalry.

Congress had authorized these latter two units in 1855 for the purpose of protecting settlers as they advanced farther west and more often encroached on Indian lands. The leadership of these five original regiments included 176 officers. When the time came to side with North or South, 104 of the most experienced cavalry officers chose to serve in the Confederate Army. This presented the Union Army with an initial deficit of skilled cavalry leadership, which resulted in battlefield superiority for the South during the early years of the conflict. But in the second half of the war (commencing in 1863), increasing Confederate shortages of men, horses, and equipment, and major improvements of Union Cavalry combined to shift the advantage to the North. As one example of this shifting advantage, by 1865 the Union Army had raised 272 cavalry regiments while the South had raised only 137. Because of the successful use of large mounted forces capable of independent and decisive action, particularly the Union Army's integration of cavalry with infantry and artillery into a combined striking force capable of sustained operations, it is clear that — in terms of effectiveness in conventional battle and stature within the U.S. Army — cavalry had reached its historical zenith during the American Civil War.

At the conclusion of the war, the Regular cavalry units of the Union Army were significantly depleted (as were the infantry and artillery units), creating an initial shortage of available military resources. Although the enlistment in the Regular Army by members of disbanded volunteer units had somewhat eased the shortage by 1866, Congress felt compelled to authorize four additional Regular cavalry regiments on July 28th: the 7th, 8th, 9th, and 10th (The 9th and 10th Cavalry Regiments consisted of Negro enlisted men and white officers). At the same time, the authorized strength of the Regular Army was increased to 57,000 officers and men and the Army was formally organized into 10 regiments of cavalry, 45 of infantry, and 5 of artillery. This authorization also provided for the creation of a corps of up to 1,000 Indian Scouts. Cavalry regiments were further organized into 3 squadrons with 4 companies each. A colonel commanded a cavalry regiment, and regimental staff included 7 officers, 6 enlisted men, one surgeon, and 2 assistant surgeons. Although not officially listed as part of the organizational structure, a civilian veterinarian typically accompanied a regiment in the field. Cavalry companies consisted of 4 officers, 15 noncommissioned officers, and 72 privates for a total authorization of up to 91 men.

Because of the subsequent growth of Congressional opposition to a large standing army, as well as national confusion about the role of the Army, the authorization of 1866 did not last. Congress reduced the number of infantry regiments from 45 to 25 in 1869. The following year, Congress reduced the enlisted force to 30,000 men. And in 1874, two years before the Battle of the Little Big Horn, Congress again reduced the enlisted force to 25,000. Because this latter reduction did not change the number of authorized regiments, the true consequence was to shrink the typical strength of an individual cavalry company to 58 men.

Among the many problems facing the peacetime Army, including enforcing Reconstruction and suppressing labor strikes, the expanding westward migration and the increasingly common occurrence of deadly conflicts between settlers and Indians demanded the most significant response. By 1868 a large majority of the Army's cavalry units were active in the west. Of the 120 authorized cavalry companies, 92 were stationed in 59 different outposts extending from the Canadian border to the Rio Grande and from Kansas to California. Although the deployment of forces in this manner served the purposes of the times, the resulting fragmentation of individual cavalry regiments rendered any meaningful training for a potential foreign war impractical. Many infantry units were also relocated to the west (it was not uncommon to find both a cavalry company and an infantry company stationed at larger forts), but the mobility and speed of the cavalry proved far more effective against the accomplished mounted warriors of the Plains Indians. Even so, cavalry officers rarely modified the conventional tactics learned during the Civil War to accommodate the unconventional tactics of the Indians.

The U.S. Cavalry did not engage in a single battle with an organized military force during the entire period of 1866 to 1890. It is therefore astonishing, when viewed from the perspective of historical hindsight, that military doctrine and training during this same period generally evolved to prepare the cavalry for just such an unlikely event. The basic principle inherent in the doctrine was that cavalrymen must be trained as infantry and fully prepared to dismount and carry the battle to the enemy on foot.[9] This doctrine, a natural consequence of the Civil War experience, was formalized in 1873 when the U.S. Cavalry adopted the 1867 Infantry Tactics manual for drill. Originally prepared by Major General Emory Upton, the manual taught movement of infantry based on groupings of four. Although the infantry system did work for drill on horseback, it was never intended for this purpose. The cavalry continued the use of this infantry system for drill until 1891 when the War Department promulgated individual drill regulations for cavalry, infantry, and artillery. It

---

[9] Although not strictly relevant to the time period of this article, it is worth noting that in 1898 the U.S. 10th Cavalry served as infantry (their horses were never shipped to Cuba) in the Spanish-American War.

is therefore useful to our understanding of events to characterize the U.S. Cavalry during the years following the war as mounted infantry, and to appreciate that they faced a lethal foe some historians have described as the best light cavalry the world has ever known.

In June 1876 a coalition of the Sioux, Cheyenne, and Arapaho Indian Tribes destroyed nearly half of the 7th Cavalry Regiment at the Battle of the Little Bighorn. In all, five companies were lost. In partial response to this tragedy, Congress authorized an increase to the cavalry forces serving in the West. In fact, the law decreased the overall size of the standing army by 5,000 men while adding 2,500 men to the cavalry units deployed against the Indians. The authorization also increased the permissible strength of individual cavalry companies to 100 enlisted men, an allowance which remained in place until 1890. In practice few units successfully reached this limit, primarily because of sickness and desertion.

The end of the Civil War produced large surpluses of uniforms, horses, saddles, weapons, and other military equipment. Because Union cavalrymen were generally armed with Spencer repeating carbines, the ten regiments of the peacetime cavalry were supplied with these relatively lightweight rifles until 1873, when replacement by single-shot Springfield rifles and carbines commenced. Testing of the .45 Colt Revolver that used metal cartridges began in 1871. This pistol soon became standard cavalry issue, and was not replaced until 1894 when the....

Muireall Anne Ravenscroft jabbed the tip of her hand trowel into the dampened soil, pushed herself up to her knees, and scanned the October skies spreading blue-gray above the distant coastal mountains. Her azure eyes drifted a little to the right and viewed northwest beyond the narrow valley flowing along the foothills of the inland mountains from San Luis

Obispo to the idyllic ocean community of Morro Bay. She recounted the many tasks she had accomplished on this pleasant day. With great vigor she had cleaned out the garden beds, dug up and replanted an area of crowded perennials, and cut two entire rows of yellowed asparagus to the ground. She had used the pruning shears John had sharpened after breakfast to attack the dead and diseased branches of the large avocado tree growing near the corner of veranda. She had turned the compost pile and replenished it with the debris of her work. And now she had returned to the garden to remove a number of errant weeds she had missed during the morning. She thought of planting some winter greens and herbs before dinner, but decided this task could wait until later in the week.

Wearing a crisp, clean, white shirt with long sleeves and rigid collar, John Ravenscroft sauntered through the front door and across the covered veranda, skipped down the steps, and strolled casually to the garden. He waited for Muireall to look up from her work, but when she did not, he proclaimed loudly, "I just finished your manuscript, less than five minutes ago."

Muireall sat back on her ankles and pressed the back of her hand against her forehead, depositing a smudge of dirt below the hairline. "You finished it? The entire thing? Just now?"

"I sure did. Every single word of it. Didn't skim or skip anything."

Muireall lifted the brim of her bonnet. "I'm impressed. I assume you read every word because you were enjoying it. I know there are still parts that could be improved by another revision … or two."

"I suppose, just like I could always redesign some aspect of one of my houses." He considered telling her that the last five percent always takes half of your time, but on second thought said, "I've given you many comments."

Muireall stood and brushed off the front of her garden apron. "And?"

After several seconds had elapsed, John answered coyly, "And … what?"

Muireall sighed deeply. "And … what do you think?"

John stroked his chin to prolong his little joke. "It's very long, even for a one-volume history. The manuscript is very heavy when one sets it on one's lap. Very weighty."

"It's very long? And heavy? And weighty? Is this all you have to say?"

"Do I need to say more? I've already said many things along the way."

Muireall frowned. "No, I suppose not."

After waiting a few more seconds, John grinned. "I'm just teasing you. I think it's a magnificent achievement. I'm so very proud of you. Well done!"

Muireall demurred. "You're just saying that because you're my husband."

John quickly protested, "Absolutely not. I'm telling you the absolute truth. And one thing more...."

Muireall gripped the hand spade with both hands and held it in front of her bosom. "Yes?"

John touched Muireall on the shoulder. "Your parents will be very proud of you too."

Overcome by his words, Muireall kissed John hard on the lips and hugged him tightly. "I love you, John." But then, when she realized her hands and the spade had smeared grubby streaks across the back of his white shirt, she jerked away. "Oh dear. My hands are filthy from the garden. I'm afraid I may have ruined your shirt."

John brushed loose flecks of dirt from his shoulder. "Not to worry my love. It was worth it."

A small boy played with a raggedy twine ball and a brown dog on the bridge north of town. The boy had fabricated the ball especially for the brown dog, although the boy did not own the dog. Over the last three weeks, the boy had wrapped found remnants of twine round and round, tying each remnant end to end with a figure eight knot—rewrapping once when he dropped the ball and it unraveled into the street—until the ball had reached sufficient diameter to qualify as a dog ball. Today the small boy had decided the ball was ready, and, after much careful thought, that the bridge was the ideal venue to try the twine ball with the brown dog.

The morning sun had just peeked over the mountains, and within the hour would shine fully on the heavy-timber structure spanning the gently flowing waters of Jordan Creek. The boy, probably eleven or twelve, tossed the ball down the length of the bridge and the brown dog chased after it with joy. The dog retrieved the ball and dropped it at the boy's feet. The boy wiped the twine ball along the seam of his tattered pants to remove some of the slobber, then threw it again. When the dog reached the ball on the other end of the bridge, the boy discerned two lines of riders approaching on horseback. He had never seen such men before—all dressed in blue and all wearing black hats—and they frightened him a little. When the dog ran back with the ball and dropped it at the boy's feet, he picked it up and held it, but did not throw it. The blue riders arrived at the opposite end of the bridge and rode across Jordan Creek. The blue riders rode right up to the boy before halting. The boy squeezed the ball in his hand and a transparent string of slobber drooled to the ground.

The man to the left addressed the boy in a pleasant voice. "Pardon me young man, but can you tell me where to find the jail?"

The boy gestured with the slobbery ball of twine. "Go down that road and turn right on Avalanche. When you get to the end of Avalanche, turn left. It's the big building across the street. It doesn't look like anything else in town. You can't miss it." The boy lowered the ball to his side. "There's a big hanging today. They built the scaffold where they're gonna hang him south of town, right near where the Chinamen live. You come to see it?"

The man peered high above the boy's head. "No, we're not here to see the hanging." He leaned forward a little and lowered his gaze to the boy. "If you and your dog don't mind moving aside, we'll be on our way so you can continue your game." The man touched the brim of his gold-braided black hat with a white-gloved hand and nodded. "Much obliged for the information, young man. You and your dog have a good day now."

The boy and the dog stepped to the side of the bridge. The boy counted each pair of blue riders out loud as they passed by. "Two, four, six, eight, ten, twelve, fourteen, sixteen, eighteen, twenty." The boy observed a yellow stripe running down every man's leg to the top of a tall black boot. The last blue rider towed an extra horse without anyone sitting on it.

The blue riders crossed the bridge and maneuvered right onto Avalanche. They ran into three men walking down the center of the street, but the men quickly scattered when the blue riders refused to give way. When the blue riders reached the end of the street, they turned left. A freight wagon slowed as the blue riders crossed Washington. When they arrived at the front of a two-story building with stone columns on the ground floor, the man who had spoken to the small boy raised his hand

and the column halted. He lowered his hand and spoke in a composed voice to the man on his left. "Sergeant, pick two men to guard the front door while you and I are inside. Position the rest of the men north and south of the jail. I don't want any unpleasant interruptions while we're conducting our business."

Sergeant O'Malley, a stout man of thirty-two who had staggered off the boat from Ireland directly into the Union Army in 1864, twisted around in his saddle and yelled with an agreeable Irish brogue, "Jones... McCauley, dismount and stand guard at the front door. Don't let anyone in while me and the major are inside conducting our business. The rest of you... I want eight to the right and eight to the left of this lovely building to keep the area clear." He grinned and cautioned, "And keep your carbines in the scabbard. I don't want you scaring anyone or causing any trouble with the lovely townsfolk."

The troopers moved to their assigned positions. The man who had talked to the boy and the sergeant dismounted and marched to the front door. Sergeant O'Malley politely opened the door, and both men strode into the jail.

Sitting behind a small desk in a wobbly swivel chair, Sheriff Boyle crumpled a sheet of paper in his hands and tossed it into a wastebasket. "What's all this, a parade or something?"

With Sergeant O'Malley smartly at his side, the man who had talked to the boy advanced to the front of the desk and saluted. "Major Ethan Plantagenet at your service, sir."

Sheriff Boyle fell back in the chair and it squeaked. He clasped his hands behind his head and lifted his boots to the desk. "I don't recall asking the U.S. Cavalry for any help. I think we got everything all sorted out by ourselves. If you want my advice, you should just get back on your horses and ride back to wherever you came from."

Major Plantagenet tipped his wide-brimmed-gold-braided hat with crossed sabers pinned to the front and then positioned it neatly on the desk. "My apologies for failing to notify you before our arrival." He pulled his gloves off and slapped them smartly on his thigh. "I considered arriving in the nick of time to further enhance the sterling reputation of the U.S. Cavalry, but finally decided such an action might provoke unnecessary bloodshed."

Sheriff Boyle lowered his feet to the floor and slid the chair forward. "I don't think I get your meaning. In the nick of time for what?"

Major Plantagenet produced an envelope with a flourish and held it up without opening it. "I have orders from General George Armstrong Custer to find and capture the former Indian Scout Joshua Hotah, and to immediately escort him to Fort Boise. I therefore request that you turn your prisoner over to me at once."

Sheriff Boyle stood aggressively, an expression of shock pulsing across his wrinkled face. "What does General Custer want him for?"

Major Plantagenet lowered the envelope to his side. "He's wanted for questioning about an incident that occurred in Kansas in 1867."

"What kind of incident?"

"A massacre, near the forks of the Republican River. Maybe you've heard of it. It was in all the papers at the time."

Sheriff Boyle harrumphed, "Not surprised. Seems like this Indian fellow just goes from one massacre to the next." The tone of his voice hardened. "But you can't have him. He's been sentenced to hang today, fair and square by judge and jury. And since I'm the law in this town, it's my job is to see it gets done."

Major Plantagenet raised his chin slightly. "Your decision to resist is understandable. Unfortunately, I have no choice but to inform you that the U.S. Cavalry has jurisdiction in the Territory of Idaho. In other words, I'm the law here, not you."

"There might be trouble if you try and take him. The rest of my deputies might come back any time now, and I've got a bunch of 'em."

"Your deputies will not get within a hundred feet of this building. And we have no intention of taking him by force, because you will simply agree to hand over Joshua Hotah without further objection."

Sheriff Boyle bluffed, "And what if I don't?"

Major Plantagenet answered crisply, "I can assure you that I will carry out the full measure of my orders, sir. I will not leave Silver City without Joshua Hotah—one way or the other."

Sheriff Boyle frowned, then slowly opened a desk door and retrieved a ring of keys. "You're taking an awful chance, if you ask me. A lot of people are gonna be mighty angry when he doesn't show up for the hanging."

Major Plantagenet donned his hat, pulled his gloves on, and ran his fingers along the front of the brim. "We'll be waiting outside. And, if you don't mind, please remove any shackles before you deliver Mister Hotah. We intend to ride at once."

Sheriff Boyle muttered, "Lot of people will be angry about this. And mighty disappointed too." He fumbled with the keys as he neared the jail door. "Lot of people."

Major Plantagenet watched the sheriff twist a large tarnished key into the lock. "Is there anyone else back there?"

"Just a couple of visitors. The Indian's our only prisoner today."

"When you bring him out, tell the visitors to stay where they are. No need to make this any more difficult than it already is."

After they had walked out of the jail and mounted their horses, Sergeant O'Malley asked in a low voice, "You really got orders from General Custer? If my memory serves me, he's Seventh Cavalry."

Major Plantagenet patted the front of his shirt, "I surely do, right here in this envelope."

After the passage of nearly five minutes, Sheriff Boyle emerged from the front door holding Joshua Hotah by the arm. "Here's your murdering savage. Now, what do you 'spect me to tell everyone when they show up for the hanging and there's no one to hang?"

Major Plantagenet motioned Joshua Hotah to mount the cavalry horse waiting by the sergeant's side. "I'm sure you'll figure out something, Sheriff. You've still got several hours to sort it out."

Sheriff Boyle glared toward the southern end of town where the scaffold stood, and muttered, "Damn."

Joshua Hotah waited until they had travelled about a half-mile beyond the bridge before saying his first words to Ethan Plantagenet. "My appaloosa is still in town."

Incredulous, Ethan asked, "Your appaloosa? Where is it?"

Joshua shrugged. "I do not know. In town."

Ethan spoke to the sergeant. "O'Malley, take four troopers and ride back to the jail. Ask the good sheriff to tell you where they've taken Mister

Hotah's appaloosa. And make it a quick trip. The word's probably already out that the hanging's been cancelled. The rest of us will ride on."

Sergeant O'Malley called out the names of four troopers, and the five men galloped back to Silver City to find Joshua Hotah's appaloosa.

The appaloosa snorted her disapproval when Joshua Hotah mounted. He bent down and patted the appaloosa on the neck, but she pulled away and shook her head back and forth. Not concerned about the twenty cavalrymen nearby, Joshua spoke to the appaloosa in a defensive tone. "It is not my fault you had to spend so much time in the stables with horses you do not know." The appaloosa snorted again and stomped its foot. Joshua explained, "I had my own problems while you lived comfortably in the stable. You should be thankful we are together again."

Ethan appeared unaware of the strange conversation. "We should get moving. Do you wish to ride with us? We can give you safe passage to Fort Boise, but no further."

Sergeant O'Malley interjected, "Begging your pardon, sir, but what about the orders from General—" He stopped short when he realized the orders did not exist. "Never you mind, sir. It's not my place to be asking such a thing."

Joshua Hotah answered pensively, "I will ride no further with you. You have done enough on this day. I thank you for it."

Ethan pushed down on the stirrups to improve his position in the saddle. "I am merely returning the favor, my friend, and many years overdue. Where do you plan to go? You surely can't stay here."

Joshua shifted his vision to the north. "I know a Nez Perce woman and her son who have made camp nearby. I will ride north, far away from Silver City. I think they will be glad to come with me."

Ethan vigorously thrust out his right hand. "Then safe travels Joshua Hotah, for you and your new family."

Joshua gripped Ethan's hand. "Goodbye, Ethan Plantagenet." He squeezed Ethan's hand without shaking it. "You are a good man."

Growing impatient to leave, the appaloosa snorted.

CHAPTER SIXTEEN

A day of confusion
May 27, 1872

S till waiting in the chair, Priscilla Kimball whirled around when the heavy door swung open and bounced against the wall. Disheartened by the unfortunate events of the day, and his utter helplessness to do anything about it, Manfred Herrmann did not react to the sound of the door. Joshua Hotah, his head still plopped against the frayed wool blanket pillow, merely opened his eyes when the door slammed and closed them again when the sheriff entered the narrow hallway fronting the jail cells.

Sheriff Boyle uttered an abusive litany of cuss words as he trudged down the hallway. He stomped metrically across the creaking wood floorboards, carefully emphasizing the cadence of each vulgar phrase with a sudden rise of voice and a vigorous shake of the key ring. His voice trailed off to a grumpy mumble by the time he arrived at Joshua Hotah's cell.

Finally aroused from his melancholy, Manfred addressed the angry sheriff in disbelief. "Sheriff Boyle. What's this about?"

Sheriff Boyle muttered a few more profanities before answering, "What's this about? I'll tell you what it's about. I'm removing this here Indian from this here cell. That's what it's about." He stabbed a key into the cell door lock. "And if you don't mind, I would appreciate it if you'd get out of my way so I can unlock this here door and get on with my business."

Priscilla jumped to her feet. "But it's not time yet. The hanging's not till the afternoon. We're still talking and saying our goodbyes. You can't take Mister Joshua now!"

Sheriff Boyle rotated the key and mocked, "Well then, little girl…if you need more time to say your goodbyes, then I guess I got no choice but to leave Mister Joshua in here and let you talk his ear off until he gets hanged." He pulled the door open with a grunt.

Manfred caught the jamb of the swinging door with his left hand. "I don't understand, Sheriff. Why are you taking him now? The execution's not until two."

Sheriff Boyle entered the cell and fumbled with the ring of keys. "It's none of your darn business why I'm taking him now." After finding the right key, he jammed it into the left barrel lock of the leg irons binding Joshua's ankles and began unscrewing. "Now that I think about it, it's none of your darn business why I do anything." When he had finished unscrewing the right barrel lock, he tossed the leg irons to the floor and snarled, "Get up. Time to go."

Joshua slid across the bed and stood. "Where are you taking me? It is not my time."

Sheriff Boyle grabbed Joshua's arm. "Here we go again. Didn't I just explain to your friends here that's it's none of anyone's darn business?"

Joshua resisted. "You did, but—"

Sheriff Boyle pulled Joshua out of the cell. "No more explaining anything to anyone. I've got to take you outside right now, and that's all there is to it."

Manfred thought of blocking the way, but instead declared, "Then we're coming with you. We want to stay with Joshua as long as possible."

Priscilla hopped to Manfred's side and wrapped her little hands around his arm. "Yes, we want to come with you."

Sheriff Boyle sneered, "The two of you aren't going anywhere. I got strict orders to keep you back here. Now sit down and shut up…and don't go anywhere until I come back."

Manfred, his patience spent, taunted Sheriff Boyle. "Strict orders from who? I thought you were the only law in Silver City."

Sheriff Boyle hesitated at the heavy door to spit out a few last words before escorting Joshua out of the jail. "None of your business who I got the orders from. Now sit down and shut up like I said, or there'll be trouble."

Priscilla shouted, "This isn't right," but Sheriff Boyle ignored her and slammed the door.

Twenty minutes before two. A crowd of several hundred locals—and a few dozen from out of town who were curious to see the man who had ruthlessly massacred an entire family and scalped innocent children—had gathered around the scaffold at the south end of town. Two unkempt men standing only a few yards from the front of the scaffold engaged in a curious conversation to pass the time.

The first man exclaimed, "Mighty fine carpentry, if you ask me. Look at how straight them spikes is lined up. Better work than most of the buildings in town, if you ask me. Mighty fine carpentry. Mighty fine."

The second man observed the neatly spaced and aligned row of nail heads. "The nailing's fine, to be sure, but the joinery's what impresses me. Take a close look at the fit of those mitered corner boards. Whoever built this took real pride in their work."

The first man countered, "The miter joints are fine too, but it's them spikes I can't get over. I seen joints as good before, but can't say I remember seeing spikes all lined up neat as a pin."

The second man looked over at the steps leading up to the platform. "Did you ever see anything like that? Here we are arguing about the spikes and joints, and it's those steps we should'a been talking about in the first place."

The first man inspected the stairway from ground to platform and back down to the ground. "You might be right. Them stairs is mighty fine work too." And then he noticed an unusual feature. "And look at the handrail. Look how he smoothed out the corners so you won't get a splinter in your hands. Mighty fine carpentry. And mighty considerate, too."

The second man asked, "Whoever heard of a handrail on a hanging scaffold? No doubt about it. Whoever built this took real pride in their work."

The first man smirked, "Never heard of a handrail on a hanging scaffold before." Then he guffawed, "Sheriff must'a been afraid the Indian might fall off and break his neck before they could hang him."

The second man slapped his thigh. "Could be. It sure would be a shame if he died before we got the chance to hang him proper."

The first man wiped a glaze of slobber from his bearded chin. "Yes sir. A real shame. A real shame for sure."

Holding Priscilla by her slender wrist, Manfred shouldered his way through the crowd until he arrived behind the two unkempt men. He pulled her to his side. "I still don't think it's a good idea for you to watch the hanging. You're too young to see such things. It might give you nightmares for the rest of your life."

Priscilla tugged at the cuffs of her sleeves. "I'm plenty old to watch the hanging. I've already seen lots of things, things no one should see. A hanging won't make any difference one way or the other."

Manfred acquiesced but still did not approve. "I understand what you're saying, but there's still time for me to escort you back to the saloon. It's bad enough to see a stranger die, but this is someone you know. I don't think you appreciate what it's like when a friend dies right in front of you. The nightmares might be the easy part."

Priscilla nearly tumbled when a woman wearing a gray dress and powder blue bonnet pushed against her back. After regaining her footing, she explained, "I'm staying *because* Joshua is my friend. I'm not worried about any nightmares."

"Easy to say now. You might think otherwise when the nightmares begin."

"I already have nightmares. They don't bother me a bit."

"These will be different. And once they start, I can assure you they won't go away. You must trust me on this."

"I do trust you. But I'm not leaving, no matter what you say."

Manfred parted his lips to offer one last argument, but someone bellowed, "Look! The sheriff's coming up the street." Manfred and Priscilla turned but could not see anything. Manfred pushed up on his toes but still could not see the sheriff.

Priscilla jumped up several times then touched Manfred's hand. "Lift me up on your shoulders. I want to see if Joshua is alright. They might've done something to him."

I'll do no such thing. Allowing you to attend the hanging is one thing, but lifting you up on my shoulders is ...."

The thickly-packed crowd suddenly parted to form a ragged path to the scaffold stairs. The sheriff and three deputies strode through the opening, tromped up the stairway to the platform, and turned around. The pathway narrowed when the crowd swelled forward.

Sheriff Boyle repeatedly pushed his hands down to quiet the boisterous mob. When the last person had stopped talking, he cleared his throat three times before speaking. "I got some unfortunate news for you." He rubbed the back of his neck before delivering the news. "There ain't gonna be any hanging today. That's all I got to say about it."

The multifarious voices of the assemblage rose and fell, and one of the unkempt men—the one who had admired the nailing pattern—yelled, "Why not?"

Sheriff Boyle scowled at the unkempt man. "Because the Indian ain't here anymore, that's why not."

The voices of the crowd rose and fell again, and the second unkempt man asked, "Where's he gone to?"

Sheriff Boyle snapped, "How should I know? The U.S. Cavalry came and took him away, and they didn't exactly take the time to explain where they were taking him." He shifted his eyes to a distant building down the street. "Seems we weren't his first massacre. I 'spect they plan on hanging him too."

Another voice in the crowd bellowed out, "You sure they'll hang him?"

Sheriff Boyle glared at the anonymous voice and jeered, "How should I know what they're gonna do with him. I told you they didn't exactly tell me their plans. Maybe they'll just shoot him on the way back to the fort. Either way, he's a dead man."

After several more unruly exchanges, the sheriff and his deputies stormed noisily down the stairs, pushed through the crowd, and marched back to the county courthouse. Within minutes only a few of the locals lingered around the scaffold—probably to admire the fine carpentry work.

Conrad Airingsail awoke early in the morning when the first glimmer of sunlight filtered through the gauzy curtain hanging over the window at the front of his cabin. The curtain obscured his view of the valley and distant hills, but also offered the seclusion he preferred. After changing the bedding (including the pillowcase) to celebrate the arrival of spring, he swept the cabin floor clean and dusted. He prepared flapjacks, scrambled eggs, and coffee for breakfast, and ate at the small square table sitting next to the potbelly stove. When he had finished washing the plate and skillet, he dressed himself in wool stockings, long-sleeve flannel shirt, and tan pantaloons. He pulled on knee-high leather boots and strapped on a pair of spurs with the rowels filed down. He squirmed into leather chaps that were knee-puckered from too much crawling around on the rocky ground and polished smooth from too much riding. To block the incessant dust, he tied a red bandana around his neck and pulled it up until it stretched across his mouth. He removed a sweat-stained wide-brimmed hat from a wood peg next to the door and scrunched it down to the top of his ears and spectacles. And he yanked on stiff leather gloves to protect his hands from splinters, sharp edges, rope burns, and other occupational hazards.

He spent the next two hours working outside in the crisp morning air and warm sun. He repaired the gate to the circular corral next to the cabin. He crawled onto the mossy cabin roof and replaced three rough-sawn wood shakes that he speculated were the source of an annoying leak, which only dripped when rain storms blew in from the east. And he shoveled manure from the corral and piled it near the perimeter of the open area fronting the cabin (for later use in the garden). When he had finished his work, he returned to the cabin and prepared to ride into Silver City for the hanging. He pulled on a shoulder holster with a small-caliber five-cylinder revolver and concealed it beneath a sweat-stained vest. He secured a 12-gauge-sawed-off-pistol-grip-double-barreled shotgun on his back in the quick-release harness he had fabricated himself. He buckled a leather belt around his waist with sheathed throwing knife and a row of eight 12-gage shotgun shells.

He walked outside and closed the door. After stretching his arms to the sky, he retrieved a bridle and his best saddle from a small storage shed and carried them to the corral. He saddled his favorite horse (the one he had used to deliver Manfred's letter to Fort Boise), lifted his left foot into the stirrup, and swung his right leg over the saddle. He opened and closed the corral gate without dismounting and rode away. He arrived at the bridge over Jordan Creek north of Silver City about an hour later. He walked the horse through town, until he could see what looked like hundreds of people gathered around the scaffold, and waited near the middle of the street. A few minutes after two, Sheriff Boyle and three deputies passed by and headed toward the scaffold. Conrad watched the four men vanish into the crowd. They reappeared on the platform below the dangling noose. Sheriff Boyle waved his arms around for a few minutes. The four men bounced down the steps, pushed through the crowd, and passed by again. With the exception of a few individuals who lingered near the scaffold, the folks who had come to see the hanging dispersed. Conrad did not know what to make of it.

Returning from the aborted hanging, Manfred Herrmann and Priscilla Kimball were surprised to find the lone rider standing in the middle of the street. Manfred greeted the rider blithely. "Good afternoon, Mister Airingsail. I was escorting Miss Kimball back to her place of employment when I noticed you standing here. Have you heard the good news?"

Conrad Airingsail folded his hands on the saddle horn and slowly shook his head.

Manfred reached out and petted the horse's nose. "Then I shall tell you. Sheriff Boyle has just informed us that Joshua Hotah was rescued by the U.S. Cavalry this morning. There will be no hanging of an innocent man in Silver City today."

Conrad Airingsail smiled broadly beneath the red bandana.

Priscilla squeezed Manfred's arm. "What do you think, Mister Conrad? Isn't it the absolutely best news you ever heard in your entire life?"

Conrad Airingsail touched the brim of his hat, pulled on the leather reins, and cantered away without expressing any particular opinion.

CHAPTER SEVENTEEN

The Basque sheepherder
June 1, 1872

J esus Azcuenaga, a Basque sheepherder from the Province of Bizkaia in northern Spain, surveyed the jumbled buildings and narrow streets of Silver City from his mountainous vantage. He tapped the side of his nose and contemplated his arduous journey to the summit of this hill in this valley on this day. In 1850, following two years of misery in Argentina, he had boarded a crowded steamer to San Francisco after hearing of a major gold strike in a place they called California. With the exception of a rather unpleasant storm off the coast of Mexico, he arrived safely and walked joyfully down the gangplank bursting with anticipation. Although the weather had proved agreeable, he discovered not gold but more years of misery. He journeyed south, and—although he had no useful knowledge of sheep at the time—found employment as a sheepherder in the San Joaquin Valley. He did not mind the hard work or lonely life of a sheepherder, but in the 1860s (he could not remember the exact year) he again followed the promise of gold to the southeastern region of a place they called Oregon. He prospected his way east. After numerous misadventures (many of them too harrowing to recount here) and more years of misery, he arrived in a place they called Owyhee County in the summer of 1870. Because he still had discovered no gold—and because he could now boast vast experience in the herding of sheep—he again found work as a sheepherder.

Jesus Azcuenaga herded his modest flock of one-hundred-and-forty-seven sheep through a shallow ravine and down a rocky slope toward an expansive patch of grass flowing around an outcrop of fractured bedrock. He climbed up the angular southern face of the outcropping after the flock began munching the grass. When he reached the top, he stood heroically and counted his sheep. He counted his sheep at least three times every day, and each time he arrived at the same number he attributed his good fortune to the boundless grace of God. Satisfied with the count, he sat on a flat spot and swiveled north to face Silver City. He used his rumpled wool hat to brush dust from his shirt sleeves and vest, then balanced the hat on his bent knee. He closed his eyes and raised his chin to feel the warmth of the sun on his face, and considered his options. He could stay here for the night, but he felt a strong desire to move on. He could guide his flock to the lands north of Silver City by following a route high up on the mountainside to avoid the town altogether, but this would require much time and effort. He could drive his noisy sheep down the hill and right through the middle of town along the main street to the bridge over Jordan Creek, but this would likely enrage the citizens of Silver City, who generally did not approve of Basque sheepherders or their sheep. He did not like any of his options. He collected a partially-eaten loaf of bread and a chunk of cheese from a shoulder bag and decided to eat while he thought of better possibilities.

When he had finished his simple meal, he noticed two horses grazing next to a clump of small Junipers about 300 feet below. He stood and spotted a man and a woman reclining on a blanket near the horses. To his astonishment, both of them unexpectedly stood and waved. At first Jesus Azcuenaga did not know what he should do, but after considering his options he waved back vigorously with his rumpled wool hat.

Alexandra Smyth dismounted from the sidesaddle. After straightening her dark olive riding skirt and tying the reins to the trunk of a small juniper tree, she removed a floral blanket from a saddle bag. She strolled in widening circles searching for a relatively level spot. When she found one to her liking, she shook the blanket until it spread out and floated evenly down to the ground. After smoothing the wrinkles by pulling at the corners, she strolled back to the saddlebag and fetched a corked whisky bottle filled with the tea she had brewed in the morning.

Manfred Herrmann, a wicker picnic basket balanced awkwardly above the saddle horn, waited until Alexandra had set the whisky bottle down. "I think you should take the picnic basket before I make my first attempt to get off this horse."

Alexandra walked up to Manfred and accepted the basket from his outstretched hand. "If I had known you were not fond of horses, I would not have asked you to carry it."

Manfred swung his right leg over the back of the saddle, dropped to the ground, and extricated his foot from the stirrup. He arched his lower back and rubbed his hip. "It's not that I'm not fond of horses. I mostly love all of God's creatures. I just don't care to ride on top of any of them, especially horses." He led the horse to the juniper tree and secured the reins. "I prefer a simple carriage pulled by an old mule, one that does not run too fast."

Alexandra held Manfred's hand as they walked to the blanket. "Did you never ride a horse during the war?"

Manfred snorted, "Not even once. I shot a few when my aim was low, but never rode one. Come to think of it, I might have shot quite a few."

Alexandra thought it best to redirect the conversation. "Do you want to eat now, or wait a little? I'm curious why you wanted to talk to me." She placed the basket in the middle of the blanket and rolled gracefully to her side. "I'm also curious why you suggested a picnic on the hillside overlooking Silver City. Mind you, I'm delighted we're here, especially on such a lovely day, but we could have met at the War Eagle Hotel if you wanted to talk."

Manfred fell to his knees and rubbed his hands together. "I didn't want people overhearing what I have to say. What's for lunch? I see you brought a bottle of whisky. I didn't know you liked the stuff."

Alexandra lifted the top of the wicker basket. "It's not whisky. It's tea. I brewed it this morning. I also made ham sandwiches with fresh butter and mustard from the general store and an apple pie."

Manfred licked his lips. "Where did you buy the pie? I love apple pie."

Alexandra took two brown-paper-wrapped sandwiches out of the basket and offered the larger one to Manfred. "I didn't buy it. I baked it yesterday. I'll leave it in the basket for now. I don't want to tempt any of the local ravens. You know how brazen they are."

The sound of sheep distracted Manfred as he unwrapped the sandwich. He scanned the slopes above and found a man sitting on an outcrop of rock some distance away. "I see we are sharing the hillside with one of the local sheepherders and his flock."

Alexandra pushed herself up and held her hand above her eyes. "Do you know him?"

"I don't think so. They usually stay away from town because it seems most folks don't particularly like them."

"Why not?"

"Don't really know, but they are God's children just like you and me. We should stand up and wave to him."

Manfred and Alexandra stood together and waved. At first the sheep herder remained still, but then he rose up to his feet and waved back.

Manfred supported Alexandra's hand as they settled down on the blanket. He unwrapped the sandwich a little more and chewed off a healthy bite. After swallowing, he said, "Delicious. Absolutely delicious. I didn't know a ham sandwich could taste this good."

Alexandra smiled. "I'm glad you like it. I bought the bread from one of the ladies in town. She makes it fresh every day. Would you like some tea? I brought each of us a cup."

Manfred and Alexandra spoke of small things while they ate the ham sandwiches and drank tea from the whisky bottle. When they had finished the apple pie, they both reclined and snoozed a little in the warmth of the sun. After an hour, Manfred rose to his feet and brushed off the front of his trousers. He offered his hand to Alexandra. "Would you like to take a walk? I have something important to tell you."

Alexandra grasped Manfred's hand and stood. "Such a lazy day. A walk sounds just right after our pleasant little nap."

Manfred squeezed her hand. "And after such a wonderful meal too. I would suggest that we do this again sometime, but you may not agree after hearing what I have to say."

As they hiked off together, Alexandra lengthened her stride and said, "You sound very serious. I can't imagine I would not agree to join you for a picnic ever again."

Manfred did not answer immediately. After walking some distance, he said, "I am about to break two solemn vows: one made to God, and one made to a friend."

"My goodness, this does sound serious."

"More serious than you can imagine."

"You don't have to tell me anything, if you don't want to."

"But I do want to."

"Alright, then. I'm listening."

Manfred guided Alexandra around a rock and pulled her closer before commencing. "Some years ago, after the war, I made a promise to God to never kill again. At the time I was sick of killing, and it was easy and natural to make such a promise."

"Sounds like an admirable thing to do."

"Yes, but there is more to it. There is a dark secret behind the promise that I have only shared with one other person."

"A dark secret? The way you say it sounds very ominous."

"It's worse than ominous. I made the promise because something terrified me more than I ever thought possible. I made the promise ... because I enjoyed the killing."

Confused and dismayed, Alexandra slowed her pace. "Enjoyed the killing? How is that even possible?" She shook her head. "I don't believe it."

"You must believe it. If you refuse to believe it, then there is no reason for me to continue."

After a long hesitation, Alexandra said, "Alright. I believe you. Go on."

"Good. Then I will continue. I had a strange meeting with Csongor the week before last. At the livery stables on Jordan. At midnight."

"I must say, a midnight meeting at the stables *is* very strange."

"Yes, it was. But even stranger is what Csongor said to me. He told me that Joshua Hotah is an innocent man."

"That is not so strange. After all, he did defend him in court."

"He did. And at the time I thought he did a commendable job. But then Csongor confessed to me that he was the one responsible for the death of the mother, not Joshua, and that was why he knew Joshua was an innocent man."

At first incredulous, Alexandra attempted a clumsy repartee. "And I suppose he admitted to killing the children too."

"No, he didn't kill the children. At least not directly. He said one of his men accomplished this...how did he put it...messy business. But what shocked me even more was his confession about the mother. Not only did he methodically slaughter her by shooting her with arrows, it sounded to me like he had taken great pleasure in it."

An ugly smear of horror abruptly twisted the rustic beauty of Alexandra's features. "This can't be true. I don't believe it."

Manfred smiled weakly. "I know, but you must believe this too, because it involves the second broken promise."

"I don't understand."

"Before Csongor made his confession, he asked me to promise that I would never tell anyone, and I agreed. I have now broken my promise by telling you."

"But surely he did not really expect you to keep such news a secret?"

"Yes, he did. And I had every intention of keeping it...until two days ago, the same day I asked you if you were interested in a picnic."

"I see." Alexandra calmed her face, but several reddish creases persisted. "But now I don't understand how you have broken the first promise."

Manfred explored the sky above the distant mountains and breathed deeply. "I haven't broken my promise to God yet. But I will break it soon...when I kill Csongor."

Alexandra gripped Manfred's hand and yanked him to a stop. "Kill Csongor? How could you even consider it?" After thinking a little more, she added, "Shouldn't you just report it to the sheriff and let him take care of it? Wouldn't that be the more sensible thing to do?"

Manfred held both of Alexandra's hands and faced her directly. "Yes, my dear Alexandra, it *would* be the more sensible thing to do. But I already thought of this, and there are two problems."

Alexandra replied acerbically, "Only two?"

"Yes. First, the sheriff would never believe me. The story is too implausible. He would probably think I've gone mad and lock me up instead of Csongor. And even if he did believe me—which he never would—there is not a shred of evidence to prove Csongor or his men had anything to do with it. Even Joshua Hotah arrived too late to see anything."

Hearing no immediate continuation, Alexandra prompted, "And the second problem?"

"The second problem is this: I now believe Csongor Toth is unrepentantly evil. In spite of my friendship with him, he is almost certainly the evilest man I have ever known or will ever know. And because of this, I believe he is profoundly dangerous and will kill again. He has already demonstrated not the slightest remorse for butchering an entire family. Although he did not say it directly, I have inferred from his subtle words and demeanor that he has murdered before. I cannot simply report his confession to the sheriff and wash my hands of it." After a few painful seconds had slipped away, he repeated, "I cannot."

Alexandra touched a threadbare spot on Manfred's sleeve and thought to herself that she should repair it before it unraveled. "I see. Is there nothing I can say to convince you otherwise?" She felt uncomfortably warm.

Manfred lifted her hands. "No. There is nothing."

"How do you plan to do it?"

"I have already set my plan in motion. I've arranged a meeting with Csongor at the same livery on Jordan Avenue, where he made his confession."

"When?"

"Tomorrow night, at midnight. I don't think he'll suspect a thing."

"And then what?"

"I've borrowed a rifle from William Sommercamp. I told him I wanted to do some hunting, and he believed me."

"I see. So not only are you breaking promises, you are lying to your friends as well."

"Just add it to my growing list of transgressions."

"I fear your list may grow even longer before the week is out."

"Maybe you're right, but it can't be helped. And one more thing—"

"Only one more this time?"

"Yes, only one more." Manfred reached inside his coat and produced a sealed envelope." If I should fail, I would appreciate it if you'd deliver this letter to Major Plantagenet at Fort Boise."

Alexandra accepted the letter without cheerfulness. "And what does the letter say?"

"I've already burdened you with too much knowledge of too many wicked things. I'm sorry, but also thankful you were willing to listen. I have no intention of telling you more. Just deliver the letter to Ethan. It's the last thing I will ask of you. I promise."

When they returned to the horses, the Basque sheepherder and his flock of sheep had vanished. While they gathered the blanket and whisky bottle of tea and the wicker picnic basket, Alexandra thought of telling Manfred her real name and the truth about the unfortunate events in Brookline and the time Csongor saved her life in Liverpool and how he helped her escape from Boston, but the right moment never presented itself.

CHAPTER EIGHTEEN

Enlightenment at Mahogany Gulch
June 2, 1872

E lijah Brown hawked up a gob of ropy phlegm and spat it to the ground. After casually observing the trajectory of the gob, he snatched his hat off and used it to fan his face. "What does the book say to do now?" Although he could only recognize a few dozen words, he attempted to read the book over Longwei's shoulder.

Tseng Longwei opened the book, taking care not to further damage the fragile binding, and turned to the table of contents. "Now that we have successfully framed the walls of our new cabin, it is time to begin work on the roof. I am confident we shall find the answers to our many questions in Mister Hatfield's book." He ran his finger down the list of topics in the table of contents, then flipped through the pages until he arrived at *Article 297—To find the dimension of common rafters.*[10] "I shall read of the common rafters so we may together find enlightenment."

Impatient to hear what the book had to say, Elijah exhorted, "Go ahead. I'm listening."

Longwei gently flexed the spine of the book and began reading. *"The following rule is for slate roofs, having the rafters placed 12 inches apart. Shingle roofs may have the rafters placed 2 feet apart. The dimensions for raf-*

---

[10] Tseng Longwei is reading from the fifth edition of *American House-Carpenter: A Treatise Upon Architecture, Cornices and Mouldings, Framing, Doors, Windows, and Stairs, Together With the Most Important Principals of Practical Geometry*, by R.G. Hatfield, Architect, published 1852 by John Wiley.

ters of other kinds of covering may be found by reference to the table at Article 286, and the laws of pressure at the first part of this section."

Elijah rubbed the back of this sweaty neck with a blistered hand. "Did we read about them laws of pressure before? I can't remember if we did or not, but it sounds like it might be sort of important."

Longwei looked up from the book. "We did not, but we shall read about the laws of pressure at a later time if it becomes necessary. For now, I shall read more of the common rafters." He lowered his eyes and continued. *"Rule—Divide the length of bearing in feet, by the cube root of the breadth in inches; and the quotient, multiplied by 0.72 for pine, or 0.74 for oak, will give the depth in inches."*

Elijah pressed the hat back on his sweaty head. "What's a cube root? Never even heard of such a thing. Have something to do with funny looking trees?"

Longwei admonished, "Wait. Before you ask any questions, there is an example of how to do what the book says. I shall read it now. *Example— What should be the depth of a pine rafter, 7 feet long and 2 inches thick? 7 feet, divided by 1.26, the cube root of 2, gives 5.55, which, multiplied by 0.72, gives nearly 4 inches—the depth required."*

Elijah rolled back on his heels. "I got a lot of questions about the gibberish you just recited, but for starters, are we even using pine to build this dang cabin?"

Longwei closed the book and pressed the top edge against his chin. "I do not know if the wood we are using is pine. I did not ask the man who sold it to us. I agree this may be an important question to answer before we worry about the cube root."

Elijah moved to Longwei's side. "Then what about them laws of pressure? Maybe we should take a look now and worry about the cube root of a pine tree later."

Longwei opened the book and thumbed through the pages until he found the relevant section. "Listen carefully as I read what Mister Hatfield has to say about the laws of pressure." He flexed the book again. *"In estimating the pressures upon any certain roof, for the purpose of ascertaining the proper sizes for the timbers, calculation must be made for the pressure exerted by the wind, and, if in a cold climate, for the weight of snow, in addition to the weight of the materials of which the roof is composed."*

Elijah snorted derisively, "No question we're in a cold climate. Just about froze my ass off more than a few times last winter. But how do we figure out how much snow weighs? Does this Hatfield fellow expect me to cart a scale up to the top of one of those yonder mountains and try to find some snow to weigh?"

Longwei contemplated the peak of Florida Mountain. "Please be patient until I have finished reading. I am confident Mister Hatfield will provide the answer." He continued reading. *"The force of wind may be calculated at 40 lbs. on a square foot. The weight of snow will be of course according to the depth it acquires. (See weight of materials, in Appendix.)"*

Elijah quietly articulated a few cuss words, then complained, "Not that stupid appendix again? The last time we read from there it confused me to tears. And what *is* an appendix, anyway? And why does Mister Hatfield keep hiding stuff in it instead of putting it where you can find it? What's he afraid of?"

Longwei soothed, "Do not fear the appendix, Elijah Brown. It has offered much enlightenment in the past, and I am sure, if we are patient and take the time to understand, it will provide the knowledge we seek once again."

Elijah snarled, "Go ahead and read from the darn appendix then, but I'm not holding my breath this time. That's for sure."

Longwei opened the book to the back. "I shall read from the appendix and we shall see." He located the weight of materials section, right after the *Table of Polygons*, and ran his finger down the various entries. "According to Mister Hatfield, these are the weights of materials in pounds in a cubic foot." He announced various materials as he searched for snow. *Cast Roman cement – 100, Crystallized quarts – 165, Mortar with hair (Plastering) – 105, Yellow beeswax – 60, Solid gunpowder – 109, Shaken gunpowder – 58, Milk – 64...."*

Elijah stomped his foot and erupted. "Why do I even care about the weight of yellow beeswax? And what does Cast Roman cement have to do with a cabin roof? And what *is* Cast Roman cement anyway?"

Longwei skimmed to the end of the list. "Wait. I have found the answer we seek." And then he announced triumphantly, *"Snow – 8 pounds in a cubic foot."* And in an unusual display of passion, Longwei snapped the book closed and grinned broadly. "As promised, Mister Hatfield has once again provided us with enlightenment."

Elijah ripped his hat off and flung it to the ground, very close to where the gob of phlegm still glistened in the sun. "That does it. I don't think I can take another dose of this so-called enlightenment from this Hatfield fellow without exploding."

Longwei's grin receded to a knowing smile. "You speak with much wisdom, Elijah Brown. Truly, the attainment of enlightenment is often an unpleasant journey fraught with pitfalls."

Perched upon his most reliable mule—a two-year-old animal named Peter the Great—Roshan Kuznetsov approached to within a few hundred feet of the new cabin. He tugged on the reins and pleaded, "Begin to whoa in the now mangy animal of a mule beast." Peter the Great trotted off five more defiant steps before unexpectedly halting and nearly throwing Roshan off. The mangy animal of a mule beast swung its head around and tried to nip Roshan on the knee. Roshan quickly pulled his knee away and laughed. "You missed of me again in the time once more. Roshan is of the quick to the much for you."

The sounds of hammer and saw echoed in Roshan's ears and drew his attention to the cabin. It pleased him to see that Elijah and Longwei had finished the walls and were now working on the roof. They had made good progress since yesterday morning when he rode off to Silver City. He kicked Peter the Great in the haunches and the mangy animal of a mule beast lurched forward. When he arrived at the front of the cabin, he spoke to Elijah and Longwei without dismounting. "I see from the look of it you have made much the work from the day ahead." He discovered the new rafters. "What do you work of the now?"

Elijah Brown used his hammer to scratch an itch on his back. "Just cutting and nailing down these here roof rafters. Took a while to figure it out, but we finally decided on a four-by-twelve ridge beam and two-by-six rafters nailed twelve inches apart."

Roshan dismounted and tied the reins to a wood stud. He climbed up to the new front deck and walked through the new front door. He inspected the framing of the new walls and the underside of the new ridge beam. "How do you know with certain it is of the strong? The snow is much the thick in the winter before today."

Elijah tapped the hammer against the top of the ridge beam. "Nothing to it. Longwei's got this book by an architect in New York City who tells you everything you need to know about building a cabin. All you got to figure is the weight of snow and your cube roots and square feet."

Longwei gripped a rafter to steady himself and pulled the book from the back of his pants and held it up for Roshan to see. "We could not have done our work without the enlightenment we have received from Mister Hatfield's book. We are truly confident the cabin will tolerate any unfortunate wind or snow pressures for many years to come."

Elijah smacked the face of one of the rafters with his free hand. "You're right about that. This here cabin's not going anywhere. Why, you could slap a thousand pounds of yellow beeswax on top of this roof and you wouldn't even know about it until spring."

Roshan rubbed his chin. "Yellow beeswax?"

Longwei intervened. "Do not worry about the yellow beeswax today. It is a long story to explain another time. Tell us of your trip to Silver City. Did you complete your business with Mister Toth? Did all go well for you?"

Roshan shoved his hands in his pockets and grinned. "Of this you are the sure. Roshan is the much success with business. You should hear about it when I say to you it is of the truth you shall know when you hear of it."

Elijah scratched his left shoulder with the hammer. "Since I don't know what you're all talking about, maybe you could just tell me about it right now."

Longwei agreed. "Yes, we are both curious of your business in Silver City. It is our hope to work for you a very long time so we may prosper in our old age and not worry about debt."

Roshan did not immediately speak. When he had prepared his thoughts, he said, "Roshan will answer in the two. In the one, it is of the good business in Silver City. And it is the no to work for Roshan the very long time. It is of the sad to say Longwei and Elijah are on fire today, and will never work for Roshan in the Mahogany Gulch more the day. To this I am of the sure."

Elijah swallowed hard and dropped the hammer to his side. "Wait a dang minute. Are you telling us we're both fired? Is that what you just said?"

This unexpected announcement stunned Longwei. "I cannot believe you are doing this thing. Have we not worked hard enough for you these many days since the miraculous explosion and the discovery of more gold than anyone thought possible?"

"Yes, you have of the sure worked in the many hard. But, as they say of it, the business is of the business, and Roshan must think of the many next days to be sure of it. It is already of the done in the deal."

Elijah released the hammer; it clattered against a rafter before falling to the floor. "We'll I'll be a horse's ass. Just when I thought things were going pretty good."

Longwei diminished his voice. "Truly a sad day. Much wealth makes men do strange things. There is nothing more to say of it."

Roshan picked up the hammer and waved it around. "Yes, you have hit the problem in the big nose. Much of wealth is the strange to be sure. I tell you of this. How can Roshan ask for the hands of Nadia to the marriage when much of the wealth is not any possible to believe of it? She can never give the hands to Roshan, if you hear my lips say of it." He hooked the hammer over his shoulder and grinned.

Longwei pushed his hands into opposite sleeves. "This time even I do not understand what you mean."

Roshan tossed the hammer to the floor and pulled an envelope from inside his vest. He opened the envelope and removed a folded sheet of paper and shook it open. "It is of the simple. Roshan cannot ask for the hands to marry of Nadia with the ridiculous wealth. It is why Mister Csongor Toth is helped Roshan give a piece of the wealth to the new partners of business to smaller up the wealth of Roshan. It makes the sense perfect to be of sure."

His expression suddenly inscrutable, Longwei implored, "Are you saying it is not possible for us to work for your new business partners? If this is what you mean, Elijah and I can promise to work equally hard for the new partners. There is no reason to fire us. We have nowhere else to go."

Elijah banged the top of the ridge beam with his hand. "Why, I'll promise to work even harder for your new partners. And I'll even take a cut in pay, if it'll make 'em happy."

Roshan shook the piece of paper more vigorously. "You can work the hard and take the cut in pay if you are happy for it. You only of the need talk to the other."

Still confused, Longwei asked, "What do you mean when you say, talk to the other?"

Roshan slowly folded the piece of paper and held it up. "Because, my friends of the dear... *you* are the new partners of equal business of more gold you can imagine in the Mahogany Gulch. Csongor Toth made the words of it true on this paper. You can now work of much the hard and the cut in pay, if it is happy to you. Fall down the roof and Roshan will show you of it before you can believe the true."

Tseng Longwei and Elijah Brown stared at each other for a surprisingly long time before climbing down from the new cabin roof to shake the hands of their new partner of equal business of more gold you can imagine.

CHAPTER NINETEEN

Shopping at The Sommercamp Emporium
& General Store
June 3, 1872

F ollowing another lively weekend—which provided the unexpected
opportunity of a particularly unpleasant incident with a persistently
demanding customer—Nadia cherished the comparative tranquility of
shopping with Priscilla at her favorite general store. After browsing a pyra-
midal stack of newly-arrived canned goods, Nadia and Priscilla strolled to
the back of the store and compared the bolts of fabric organized in a partitioned bin near the end of a glass-fronted counter. Nadia touched her lips
(to signal deep contemplation) before extracting a thick bolt of cotton
fabric from the bin. She tugged on her ear (to signal critical thinking)
as she examined the delicate floral pattern. She looked up when a pair
of women entered the store, and the one wearing a plaid bonnet scuffed
her shoe along the side of the cask of nails holding the front door open
and nearly fell. Ignoring the commotion, Nadia held the bolt in front of
Priscilla and pulled back a corner of the fabric. "What do you think of this,
Priscilla? If you want my opinion, it's very pretty. I think it would make a
fine dress. Do you like it?"

Priscilla stroked the fabric with her fingertips. "It's very pretty. And very
soft too." She pulled her fingers away and clasped her hands behind her
back. "But it's probably really expensive. If you want my opinion, I don't

think we can afford such nice fabric for a new dress when I don't really need a new one."

Without hesitation, Nadia addressed the dark-suited man waiting by a display of assorted hammers, saws, screwdrivers, and hand drills. "How much for this lovely floral pattern, Mister Sommercamp?"

William F. Sommercamp maneuvered artfully around a table piled with flannel shirts and wool socks, and advanced with long strides to the fabric bin. He propped his right hand on the top of the bin, crossed his ankles, and leaned jauntily to the side. "That's a mighty fine fabric, if you want my opinion. Normally sells for a dollar a yard, sometimes two depending on availability." He winked furtively at Nadia. "But today only, it's on sale for twenty-five cents a yard. You won't find a better price anywhere in Silver City. Probably can't find a better price in Boise City either."

Nadia addressed Priscilla, who appeared more interested in the woman with the plaid bonnet than the bolt of cotton fabric. "Did you hear that, Priscilla? Mister Sommercamp says this fabric's on sale today. What a happy coincidence. If you like it, we can buy it right now and I can get started on your new dress after lunch."

Priscilla briefly glanced at the fabric. "Looks fine to me, but I don't know why I need a new dress. As far as I'm concerned, the one I'm wearing is perfectly fine. Joniah Tucker gave me this dress. She even fixed the sleeves for me and hemmed it while she was riding in the wagon. I don't think I'm quite ready to part with it."

Nadia hugged the bolt of cotton against her bosom. "Now Priscilla, we've already talked about this. I know you're really fond of that dress, but it's getting a little threadbare in a few places. And it doesn't really fit you anyway, even if Joniah did hem it for you. But you don't have to part with it. You can still wear it to do chores, if you like." She turned to William Sommercamp. "Don't you agree, Mister Sommercamp?"

William Sommercamp followed his cue perfectly. "Why yes, I certainly do agree." He spoke to Priscilla. "Miss Nadia's right. You can still wear it for chores and similar activities, but a pretty young lady like you should be wearing a new dress without tears and other improprieties, especially when you're out in public."

Priscilla frowned. "What's … other improprieties?" She smiled playfully and asked, "Are they something really bad?"

William Sommercamp uncrossed his ankles and raised his fist to his mouth and coughed. "Well, I wouldn't say they're bad, exactly. What I mean when I say improprieties…is…well…for example, if you consider the—"

Nadia interrupted, "Never you mind about other improprieties. What Mister Sommercamp is trying to tell you is …."

Ned Nordmeyer—a seasoned curmudgeon of a miner wearing knee-high black boots, a crumpled hat caked with ore dust, and a faded plaid shirt with both sleeves rolled up above his sunburned forearms—stumbled into the general store after catching a toe on the cask of nails holding the front door open. He staggered to an awkward pose next to the pickle barrel. After stomping both feet on the floor boards, he tore the crumpled hat off and shouted, "Have you heard about the big news from Mahogany Gulch?"

William Sommercamp yelled from the back of the store, "Calm down Ned. You're scaring my customers."

Ned yelled even louder, "But I've got big news!"

Annoyed by the ruckus, William Sommercamp shouted, "I don't care what you've got, Ned. You need to quiet down right this minute or I'll personally throw you into the street."

Ned twisted the crumpled hat with his sunburned hands and lowered his voice. "Big news. You'll never believe it when I tell ya. It's spreading all over town like wildfire."

William Sommercamp lowered his voice too. "What are you talking about? I haven't heard any big news for a month. And even then, it wasn't all that big."

Ned slapped the top of the pickle barrel with the crumpled hat and a haze of ore dust erupted into the air. "Big news. I'm surprised you haven't already heard about it."

A little testy this time, William Sommercamp implored, "Ned, stop beating around the bush and tell me what you're talking about."

Ned slapped his thigh with the hat and another plume of dust squirted to the side. "Big news. Why, it's hard to believe, if you ask me, but it seems these three fellers up at Mahogany Gulch were—" A woman shrieked outside. Ned spun around, jammed the dusty hat on his unkempt head, and yelled as he headed out the front door, "I'll be right back. I gotta check on my mule."

William Sommercamp spoke to Nadia and Priscilla. "I guess we'll have to wait for Ned to come back to hear about this big news."

Priscilla sensed a chance to get away from the bolts of fabric. "Maybe I should go help Ned with his mule. I'm pretty good with horses and mules."

Nadia held Priscilla by the arm when she tried to step away from the partitioned bin. "You stay right here young lady and help me decide on this fabric. Ned Nordmeyer can take care of his own mule without any assistance from you."

The cask of nails holding the front door open tumbled over and skittered across the floor boards until it thumped against the base of the pickle barrel. Roshan Kuznetsov blundered into the general store and fell to his hands and knees. He quickly spotted Nadia. Without getting up, he declared, "Oh my Nadia, I have found you of the store of generals just like the woman who lives in all the black dress said of it in the saloon who you work on the many nighttime to be sure." When he had finished his rambling sentence he jumped up, patted the front of his legs, rushed to the back of the store, and kneeled in front of Nadia. "Roshan must tell of you the important story most you cannot believe of it until you hear my lips speak to it."

William Sommercamp exclaimed, "This day is swiftly turning into a veritable circus."

A little embarrassed, Nadia broke into Russian. *"What are you doing here, you silly fool? I'm trying to buy some fabric so I can make Priscilla a dress. Can't this wait until our scheduled grammar lesson?"*

Roshan stood and answered in Russian. *"I am sorry, dear Nadia, if I have upset you. It's just that I have a very important question to ask you, and I cannot wait any longer. The news of the unusual incident at Mahogany Gulch will soon get out, and then it will be too late to ask the question."*

Nadia's voice calmed. *"What is this news of an unusual incident at Mahogany Gulch?"*

Roshan drummed his fingertips together. *"I cannot tell you about the news until I first ask the question."*

Nadia fiddled with the bolt of fabric. *"Then ask me the question. I would like to hear of this unusual incident at Mahogany Gulch."*

Roshan dodged. *"First I must ask you the question. Then, if you give the answer I am hoping for, I will tell you of the news from Mahogany Gulch."*

"*Then ask the question. I would like to hear this news.*"

"*Alright. Since you insist, I will ask the question.*"

"*I'm waiting.*"

"*I can see that you are waiting.*"

"*Roshan, please ask me the darn question. I am very busy today and do not have time for silly games.*"

"*It is a good thing we are speaking in Russian. Otherwise, Priscilla would have heard your unfortunate choice of words.*"

"*Roshan!*"

Roshan dropped to his knee a second time. "*Alright. I can see your patience has ended. I will ask the question.*" He took a deep breath and exhaled slowly. "*Nadia, will you marry me?*"

Nadia had not expected such a question, and she groped for words. "*You're asking me… you're… what are you asking me?*"

Roshan clarified his question. "*I'm asking you to marry me. I love you. I want to spend the rest of my life with you.*" After hearing no response from Nadia, he asked, "*Nadia, do you not love me too? You are taking a very long time to answer the question.*"

Nadia snapped, "*Of course I love you. I'm surprised you thought it necessary to ask. It's just… it's just that I had other plans.*"

Roshan stood and pried one of Nadia's hands away from the bolt of fabric. "*I asked if you loved me because you are hesitating to answer. Do you not want to marry me?*"

Nadia squeezed Roshan's hand. "*It's not that I don't want to marry you. I just have so many other plans. If I say yes, where will we live? Will we have enough food to eat and a roof over our heads? Will I still have to work at the saloon? Will we have to stay here in Silver City the rest of our lives?*"

Roshan insisted, "*If we love each other, what does any of that matter?*"

A tear rolled down Nadia's cheek. "*But it does matter. Who will take care of Priscilla? She is like a daughter to me. I cannot abandon her.*"

Roshan answered, "*If she is like a daughter to you, then she will be our daughter. We can adopt her after the wedding and she can stay with us wherever we may go.*"

Nadia inhaled deeply and released Roshan's hand. She faced Priscilla and spoke in English. "Priscilla… Roshan and I are thinking about getting married. What do you think of the idea?"

Priscilla clapped her dainty hands. "I think it's a really good idea! I've been praying all along for Mister Roshan to ask you to marry him. I just didn't tell you about it."

With tears glistening on both cheeks, Nadia spoke to Roshan in English. "I'm sorry I took such a long time to answer the question. It was not my intention to appear unappreciative. Yes, I will marry y—"

Ned Nordmeyer burst into the general store again, this time taking care to avoid the cask of nails, which had since rolled over by the pickle barrel and no longer posed a tripping hazard. He raised both hands high and shook them above the crumpled hat streaked with ore dust. "Have you heard the big news?"

William Sommercamp begged, "For heaven's sake, Ned. Just tell us the big news or get out of my store."

Ned Nordmeyer lowered his hands and his voice. "Them three fellers working Gustus De Angeles's claim up at Mahogany Gulch…they just struck it rich. Found a huge vein with more gold than you can shake a stick at. The news is spreading like wildfire. Wildfire!"

Roshan muttered sheepishly, "I meant to tell of it to you if you believe my lips is true."

Nadia lifted Roshan's chin, peered into his eyes, and asked, "Now that I've agreed to marry you because we love each other and nothing else matters, what do you think of moving to California after the wedding?"

Roshan quipped, "I heard of the California has nice view from the oceans if you believe it. It is of the possible Roshan has seen in the view when he arrived in the San Francisco."

Nadia lowered her hand. "Yes, I do believe it."

Priscilla touched Nadia on the shoulder to gain her attention. "Mind if I take another look at that fabric? Guess I'll be needing a new dress after all."

Nadia patted Priscilla's hand. "There's something more. Roshan and I would like you to come to California with us. If you'd like, we could even adopt you as our very own daughter."

Priscilla answered wistfully, "It would be an honor to be your daughter, but I've been thinking it's time for me and Ezekiel to return to Salt Lake City." She caressed the bolt of fabric. "My family…and my husband…are probably worried sick about me."

Nadia dropped the bolt of fabric to the floor and embraced Priscilla. Nadia's tears dampened Priscilla's dress. "We love you, Priscilla." Nadia backed away and held Priscilla by the arms. "Promise you will not leave until after the wedding. If you can't be my daughter, then I want you to be my maid of honor."

Priscilla twitched her nose impishly. "You don't have to worry one little bit about me. I never leave until after the wedding."

CHAPTER TWENTY

Final words in a diary
June 3, 1872

P rescient thunderstorm aromas soaked the muggy breeze. Brooding
clouds streaked silver-gray with moisture ascended the southern
skies beyond War Eagle's soaring pinnacle. Still glowing the angular
slopes of Florida Mountain, shredded boarders of sun-splashed blue
retreated to the north. A gust of fragrant air fluttered the leaves overhead and shimmered the mystic light. Two ravens tumbled acrobatically
before alighting on a scrawny branch together, angrily squawking their
defiance of the nearing tempest.

His mind troubled by visions of things to come, Manfred Herrmann
trudged along the meandering trail without taking notice of the
impending storm. When he arrived at his cabin, he rested his foot upon
the uneven edge of the front deck and considered that he had not a single
recollection of his long walk from town. This insight would normally
have troubled him even more, but after stepping across the deck, and just
as his hand touched the wood door handle, the cat arrived to provide a
timely distraction.

Manfred felt the cat rub against his leg. He spoke affectionately to the
manipulative animal. "Where have you been for the last two days, you
horrid little beast?" Manfred picked the cat up and stroked it behind the
ears. The cat flicked its sensual tail and purred noisily. "Off slaughtering
innocent shrews, I suppose. Or maybe a few harmless birds." Manfred
opened the door and walked into the small cabin. He deposited the cat

on the bed and the horrid little beast immediately jumped to the floor and darted beneath the small table.

Manfred consulted his pocket watch. A few minutes after seven—more than an hour past his customary dinner time. He placed the watch on the small table. He removed his coat and draped it over the back of the chair. The cat reappeared and jumped onto the chair and began rubbing its face against the coat. The cat looked up, and Manfred gently touched its pleasantly-moist nose. "I'm afraid you'll have to sit somewhere else. I'm about to write a few words in my diary before dinner, and that's my favorite chair." The cat did not move. "Do I have to get the broom?" The cat began licking its paws and cleaning its face. "I really mean it. I'll get the broom if you don't move. This time I'm not bluffing." The cat pierced Manfred with its crystal blue lizard eyes (a bit crossed), yawned luxuriously, and hopped down. The cat sauntered over to the bed, jumped up, and nested into a furry ball against the pillow.

Manfred grabbed the diary from the narrow shelf he had built above the bed. He opened the diary to the final pages as he sat in the chair. After scooting the chair forward, he pressed the journal flat on the table. He spoke to the cat as he counted the remaining pages. "Only a few pages left before I'm finished." He rubbed a thumb along the worn spine of the leather cover. "But I might not need another diary after tonight, so maybe it doesn't really matter." The cat raised its head and meowed once. Because the sky had darkened, Manfred lighted the brass kerosene lamp he kept on the small table—a local miner had given it to him as a gift after an especially good sermon—and adjusted the wick until the flame burned efficiently. He took a pocket knife and pencil from a metal cup sitting next to the kerosene lamp, opened the pocket knife, and positioned the cutting edge of the blade against the side of the pencil. When he had sharpened the pencil to his satisfaction, he closed the blade, set the pocket knife down, and began writing.

> *June 3, 1872*
>
> *I remain deeply troubled by what I believe I must do tonight, even though I am now convinced there is no other choice. I have not talked to Alex since our picnic a few days ago. Nor have I seen her from a distance. We had*

such a wonderful time. She brought tea in a whisky bottle, ham sandwiches, and homemade pie. We waved to a shepherd like little children. We held hands, and her touch reminded me that I care for her very much. Although I can no longer deny my deep love for her, I fear our time together will come to an end after tonight. But this is not my greatest concern. I also fear that killing Csongor may almost certainly separate me from the love of God. In any event, I will have to leave the clergy. If I survive. This is the only certain thing on this terrible day.

How strange it is to befriend a man who is both the most generous and most evil person I have ever known. How tragic it is that he confided in me with his darkest secret simply because of our friendship. I must confess that I still love him as a brother, even with the knowledge of what he has done. It breaks my heart to think that before this day is over I will be the one to end his life. Unless he ends mine first, because I now understand how dangerous he is. If this should be God's will, then Alex will deliver the letter I wrote, and we shall see what the new day brings. She is such an innocent child. I pray no harm will come to her because of my actions.

Manfred opened the pocket knife and whittled off the end of the pencil until he had re-sharpened the point. Curly wood shavings fell on the tabletop next to the diary; he brushed them to the floor with the back of his hand. He arched his back and looked over at the cat. "Sound asleep, I see. But I suppose you'll want to go out later to hunt for your supper. God knows I don't have much to give you, at least anything you'd probably like." He twirled the tip of the pencil against his tongue, cracked his knuckles, and continued writing.

I have many regrets on this day. There are so many that it may be impossible to write them all down on these remaining pages. I regret that I shall break my vow to never kill again. I regret telling Csongor's secret to Alex

after I promised to never share it with anyone. Not only
have I broken another vow, but I may also have put Alex
in great danger. I regret that I did not find the courage
to do more for Joshua. He is a good man and deserved
better. I regret my failure to start a real Lutheran church
in Silver City with a large congregation. If you want to
know the truth, I regret having gone into the clergy in the
first place. The foolishness of this decision is now clear to
me. I am ashamed to have ever thought myself worthy to
do God's work. When you get right down to it, I am not
really much different from Csongor. The only difference
is, well, I don't really know what the difference is. That's
the honest truth of it. And I must write of this, because it is
the truth: I regret how I may feel after I kill Csongor and
ask God's forgiveness now as I write in this diary because
it may be too late to ask later.

Manfred set the pencil down and stood. He clasped his hands behind
his head and stretched his shoulders back. He considered firing up the
potbelly stove and making a fresh pot of coffee, but then decided it was
already too warm in the small cabin. He walked over to the potbelly
stove and poured himself a cup of tepid coffee leftover from breakfast.
When he returned to the chair, he sharpened the pencil and threw back a
large swallow of the pungent brew. He grimaced at the taste, then threw
back another large gulp. He picked up the pencil, rolled it back and forth
between thumb and finger, and licked the tip. After pondering for a good
minute what he should write next, he adjusted the wick on the kerosene
lamp and started a new paragraph.

Alexandra has been such a blessing to me. I think I fell
in love the first time I saw her in Chicago, when I watched
her running along the train platform leaping over things. I
know I should be seeking out a common woman of simple
virtues, but I am drawn to her mysterious habits in ways
I cannot describe with simple words. It is a shame I shall
never get to know her better. But I can still express my deep

love for her by praying that she finds a good husband who will cherish her and take care of her. Someone who has not condemned himself with a sinful nature and impure thoughts. Someone who keeps his promises. Someone who does not put her in danger by asking her to deliver silly letters after he is dead.

On the other hand, there have been many good things about Silver City. Alex for one. William Sommercamp and his silly pickle barrel. Roshan and Nadia. Meals with Father Nero Aguilar at the War Eagle Hotel. And yes, Csongor too, at least before he told me of his part in that horrible massacre. I would find it hard to believe such evil is possible if it were not for my own frailties. And the way he spoke of it, calm and without any emotion. It chills me to the bone to think about it. I did not suspect it. I would not have asked him to defend Joshua if I had even thought it possible. Another regret to add to the list. Nothing to do about it now. It is fortunate that Conrad delivered the letter. He is odd to be sure, but always keeps his word. If the town had hanged Joshua? I can barely think of it.

Manfred finished the last of the lukewarm coffee and slumped back in the chair. He recognized that his writing had begun to ramble, but he had only filled the top half of the last page and he thought he should end with something a little more eloquent. He tapped the pencil against his forehead and reflected. He checked his pocket watch. Almost ten. Getting late, but still time for a little dinner. What to eat? Not really hungry, but should eat something. There's some bread left. A little jam. Maybe a potato or two. He stood and walked over to the potbelly stove and poured the remaining coffee into his cup. When the cat heard him, it jumped off the bed and strolled to the door. Manfred opened the door to let the cat out. "Good hunting, my friend. I don't know if I'll be here in the morning to let you in. I'm afraid you might have to fend for yourself when this night is over." After the cat scurried away, he closed the door and returned to the table. He sharpened and licked the pencil one last time.

And now I conclude with these final words on this third day of June in the year 1872. Although I am filled with regret and may not survive the night, in many ways I have lived a good life and I thank God for my time on this earth. I am thankful for my time with Alex. She has been a treasure to me. I am thankful to have called Csongor my friend, for we are all sinners. I am thankful for the many good people I have met in Silver City. I am thankful the man once my bitter enemy on the gory fields of Shiloh and now friend chose to save Joshua Hotah from certain death. And as for myself, as it says in Romans 1:32, "Who knowing the judgment of God, that they which commit such things are worthy of death, not only do the same, but have pleasure in them that do them." Bless you who read these humble words written by a pitiful sinner. My only hope after tonight is the grace of God.

Manfred laid the pencil down and gradually closed the diary. He thought about putting the diary back on the shelf above the bed, but decided it would be easier for Alexandra to find it if he left it on the table. After waiting quite a while, he pushed himself away from the table, stood, and shuffled to the side of the bed. He fell to his knees and seized a leather scabbard and a box of cartridges from beneath the bed. He pushed himself up, pulled out the Spencer Repeating Carbine, and tossed the scabbard on the bed. He opened the box of cartridges and positioned it on the table, next to the diary. He twisted the rectangular metal plate at the back of the stock, pulled the tube magazine out, and loaded it with seven .56-50 caliber black powder cartridges. He pushed the tube into the stock and rotated the rectangular plate to lock it in place. After laying the carbine on the table, he snatched his coat from the back of the chair and shoved his arms into the rumpled sleeves. He picked up the weapon and rested the barrel on his shoulder.

Manfred brooded. Should really eat something, but my appetite's completely gone. Actually, feeling a little sick. Some target practice might be a good idea. Make sure I remember how to shoot. Pull the lever, cock the hammer, pull the trigger. Don't forget to cock the hammer. Pull the lever before I go inside the livery. Maybe eat something after target practice. How many shots? Only need one. No more than two. Or three. Three at most. Four shots for target practice and three for later. That should do it. Pull the lever, cock the hammer, fire. Don't forget. Pretty late to be shooting off a rifle. Might wake up a few. Shots all the time around here. Shots at night all the time. No one will know the difference. Shouldn't need more than one, but....

Manfred picked up his watch. Almost eleven. He slid the watch into an inside coat pocket. He turned a full circle and inventoried the meager contents of his small cabin: bed, table, chair, potbelly stove, some books, plate, eating utensils, coffee pot, skillet, two metal cups, rusty shovel, a broom (mostly used on the cat), a pair of boots, kerosene lamp, all of his worldly possessions. Not much of a legacy to leave behind. Not much at all.

The approaching storm's first lightning sizzled to the ground a few miles away; seconds later thunder crackled off the mountains. Manfred did not notice the thunder as he walked away from the cabin with the fingers of one hand curled beneath the bale of the kerosene lamp and fingers of the other squeezed tightly around the trigger guard of the carbine. The cat followed him a short distance before veering sharply toward the creek.

Chapter Twenty-One

Manfred discovers the truth
June 3, 1872

The downpour commenced after the first shot. Manfred held the rain-slicked stock of the Spencer Repeating Carbine against cheek and shoulder and prepared to fire the last practice round. Before he squeezed the trigger, a seething gust of wind extinguished the lantern flame and plunged the fencepost into gloom. Manfred held his position—and waited. Rain streamed down his back and pelted his face. Another flash of lightning. The fencepost blazed into clear view and Manfred squeezed the trigger. A ragged chunk of splintered wood exploded into the air. The electrified radiance vanished into darkness. Manfred stumbled twelve paces to the fencepost and leaned the carbine against a gnarled rail. Squatting down and turning his back to the storm, he fished a box of matches from inside his sodden coat. The wick ignited on the fourth match. He stood and held the lantern close to the top of the shredded fencepost. Two out of four. And the two misses were likely close. Not too bad, really. Better than he had expected after the passing of this many years. Surprised to hit the darn thing at all, if the truth be known. Another flash of lightning. Manfred Herrmann lowered the lantern and lifted the carbine to his shoulder. He pivoted smartly heel and toe in the soggy ground and resumed the long hike to town.

Csongor Toth shoved two bales of hay into place about seven feet apart and positioned the lantern on the floor midway between. As was his custom, Hector Faure remained hidden in the shadows and refused to assist with the arduous task. Csongor sat on one of the bales, crossed his ankles near the glowing lamp, and fanned his face with his hand. His words dripping with sarcasm, he addressed Monsieur Faure without facing him. "Very thoughtful of you to help. The sweat has now soaked completely through my clean shirt. Since my friend should arrive only minutes from now, I have no time to change. Have you nothing to say for yourself?"

Hector Faure reminded Csongor of his primary role as an advisor on complex intellectual matters, and emphasized that it was not his job to push dusty bales of hay around the urine-soaked floor of a filthy livery stable. When he had finished his remarks, he tapped his cane three times on the urine-soaked floor.

Csongor stared into the flame of the lantern. "What you say may be true, yet I still find your reluctance to lift a finger quite annoying. Would that we all enjoyed the luxury of avoiding physical labor whenever it suited us."

Hector Faure remarked brusquely that many men, and even a few women, would likely appreciate his counsel if Csongor did not find the arrangement satisfactory. He told Csongor to say the word, and he would immediately offer his services to a more appreciative client.

Csongor presented the palm of his hand to the lantern. "No, no, no. Of course not, my esteemed advisor on complex intellectual matters. I did not mean to imply that you should leave. But I must ask: am I not allowed to speak frankly from time to time? Must you take offense at such a small complaint?"

Indifferent, Monsieur Faure tapped the cane once and shrugged.

A dark rider braved the storm. Turbulent skies glowered above the mountaintops. Rivulets of icy water streamed off the curled brim of the dark rider's hat and splashed across his back before dribbling down the saddle. Lightning pulsed raggedly behind angry clouds, briefly illuminating the trail with brilliant flashes. Ominous waves of rumbling thunder rolled down the valley and broke against the craggy slopes. The dark rider lowered his chin, pulled the brim of his hat down, and gently touched spurs against the horse's loins. The shifting darkness prevented him from clearly seeing the path ahead, but the horse had not yet faltered and appeared to know the way. The dark rider pushed down on the stirrups and shifted in the saddle, and the intrepid steed advanced.

Frenzied currents of chilly air extinguished the lantern a third time. Manfred remembered that he had already used the last match. He checked the empty matchbox anyway to allow the possibility of a miracle. Finding no miracle, he cradled the carbine across his soggy forearm and dumped the useless device next to the glistening roots of an oak tree. When he straightened up and rubbed his eyes, he spotted a glowing window some distance ahead. As his vision adjusted to the darkness, he narrowed his view and noticed a few more scattered lights. To his right he could barely hear the churning waters of Jordan Creek. Strangely comforted by the sound, he swung the carbine to his shoulder and cautiously stepped off. After a few muddy strides he thought about something he had written in the diary—on the next-to-last page—the diary which he had conveniently placed on the small table for anyone to find. Fortunately, he had made the entry in pencil and could still erase it. He nearly turned to walk back to the cabin, but decided not to because of the time. Instead, he marched ahead toward the lighted windows. He could expunge the thoughtless sentence later, that is, if he survived the night.

Although he could not discern the man's countenance in the darkness, Csongor stood and faced Hector Faure. "Why should I have any idea of Manfred's intentions? He asked me to meet him here at midnight. Nothing more, nothing less."

Monsieur Faure advised Csongor of his apparent naiveté. When he had concluded his unpleasant lecture, he suggested an ominous possibility.

Csongor scoffed, "Don't be ridiculous. Manfred Herrmann is a man of the cloth. He is not allowed to even consider such things."

Monsieur Faure listened politely, then repeated his accusation of gullibility, this time using blunter words.

Csongor sniffed and waved the indictment off with a flick of his hand. "I must protest your unsubstantiated allegation. This time you have surely miscalculated. There is no possibility—"

Monsieur Faure interrupted to ask a follow-up question.

Csongor patted the right side of his coat. "You, of all people, should know I'm armed. I have my favorite pistol hidden away here. It is foolish of you to think I would go anywhere without affording myself a means of protection. One cannot be too careful these days, especially in a town like Silver City."

Hector Faure nodded approvingly before dissolving into the shadows.

Mercifully, even though a few random lightning strikes persisted, the intensity of both the rain and wind began to weaken. The dark rider released his hand from the brim of his hat. He reached beneath his chin and loosened the hat's leather drawstring. His courageous horse trudged ahead through muddy puddles and the dark rider soon crossed over the bridge above Jordan Creek north of town. The dark rider dawdled next to a hay storage building, just south of the bridge, and observed the flickering lights of the Idaho Hotel off to the left. Should have left earlier. Slowed down by the storm. *What's the plan?* There is no plan, because I don't really know what I'm getting into. *If there's no plan, then what's the point?* I'm not sure of that either. Well, that's not really true. There is a point, I'd just rather not talk about it right now. *If you know the point, then surely it is possible to make a plan. You can't go into the livery without a plan. To do so is pure insanity.* Maybe, but that is exactly what I plan to do. *Then, you do have a plan!* I already told you I don't have a plan. *But you just said*—shut up and ride. Plan or no plan, because of my indecision it may already be too late.

Manfred arrived at the front of the two-story livery stable where Csongor had made his earlier confession. As before, someone had already pulled the large sliding door open a few feet. When he peered through the narrow slit, he could discern a warm glow at the far end of the narrow building. He shuffled through the opening; muddy water squeezed from his shoes. As he walked toward the distant light, he grasped the Spencer Repeating Carbine in his right hand and used his left to operate the lever beneath the trigger. After he had loaded a fresh round, he pressed the butt against his right shoulder and raised the barrel midway with his left hand. His finger twitched when it touched the trigger. His pace slowed when he neared the two bales of hay and the glowing kerosene lantern. He stopped about ten strides from the lamp. His dilated eyes searched for Csongor Toth, but did not find him. The metallic click of a pistol hammer issued from the shadows to his left. Manfred turned and raised the carbine to his cheek. Then he remembered something rather important: he had forgotten to cock the hammer.

The dark rider dismounted around the side of the livery stable and tied off the reins to the remnants of a weathered fence. He walked to the front. Before entering the building, he reached back and retrieved a 12-gauge-sawed-off-pistol-grip-double-barreled shotgun secured between his shoulders in a quick-release harness. He pulled back the hammers of both barrels until they locked into place before proceeding through the narrow opening.

Csongor Toth appeared from the shadows with a small caliber pistol raised in his left hand, the polished sights aligned with the center of Manfred's chest. He walked forward and stopped about five yards from the nearest bale. "I'm surprised to see you have chosen to bring a weapon to our little meeting. But then, one might argue, who am I to criticize such behavior? As you can plainly see, I have done the same."

"I will not lie to you, Csongor. I have come here to kill you." After cocking the hammer, Manfred acquired Csongor's heart.

Csongor took one more step. "How droll. I had foolishly imagined that you arranged this meeting as an opportunity to proffer your own confession."

Sweat dribbled from Manfred's trigger hand. "No. Although the thought has occurred to me, I'm not sure you're the right person to hear it."

"Oh dear. Then what are we to do now?"

Manfred's finger quivered against the trigger. "I told you what I came to do. Have no doubt that I intend to do it."

Csongor queried politely, "I have never doubted you, my friend, but what if I should decide to kill you first?"

Manfred's aiming eye twitched. "I'll just have to take that chance." His eye twitched again. "But I don't think you will."

Csongor opened his mouth to speak, but the sound of chinking spurs distracted him. He probed the blackness to Manfred's side. "Pray tell, what is this? Has the cavalry arrived to save the day once again?"

Manfred did not move or take his sights off Csongor's heart. "I have no idea who it is. No one else knew about this meeting."

The chinking spurs continued their approach until the dark rider appeared in the light of the lantern. The dark rider raised the shotgun and pointed the barrels at Csongor.

Csongor swung the pistol smoothly to the right and took aim on Conrad Airingsail. "Mister Airingsail. What a disagreeable surprise to find you here tonight. And just when I thought Manfred and I were coming to an understanding."

Conrad Airingsail began to squeeze the triggers to fire both barrels into Csongor's belly but, suddenly overcome by indecision, jerked his finger away.

Csongor detected the movement of Conrad's hand and fired his pistol. The bullet ripped into Conrad's right shoulder and wedged against a bone. Conrad staggered back, then lowered the shotgun and dropped it to the floor. He collapsed to his knees and flopped forward. Blood spread across the filthy floor.

Manfred lowered the carbine and shouted, "What have you done?"

Csongor slid the pistol into his shoulder holster and quipped, "Just defending myself from an obvious madman. I've always thought Conrad Airingsail was an odd duck, and now he's proven it."

Manfred pitched the carbine to the ground and rushed to Conrad's side. He rolled Conrad over to his back, then yelled at Csongor, "Don't just stand there like a fool, help me get him up."

Csongor strolled over and examined the wound in Conrad's shoulder. "He is definitely bleeding. What would you like me to do?"

Manfred barked, "We have to get him to the doctor before he bleeds to death. Help me get him up on my shoulder."

Csongor kneeled down. "If you wish." He removed Conrad's hat and lowered the bandana. When the light flashed across Conrad's face, Csongor hissed, "Good heavens, what *have* I done?"

Manfred stared down into the passive face. "Oh my! You have just shot Alexandra Smyth! That's what you've done."

Csongor stammered, "It can't be. How could…if I had known…I would not…not have pulled the trigger. You must believe me."

With renewed strength, Manfred hoisted Alexandra up and shifted her limp body over his shoulder. "Too late to worry about it now. Help me get her to the doctor."

Csongor stroked Alexandra's damp hair. "If only I had known it was sweet Alexandra, I would have lowered my pistol and gladly accepted my fate."

Guinevere Dupree opened the door of her small clinic and discovered Manfred Herrmann with a small man slung over his shoulder and Csongor Toth looking like he had seen a ghost. She held up a small glass oil lamp. "What's this about, gentlemen? It's after midnight."

Csongor declared, "Alexandra Smythe has been shot. She urgently needs your help."

Manfred pushed through the door and forced Guinevere to step aside. "She's lost a lot of blood. We don't have time to explain how it happened. Tell me what to do."

Guinevere scurried across the small room and quickly opened the door at the back. "Set her down on the table. I have to stop the bleeding first. Then I'll try to remove the bullet."

Manfred carried Alexandra into the room. Csongor followed behind, and together the two men lowered her onto the table.

Guinevere entered the room and set the glass lamp on a small side table. "I'll have to remove some of her clothing. I want both of you to wait outside."

Stunned by the calamity they had jointly caused, neither man moved.

When Guinevere rested her fists on her hips and glared at them, Manfred offered, "We'll wait outside. Please let us know if we can do anything to help."

Csongor added, "Yes, please do not hesitate to ask. I would never forgive myself if precious Gordania were to die at my own hand."

Guinevere poured water into a porcelain basin and began washing her hands. "I won't need any help. Now, the both of you get out. I have work to do."

The two men nodded and retreated from the clinic. They blundered through the front door of the building and waited outside beneath the shelter of the canopy. A light drizzle proclaimed the death of the storm. After the passage of several awkward minutes, Manfred finally said, "I have a question to ask you, Csongor."

Csongor focused on a jittering reflection of the moon in a wide puddle near the middle of the street. "Ask anything you wish, my friend. I promise that I shall do my best to provide the answer."

Manfred leaned against one of the wood posts supporting the canopy and crossed his arms. "Why did you call her … *precious Gordania?*"

EPILOGUE

Mendota, Illinois
May 1882

A crisp breath of springtime pulsed through the open window and fluttered the wispy linen curtains. Rising grandly from the rich land beyond the window, an ancient black walnut tree shimmered in the radiance of the fading afternoon. A Northern Flicker hopped along the verdant ground searching for ants and beetles, then ascended vertically with heavy wing flashes to an outstretched branch of the black walnut, announcing its presence with a loud rolling rattle. An errant dog barked far away. The muffled voices of students walking across the green drifted through the window and—

"Reverend Herrmann?"

Manfred Herrmann shifted his gaze from the open window to the young man sitting stiffly on the other side of his desk. "Yes Matthew. What is it?"

Matthew politely answered, "I was asking you about California, but you appeared to be deep in thought."

"I apologize, Matthew. I was thinking of another place...another time. What was the question you were asking? I promise to pay attention this time."

"I was asking what you thought of San Francisco. I've heard it's in desperate need of a Lutheran mission."

Manfred's thoughts drifted briefly to Silver City. "I'm sure it is. Probably a pretty wild place, especially these days. Think you're up to the challenge?

You do know the Catholics are already there. They established the first mission in 1776. A fellow named Father Serra, if I remember correctly."

Matthew answered confidently, "I know about Father Serra and the Catholics. And yes, I believe I'm up to the challenge."

Manfred admired the young man's sangfroid. "I believe you're up to the challenge too. I think San Francisco would be an excellent choice for a man of your temperament. I may even have a few contacts to suggest, to make the trip a little more interesting. Now, if you don't mind, I have to meet my wife and daughter in a few minutes. We can talk more about it tomorrow, if you wish." He recalled his own youthful self-assurance ten long years ago.

Matthew stood. "I would like that. I'll drop by again tomorrow afternoon." He shoved the chair to its original position and walked from the small office in silence.

Manfred Herrmann checked his pocket watch. He arranged a few papers on his desk, closed the window, and retired from the office without locking the door. After chatting briefly with a student in the hallway and another near the front doors, he arrived beneath the ancient black walnut a few minutes early. He looked out over the sprawling lawn. A slender woman and a small girl approached. The woman wore a sunny white dress with a modest neckline. The brim of her hat drooped provocatively above her lovely auburn hair (braided in a loose ponytail that hung below her waist). Manfred waved and shouted, "Gordania, I'm over here."

The little girl broke into a full sprint toward her beloved father. Gordania Herrmann began to chase after her daughter, but quickly gave up and admonished, "Muireall Anne! Walk!" She smiled and asked, "How many times have I told you not to run in your Sunday dress?"

Excerpt from A Concise History of the West
by Muireall Anne Ravenscroft
Epilogue: The End of an Era

Several notable historians warned me before I began this book that the idea of writing a meaningful one-volume history of the American West was, if not presumptuous, almost certainly a fool's errand. Although I have com-

pleted this concise accounting of the west as I originally intended — more or less — I did not ignore or take
this sage advice lightly. Fully aware of the pitfalls of
my own arrogance, I worked diligently throughout my research and writing to include events, people, and facts
that I felt were particularly important to tell the true
story of the American West in a straightforward manner
that did not needlessly embellish or fall short of reasonable completeness. Nonetheless, to condense such a
vast and complex history into a single volume did require countless decisions about what to include and what
to leave for another time. But I cannot end this effort,
which has consumed so much of my time during the last
five years, without offering some final thoughts concern-
ing the end of this fascinating era — if it can be argued that it has ended at all. To understand the end of
anything, one must appreciate the key events preceding
the end. The starting point and particular events are up
to the capriciousness of the historian: anyone who ar-
gues differently is simply uninformed. With this assertion in mind, I have chosen to begin this chronology in
1803, and to include an abridged sequence of events of
my choosing to support my conclusions. If you have read
this book thoughtfully, the following chronology will
serve merely as a reminder. If you have not, then you
may find new material here that deserves further study.

   (1803) One of President Thomas Jefferson's greatest
achievements, the Louisiana Purchase adds over 828,000
square miles of former French territory to the United
States, doubling the size of the country at the stroke
of a pen. A few weeks after this purchase, and at the
urging of Thomas Jefferson, Congress appropriates $2,500
to fund the exploration of the western wilderness all
the way to the Pacific Ocean. Jefferson selects 28-year-
old Army Captain Meriwether Lewis to lead the expedition, and he in turn selects former Army associate

William Clark, then 32, to co-lead. The expedition of approximately 40 men sets out on May 14, 1804, and does not complete the 8,000-mile roundtrip until September 23, 1806.

(1820) Congress passes the Missouri Compromise, which admits Missouri as a slave state and Maine as a free state. This action maintains the balance of free and slave states at 12 each. The law includes a provision drawing an unseen east-west line across the former Louisiana Territory to establish a boundary between free and slave regions. The boundary is not abolished until passage of the Nebraska-Kansas Act of 1854.

(1836) On February 24th, about five months after the beginning of the Texas Revolution, Mexican forces (under the leadership of General Santa Anna) lay siege to the Alamo near San Antonio. Over the next 13 days the Texans holding the Alamo fight heroically until overwhelmed in a final assault on March 6th. Approximately 180 Texans and between 400 and 600 Mexican soldiers are killed during the siege. Among the dead are Jim Bowie, Davy Crocket, and William Travis.

(1842) The first organized wagon train successfully traverses the Oregon Trail. Led by Elijah White, approximately half of the more than 100 pioneers who complete the trip settle in Oregon, while the rest travel south to California.

(1847) On July 24th, Brigham Young and his exhausted band of Mormons arrive in Utah's Great Salt Lake Valley. By the end of the year, nearly 2,000 Mormons settle in the valley.

(1849) The non-native population of California increases from around 20,000 to an estimated 100,000 people after gold is discovered at Sutter's Mill the previous year. These gold seekers are dubbed the "49ers."

(1854) The Gadsden Purchase is finalized, in which the United States agrees to pay Mexico $10,000,000 for a

29,670 square-mile portion of Mexico that later becomes part of Arizona and New Mexico.

(1860) In April, the Pony Express begins using horse-and-rider relay teams to carry mail between St. Joseph, Missouri and Sacramento, California — an approximately 2,000-mile route. The company's best time is achieved in March 1861 when riders transport a copy of Abraham Lincoln's inaugural address from Nebraska to California in 7 days and 17 hours. However, after significant financial losses, the company folds in October 1861.

(1861) Early in the morning of Friday, April 12th, Confederate batteries open fire on Fort Sumter in the middle of Charleston Harbor, thus commencing the Civil War. Major Andersen, commander of the fort, surrenders to the Confederates on Saturday, April 13th.

(1864) Under the direction of General James H. Carleton, Kit Carson leads hundreds of men into Canyon De Chelly to destroy crops, seize livestock and food caches, and burn down homes. Nearly 3,000 Navajos surrender, thus ending pacification efforts that began in the spring of 1863. After incarceration at Forts Canby and Wingate, over 2,000 Navajos begin the infamous "Long Walk" across New Mexico to Fort Sumner, 165 miles southeast of Santa Fe.

(1865) On April 9th, General Robert E. Lee and the Army of Northern Virginia surrender at the McLean House in the village of Appomattox Courthouse, Virginia, thus ending the Civil War.

(1866) Following service with "Bloody" Bill Anderson's guerilla band and Quantrill's Raiders, respectively, Jesse and Frank James (along with eight other men) begin their outlaw careers by robbing a bank in Liberty, Missouri. Eventually the gang will rob banks from Iowa to Alabama and Texas. The gang will begin robbing trains in 1873.

(1869) On May 10th at Promontory Summit, Utah, the final spike is driven to join the Central Pacific (west) and Union Pacific (east) rail lines, thus completing the Transcontinental Railroad that began construction in 1863.

(1876) After working as a part-time policeman in Wichita, Kansas, Wyatt Earp moves west to Dodge City in the spring and is offered the job of Chief Deputy Marshal by the mayor. On June 25 and 26, a battalion of the U.S. Army's 7th Cavalry, led by Lt. Colonel George A. Custer, confronts thousands of Lakota Sioux and Cheyanne warriors — led by Sioux Chiefs Sitting Bull and Crazy Horse — at the Little Bighorn River in the Montana Territory. All 263 soldiers are lost in the battle, which has come to be known as "Custer's Last Stand."

(1878) Born William Henry McCarty in the slums of New York City in 1859, Billy the Kid begins to acquire a reputation as a ruthless killer during the Lincoln County War in the New Mexico Territory.

(1881) On the night of July 14th, Sheriff Pat Garret shoots and kills Billy the Kid at the abandoned Fort Sumner, about 140 miles west of Lincoln, New Mexico Territory. On July 19th, Sioux Chief Sitting Bull returns from Canada and surrenders to U.S. forces. He is held as a prisoner of war at Fort Randall, South Dakota Territory. On the afternoon of October 25th in Tombstone, Arizona, Wyatt Earp, his brothers Morgan and Virgil, and Doc Holiday confront five members of the Clanton-McLaury gang in a vacant lot behind the OK Corral. Although it is unclear who fired the first shot, when the 30-second gunfight has finished the two McLaury brothers and Billy Clanton are dead, and Morgan and Virgil Earp and Doc Holiday are each wounded. Wyatt Earp escapes the event without a scratch.

(1882) On the morning of April 3rd, Jesse James is shot in the back of the head (while standing on a chair to clean a dusty picture on the wall of his home in St. Joseph, Missouri) by Robert Ford. Born Phoebe Ann Moses in Ohio in 1860, Annie Oakley begins her professional career as a trick shooter.

(1883) In September, Theodore Roosevelt travels to the North Dakota Badlands to hunt Buffalo. At the end of the 15-day hunt, he buys the Chimney Butte Ranch, effectively entering the cattle business.

(1886) After more than a decade of guerrilla warfare, the Apache leader Geronimo surrenders to the U.S. Army on September 4th in Skeleton Canyon, Arizona. He is imprisoned at Fort Pickens in Florida, along with nearly 400 of his followers.

(1889) Born Robert Leroy Parker in 1866 in Beaver, Utah — and the oldest of 13 children in a poor Mormon family — Butch Cassidy robs his first bank, the San Miguel Valley Bank in Telluride, Colorado. He and his three cowboy companions escape with more than $20,000.

(1890) Because of concerns over the growing Ghost Dance movement, Chief Sitting Bull is seized by Lakota police at Standing Rock Reservation on December 15th. He is killed when his warriors attempt to rescue him. On December 29th, soldiers of the 7th Cavalry massacre over 150 Lakota Sioux warriors, women, and children near Wounded Knee Creek in South Dakota. Twenty-five soldiers also die in the action. This event is generally considered to mark the official end of the long and bloody war between the United States and the Plains Indians.

(1896) Butch Cassidy recruits Harry Longabaugh, aka The Sundance Kid, to join his newly formed gang: The Wild Bunch. During the ensuing years the Wild Bunch will rob banks and trains in South Dakota, New Mexico, Nevada, and Wyoming, igniting a massive manhunt by many famous lawmen of the day.

I will conclude my summary here, because many historians, myself included, would argue that the era under consideration ended at Wounded Knee in 1890. Other scholars might assert that the era is simply in a state of rapid decline, because Butch Cassidy and the Sundance Kid are purportedly still alive and still robbing banks and trains in South America. However, even if this assertion were true — which is difficult to verify based on my review of recent newspaper articles — I would contend that they are certainly no longer consequential to the story of the American West. But there is another issue in play, something far more important than the selection of an artificial date. Even though one can make a compelling argument that one era ended and another began in 1890, one cannot deny that the events preceding the end will live on in the American spirit and will therefore always shape the American character. This then, is the primary point of my analysis: the end of an era may or may not have officially occurred in 1890, but the spirit of that era will forever define the American spirit, and therefor forever temper America's destiny.

Muireall Anne Ravenscroft
San Luis Obispo, 1907

Azure eyes searching the distant sun-dappled hills above the polished rim of a porcelain cup, Muireall Anne Ravenscroft sipped green tea. She set the cup on the wide arm of her Adirondack chair, pulled her favorite cardigan snugly around her neck to fend off the chill of an otherwise pleasant November morning, and gazed wistfully at puffy cumulus clouds floating somewhere in the distance above the comforting waves of the Pacific Ocean.

John Ravenscroft, who had chosen to drink coffee instead of tea on this tranquil morning, rested the cup on his knee. "What's next, now that the book is in the hands of the publisher? Is there another history book on the horizon?"

Muireall extended her arms and yawned without covering her mouth. "There is still work to do on the current book. The publisher will create a galley and assign an editor who has never written a book. The editor will suggest numerous changes, many of which I shall find objectionable. This will go on for months until the final galley is approved and printing begins." A gray squirrel perched in a tree near the front of the veranda chirped hoarsely.

John sipped some coffee and warmed his hands on the cup. "It sounds very much like the design process. I spend weeks creating a building design based on the client's program and budget. I meet with the client, who has never designed anything, and they immediately want to change things that violate their own program or that they cannot afford or both. When I object—gently and professionally, of course—they often grab a pencil and try to draw what they are thinking of, even though they do not know how to draw. I explain why what they just drew will not work, but usually agree to go back to the office and try to make it work. Sometimes I win and sometimes I don't. I believe it's called *compromise*."

Muireall released the cardigan and stretched her shoulders back. "I didn't mean to imply that an editor does not know anything about writing in the same manner that your client may not know anything about design. But the act of actually finishing and then publishing a book is an accomplishment very few achieve. I just find the process is sometimes…what's the word I'm looking for?"

"Ridiculous?"

"No, that's not even close."

"Obnoxious?"

"That's even less close."

"Disgusting? Aggravating? Preposterous?"

"That's it! Presumptuous. I don't mind a good proofreading by an accomplished editor, but I find it presumptuous when they try to rewrite my prose in their own style for no other purpose than to put their hand on the book."

The squirrel suddenly appeared on the veranda railing. Spotting the squirrel, John said, "That darn squirrel is getting more…*presumptuous* every day. Next he'll be trying to get into the house and help himself to our pantry." John clapped and the squirrel darted along the railing and vanished behind the downspout. "I see your point, but since the publisher is paying you for your book, I suppose they have some rights to edit the book as they see fit."

"Historical fiction. Now that I've done all of this research, I'm thinking of writing a novel based on the American West. Maybe I'll even try to write a trilogy, although such an endeavor would likely require a crushing amount of work. Of course, it would be historically authentic in every way possible. I might even try to work some of my parents' more exotic experiences into the storyline. It could certainly add a dash of color."

"Are you thinking of Csongor Toth?"

"Among others."

"Wouldn't this be quite a departure from nonfiction? From what I've read, the problem with fiction is that it has to be believable."

"I understand, but I think I'm up to the task."

"Don't misinterpret my words. I have no doubt you are up to the task. No doubt whatsoever. And where, might I ask, would you start this fictional story?"

Muireall smiled nostalgically. "That's easy. I would start at the beginning."

THE END

CHAPTER NOTES

CHAPTER ONE

1. Because of name recognition (and because my heritage is half-German), I initially wrote that Csongor had purchased Zeiss binoculars, but after further research discovered that Carl Zeiss did not manufacture binoculars until the 1890s. More precisely, the Carl Zeiss Company first sold high-performance Porro prism binoculars in 1894. However, the G. & S. Merz Company of Munich manufactured twin-telescope binoculars as early as 1860. These rather longish (some models up to 750 mm in length with the sunshades extended) binoculars were sold with either aluminum or brass tubes, and incorporated both a central focus knob and a central hinge to allow adjustment of interpupillary spacing similar to modern binoculars. The magnifying power of these early devices ranged from 5X to 20X, and they presented the advantage of a wider field of view than did telescopes. Although a technological tour du force of the times, the manufacture of twin-telescope binoculars ended abruptly with the advent of modern prism binoculars in the 1890s. (A Plenary Paper by John E. Greivenkamp and David L. Steed, *The History of Telescopes and Binoculars: An Engineering Perspective,* College of Optical Sciences, University of Arizona)

2. I used the following primary Internet resources to write Muireall Anne Ravenscroft's excerpt in Chapter 1 titled *Lawmen, Judges, and Vigilantes*:

    www.legendsofamerica.com, article by Kathy Weiser titled *Big Dave Updyke - Crooked Sheriff of Ada County, Idaho,* www.desertusa.com, article by Bob Katz titled *The Law West of the Pecos: Judge Roy Bean*,

www.legendsofamerica.com, article by Kathy Weiser titled *The Fierce Missouri Bald Knobbers*,

www.nps.gov/fosm/historyculture/judge-parker

CHAPTER TWO

1. The 1903 Sanborn Map Company map of Silver City (referenced earlier) illustrates a two-story county courthouse across the street and southeast from the saloon on the corner of Avalanche and Washington. The floor plan for the building indicates two ground-floor offices facing the street with a jail in the back, and courtrooms (plural) on the second floor. The plan does not show the layout of jail cells. I have therefore made assumptions based on my knowledge of other facilities of the era. The second-floor courtroom will come into play in later chapters. In Chapter 12 of *Gold Town to Ghost Town*, Julia Conway Welch describes the structure as the only well-constructed building in town and notes that the cut stone arches gave the facade the appearance of a "Roman Forum of the West." She does not say when the building was first constructed, but indicates that it housed various businesses on the ground floor and a miners' meeting hall on the second prior to its conversion to the county courthouse in 1884. Before this date the courthouse was located across Jordan Creek on the east side of town. She adds that an exterior stair provided the only access to the courtroom (singular). In the pamphlet *Interesting Buildings in Silver City, Idaho*, Helen Nettleton refers to the building as the Granite Block, and explains that a one-story stone building was built in 1868 and that it housed several businesses at different times including a saloon, post office, two general stores, and a drug store. The second story was completed in 1873 and provided space for miners' meetings, stage plays, and general gatherings. She confirms that the original courthouse burned in 1884, and remarks that the county records were moved to the second floor of the Granite Block and the District Court began using the same space for a courtroom (singular). She writes that the county also purchased the first floor for use by the sheriff and county recorder (the county records were moved to a vault on the first floor), but she does not mention a

date. Although the basic two-story structure existed in 1873, I have fictionalized use of this building as the county courthouse housing the sheriff's office, jail, and a courtroom earlier by 12 years. In 1935 the county seat moved to Murphy. The county sold the building in the 1940s and major portions were demolished and the materials salvaged for use elsewhere. Today only the stone arches, the door to the vault, and a remnant of the exterior wood stair have survived.

CHAPTER THREE

1. In 1872 the majority of Americans would have played *American Four-Pocket Billiards*. This game required a 12-foot long table with four pockets and four balls (two white and two red). The rules of the game were similar to English Billiards (the leading game in Great Britain from around 1770 through the 1920s), with points scored by pocketing balls, scratching the white cue ball, or by achieving caroms off two or three balls. By the late 1870s two new games had surpassed American Four-Pocket Billiards in popularity: *Straight Rail*, played with three balls on a pocketless table and the ancestor of all carom games; and *American Fifteen-Ball Pool*, the precursor of modern pocket billiards. The 1903 Sanborn Map Company map of Silver City shows that the Idaho Hotel maintained a billiards room and a dining room on the ground floor, both directly accessible from the back of the main lobby. A narrow stairway to the second floor separated the two rooms. (www.thebilliardshop.com/history-of-pool-and-billiards)

CHAPTER FOUR

1. According to the *War Eagle Mountain Field Guide: Historical and Mining Road Log* by Wilma Lewis Statham with H.R. 'Rusty' Statham and William P. Statham (Owyhee County Historical Society, Revised Edition, July 2003), the first major period of mining on War Eagle Mountain spanned the years 1863 to 1875. The discovery and development of placer mines at Jordan Creek, Ruby City, Blue Gulch, Purdy Gulch, as well as other areas, and the initial discovery of several load claims on the slopes of War Eagle Mountain, occurred from 1863 to 1865. Individual prospectors typically exploited these early gold and silver veins, but because of limited financial resources they

usually mined only the more accessible surface deposits. The discovery and initial development of the major lode claims on War Eagle Mountain including Oro Fino, Poorman, Ida Elmore, Golden Chariot, Minnesota, Mahogany, and the Morning Star in Silver City, had occurred by 1866. During the latter years of this period, from the late 1860s to 1875, the cost of mining on War Eagle Mountain remained relatively constant at $40 to $60 per ton of ore, but the value of the ore decreased as the depth of the mines increased, reducing potential profit. To illustrate this trend, the value of ore per ton at the Oro Fino Mine ranged from $160 at the surface level to $45 at the lowest level. In 1875 the financial collapse of the Bank of California and the failure of the San Francisco Stock Exchange Board forced the mines on War Eagle Mountain to either dramatically reduce operations or close entirely. Nonetheless, it is estimated that the total value of gold and silver produced during this first mining period was approximately $12,400,000. Fifteen years later, in 1890, a new period of profitable mining and great prosperity commenced with the discovery of rich veins on Florida and DeLamar mountains.

Chapter Five

1. Reserved.

Chapter Six

1. Reserved.

Chapter Seven

1. Reserved.

Chapter Eight

1. As I explained in my notes to Chapter Two, the 1903 Sanborn Map Company map of Silver City illustrates the ground floor plan for the county courthouse but does not show the layout of the second-floor courtroom. I have also found only exterior photographs of the courthouse, including one with a stagecoach parked in front on a sunny day. I have therefore relied on a tourist photograph of the interior of the historic courtroom in Idaho City to write the descriptions contained in this chapter. Although the photographer did not provide any specific information or dates, the courtroom has the look of the 1870s to me.

CHAPTER NINE

1. Reserved.

CHAPTER TEN

1. The history of the sidesaddle begins in the 1400s with designs that variously incorporated stuffed pillows, a foot and back rest, and handholds in front and back—all requiring a woman to sit completely sideways on the horse. The timing of the introduction of the first upright horn (around which the woman hooked her right leg, allowing her to face completely forward) is unknown, but the advent of the second horn (which provided a more secure ride by cradling the woman's right leg between the two horns) is attributed to Catherine de Medici in the 1500s. Both the English and French claim responsibility for the development of the leaping horn (a third horn positioned above the left leg) in the early 1800s. The balance strap, which stabilized the saddle from the added weight on the left side, was also developed during this period. Charles Goodnight (a prominent Texas cattleman) is credited with developing the first western sidesaddle—a more rugged design better suited to the daily rigors of the American West—for Mary Dyer Goodnight, his first wife. The two Internet sites I used to research this topic offered conflicting dates for the timing of the Goodnight sidesaddle: the first claimed 1860s and the second 1870s. But both claims may be accurate because the second site also claimed that Charles Goodnight commissioned a sidesaddle with SC Gallup of Pueblo, Colorado in June 1870. It is therefore likely that he first worked on the new design in the 1860s. A number of American companies soon adopted the Goodnight design and manufactured several versions of his sidesaddle during the ensuing decade. (www.hoosierladiesaside.com/sidesaddlehistory.html and an educational article titled *Goodnight Western Side Saddles* by Linda Flemmer)

2. According to the *Idaho State Historical Society Reference Series Number 150*, the stagecoach travel time from Ruby City (about a mile from Silver City) to Boise City was 10 to 12 hours in 1866. The reference did not list a schedule of departure and arrival times for the route between Silver City and Boise, so I have assumed a daily early-morning

departure to support the storyline. Although the distance from Silver City to Boise is a little more than 70 miles, it is not unreasonable to assume that a skilled rider on a well-conditioned mixed-breed horse could have completed the trip in 10 hours or less.

CHAPTER ELEVEN

1. Alfred Nobel first acquired patents for his invention of dynamite in 1867. Originally consisting of a mixture of nitroglycerine and diatomaceous earth, the resulting paste could be formed into cylindrical rods suitable for insertion into drilling holes. Nobel's combination of materials rendered nitroglycerine—which by itself was dangerously sensitive to shock—much safer to transport and use while also providing a manageable explosive more effective than black powder. Unless the nitroglycerine has leached out over time, dynamite is generally safe and will not explode when subjected to heat or shock: both a fuse and blasting cap are required for detonation. An English leather merchant named William Bickford invented the first practical fuse in 1831, later called the "safety fuse." He fabricated the fuse from jute yarn spun around a core of gunpowder and varnished with tar. Bickford's fuse was supplied as a "rope," and burned at a consistent rate of approximately 30 seconds per foot. Alfred Nobel also invented a blasting cap specifically for use in detonating dynamite. To achieve a controlled explosion, the fuse is cut to length based on the required time delay, the blasting cap is crimped to the end of the fuse (using a special tool) and inserted into the end of the dynamite, and the opposite end of the fuse is ignited. (www.nobelprize.org/alfred_nobel/biographical/articles/life-work/index.html, www.cornwall-calling.co.uk/famous-cornish-people/bickford.htm, and various other sources)

CHAPTER TWELVE

1. The livery, also called the livery stable, flourished across America from the 1800s well into the 1900s. Primarily a "hotel" for horses, the livery provided a place for travelers to leave their animals while visiting a town. The horses were fed, watered, and furnished with an individual stall. Other services often included the rental of horses, carriages, and wagons to those who did not own such advantages. Many liveries incorporated a blacksmith shop. The blacksmith was

a highly-skilled individual who used his knowledge of metal craft to fabricate tools, horseshoes, wagon wheel rims, and other implements from raw iron. The need for liveries and blacksmiths faded with the advent of the automobile. (www.iptv.org/iowapathways/mypath. cfm?ounid=ob_000130&h=no)

Chapter Thirteen
1. Reserved.

Chapter Fourteen
1. Saturday, April 20, 2013. After four weeks of daily high-dose interferon and over three weeks of physical and intellectual recovery, I will begin work on Chapter 14 today. It pleases me to report to you, dear reader, that I have now finished my full chemotherapy regimen. Although I am deeply thankful for the talented and compassionate doctors, nurses, and medical personal who cared for me during the last 11 months, I am also thankful for the end of this long process of biopsies, surgeries, physical therapy, blood tests, and chemotherapy. I still have to visit the dermatologist every three months for three years, then every six months for two years, and finally every year for the remainder of my life, but such vigilance is necessary. I should also report to you that I had a major CT scan (from chin to crotch) around 7 weeks ago, and the doctors found no tumors—the best possible news. I will require a similar CT scan every 6 to 8 months, but only for five more years. From vacation photographs, my wife and I have now verified the existence of the malignant melanoma tumor under my right thumbnail for at least 18 months (and possibly up to 2 years) prior to discovery, not 6 months to a year as I originally told the oncologist. It doesn't matter now. I am thankful for each new day—even the stormy ones.

Chapter Fifteen
1. Although exceptionally uncommon, white ravens do exist. An article in the *Digital Journal* titled "Another Rare White Raven Born This Year on Canadian Beach" (Stephanie Dearing, July 5, 2010) discusses the annual appearance for the preceding ten years of white ravens at Qualicum Beach, a small town on Vancouver Island. The article

quotes from several other sources. From the *Globe and Mail*: "The birds are thought to be leucistic and not albino, the result of a genetic defect producing chicks lacking normal pigmentation." And from the *Times Colonist*: "White ravens are the result of the mating of two common ravens with the same genetic defect. The same pair could produce many generations of white ravens, since common black ravens are monogamous and long-lived." If you remember, a white raven first appeared in Book 2, Chapter 14. Because this particular white raven occurred in the context of Joshua Hotah's strange dream, I did not feel compelled at the time to research the actual existence of such birds in the wild.

2.   I used the following primary resources to write Muireall Anne Raven-scroft's excerpt in Chapter 15 titled *The U.S. Cavalry: 1865 to 1890*:
   The U.S. Cavalry: Soldiers of a Nation, Policemen of an Empire, an article by Dennis Showalter, *Army History* (magazine), Fall 2011,
   Armor-Cavalry Part I: Regular Army and Army Reserve, from the Army Lineage Series, by Mary Lee Stubbs and Stanley Russell Connor, 1969,
   Chapter 14: Winning the West, the Army in the Indian Wars, 1865-1890, Army Historical Series, Office of the Chief of Military History, United States Army,
   The Indian Wars and U.S. Military Thought, 1865-1890, a report by Clyde R. Simmons, U.S. Army War College, 1992,
   http://ehistory.osu.edu/uscw/features/regimental/cavalry.cfm.

3.   Gardening is not my strong suit. In fact, I have eventually killed every potted plant my wife has brought into my office. It's not that I don't like plants. I do. But if they are to survive, then someone who knows what they are doing should take care of them. I was therefore thankful to find an article on the website SanLuisObispo.com by UC Master Gardener Maggie King titled *October Gardening Chores Center on Cleaning Up*. I can assure you of this: Muireall has assiduously followed every one of Ms. King's recommendations.

CHAPTER SIXTEEN

1.   Reserved.

CHAPTER SEVENTEEN

1. When I visited the Owyhee Museum in Murphy, Idaho in August 2011, Joe Demshar (the Director and Curator), suggested that I incorporate a Basque sheepherder into the storyline of my novel. I have honored his request in this chapter.

CHAPTER EIGHTEEN

1. Reserved.

CHAPTER NINETEEN

1. Reserved.

CHAPTER TWENTY

1. When my wife and I stayed with our friend at her Silver City "cabin" in August 2011, we were presented with a thunderstorm after dinner the very first night. We sat in the open air of the front deck, drank wine, watched the lightning flashes some distance beyond the summit of Florida Mountain, and listened to the thunder rumble across the valley and echo off the mountains. We retreated inside when the downpour began, but the rain only lasted about twenty minutes. I love the fragrance of the air just before a thunderstorm.

2. For a detailed discussion of the .56-50 caliber Spencer Repeating Carbine, see Chapter Notes, Part 1, Chapter 17, Note #8. In case you are too lazy to look it up, I will remind you here of these basic facts: the carbine had a capacity of seven rounds, weighed 9 pounds 6 ounces, and had a length of slightly over 39 inches.

CHAPTER TWENTY-ONE

1. I completed this final chapter of my third book on July 16, 2013. I will begin work on the epilogue tomorrow. Or maybe the day after tomorrow.

Update: I completed final revisions on July 19, 2014. Since I began working on the story outline in February 2010, it has required four years and five months to write *Nor Things to Come: A Novel of the West*. But I'm not done yet. I'm confident the publisher will suggest more revisions before sending the book to the printer.

Second Update: After reviewing the initial manuscript, my publisher concluded that no one would buy a book this large and expensive from an unknown author. Since the novel was already organized in three parts, my wife suggested publishing the book as a trilogy. My publisher declared the idea brilliant, and *Nor Things to Come: A Trilogy of the American West* was born.